Stay

At

Home

Sarah Phelan

Blanket Fort Publishing

Stay At Home
by Sarah Phelan

Published by
Blanket Fort Publishing
117 Lakeview Avenue
Lynn, MA 01904 U.S.A.

Library of Congress Cataloging-in-Publication Data
Library of Congress Control Number: 2006900926
Phelan, Sarah, 1973-
Stay at home.
ISBN 0 9779927 0 5

Printed At King Printing, Lowell, MA
Set in Times New Roman

Cover Art by Peter Phelan

ISBN 0-9779927-0-5

www.billysmitts.com

For Eunice and Jim Blatchford

Chapter One
A Night Out

Janie couldn't, and honestly didn't want to imagine what type of substance it was that she had just stuck her hand into. She was doing a quick sweep, investigating for toys possibly stuck in the No Man's Land between the kitchen cabinet and the fridge. And before she left for the evening, she needed to find Brian's most precious item - a teeny, tiny plastic Happy Birthday Troll Janie had stuck on top of his third birthday cake over six months ago. The fuzzy-haired centenary prize rarely left her son's hands and on today of all days, it had gone missing, for almost two hours. And poor little Brian was approaching critical mass.

If Janie had any chance of actually being able to leave the house tonight without a coda of pitiful wails following her out the door, never mind first making that date with the hot shower, the at-home waxing kit and the weapons-grade pink Daisy Twin Blade that she would definitely need to put to use before stepping foot in public, the troll would need to be back in her son's eagerly awaiting hands.

So right now, Janie needed to see what cool, gelatinous slime she had just unseeingly plunged her fingers into. She closed her eyes, pulled out her hand and looked.

And her worst fears were realized.

It was brown.

Please, please, please, please let this be chocolate. She held her hand as far away from the rest of her body as the length of her arm would allow, unable to take her eyes off of the oozing sludge. Now, she would not only have to clean her hand but move the fridge, get a cloth, immerse it in some type of bleach/soap solution and completely sanitize the entire area between the cabinet and the refrigerator. Although she did realize that no one else in the world would ever look there, or have an opportunity to run their hand in the tight spot in their improbable quest to find out how disgusting her house might actually be, Janie, for her own sanity, needed to know that the offending substance, whatever it was, was gone. *Otherwise, I'll be at this concert all night, thinking about festering, brown slime.*

"Katie!" She called to her five year old, as she fanatically scrubbed off the glutinous grossness, "Can you keep Brian in the living room for a few minutes?"

"Yes, Mama!"

"Thank you!" Janie called back, snapping shut the safety gate between the dining room and the kitchen, just to be sure. Despite the promise of youthful cooperation, Janie had to realize that invariably her two little children's curiosity would get the better of them. And soon, she would be pinned behind the fridge answering a litany of "Mama,whatareyoudoing? Whatisthat? Thesoapisstinky. Ismytrollinthere? CanIhaveajuicebox?" while being baptized in both bleach and disgusting, unidentified-*but-I-sure-still-hope-it's-chocolate* goo.

Janie ran the hot water and grabbed a bucket and her old reliable Clorox. She dried off her hands, stepped to the refrigerator and placed them against the only side not covered in fingerpainted artwork and shoved. The big appliance wouldn't budge. *Bad leverage?* She lowered her hand position, dug in with her sneakers and rammed it again.

Nothing.

"Come on, you big, ugly bas…" Before she ended that particular sentence, mama-instincts kicked in, she glimpsed over before beginning what would have most assuredly proved to be a very satisfying catalogue of curses. Her two little darlings were peeking over the safety gate.

"Hi Mama," they chorused.

"Hello sweeties," she chimed, with a wave and a little smile, glancing up at the clock over the doorframe. *Stacie's gonna kill me.* Janie stood back, cracked her knuckles, put her hands in optimum leverage position upon the plastic exterior, threw her weight up into her shoulders, dug her toes into the tile grout on the floor, grunting and heaving against the largest appliance in her house. Her t-shirt rode up on the side where her skin was sliding hard against the edge of the counter, "Ow… jees… godda… sonofa… ow." *Little ears, Janie.*

But, wait, she could feel it. There it was - the giant almond bisque elephant of a refrigerator was moving! She was doing it!

It wasn't much, but it was at least enough to slide a bleach-laden sponge, a hand, an arm and a shoulder in far between so she could clean that disgusting whatever-it-was up. She went to the sink, grabbed her bucket, her sponge, *no time for gloves, screw the gloves*, and some paper towels.

After a quick but effective sterilization that would have made a member of the CDC beam with pride, the entire area was clean and dry. And Janie was light-headed – Bleach Buzz. All vestiges of the sticky, brown, still unidentified and hopefully-will-stay-that-way substance were eradicated. Janie scrambled up, went to the opposite side of the fridge, cleared a spot in the magnetized art gallery and placed her back against it. She shoved and heaved and hoisted until beads of sweat formed in the hollow of her chest and upon her brow and the fridge slid slowly back in to place.

Whew. "Ah, now, let's go upstairs," she sighed to her two little cherubs still watching this interesting show over the top of the gate, "You little pumpkins need to get ready for bed."

"But Mama," Brian's face took on a very distraught look, and his voice climbed up two anxious octaves, "Happy Birthday Troll?"

Janie picked up the bucket, the sponge, the wet paper towels, and dumped them all into the sink, "Oh honey," she said sympathetically over her shoulder, "I promise we'll keep looking."

Turning back towards her audience, she felt her foot kick something small and hard. She only caught a brief glimpse of the punted item as it skittered across the floor before finally wedging itself deeply in between the dark, yet fully disinfected, half-inch of space between the refrigerator and the kitchen cabinet.

It was the Troll.

Of course.

Janie looked to the ceiling and sighed. *I can't say this out loud. There are children here. Not out loud. As much as I would really, really, really like to.*

Shit.

And Brian and Katie chirped over the barrier, "Can we have a cookie?"

Stacie's ass fat jiggled as she swung a leg over the safety gate, only adding to her annoyance. The birth of her second, Marco, had left her with about two inches of baby bulk that she had yet to get rid of. She had to know in the depths of her heart, that she couldn't blame her two year old for the roundness of her tummy and thighs – she knew she hadn't exactly been a conscientious eater while pregnant, noshing mostly on Oreo cookies dipped in butterscotch - but she liked to say that it was the baby who had craved the sugar.

But after giving birth to the little darling, that excuse had gone a tiny bit lame. Clearly that glycemic coma-inducing snacking had flung her metabolism so out of whack that despite the fact that she continued to surreptitiously down stack after stack of them late into the night when Marco, her oldest Benjamin, and even her husband Frankie had fallen fast asleep, the extra little jiggle could not really be her fault. Plus, Stacie mused, if she was to really buckle down and lose the couple of pounds, there was a distinct chance that she'd lose some valuable real estate in the boob area. And she just wasn't willing to give that up yet.

But her problem right now, the thing that was really twisting Stacie's prettiest thong into a big sequined bunch was the fact that when she pulled up, only Janie's white minivan was parked in the driveway, which could only mean that Frankie's stupid brother, Scott, was late. Again.

His wife goes out once a year, plans the date for six months in advance, notifies the jackass by cell phone, PDA, laptop, as well as in some ancient form of actual writing, and he still can't get his workaholic butt home in time to watch the two kids, Stacie fumed. *And it's my fricking night out! My birthday present. Selfish asshole.* "Janie!" Stacie bellowed, plopping the gallon of milk onto the shelf and kicking the fridge door shut, painted papers fluttering on their magnets. She shifted her armload of clothes, the hangers clanking against her knuckles. Stacie wiggled over the barricade, stalked through the dining room, still hollering, "Please tell me you have at least showered!"

From up the stairs, Janie called back, "Haven't had a second yet! But if you could watch the kids, I can go in now!"

"Where is he?"

"He just called from the car. He shouldn't be more than fifteen minutes."

"He better not be," Stacie warned.

"I'm sorry, Stace, we won't be that late, I promise. The kids are fed and this way I can get them off to bed and then Scotty will..."

"Scotty can't put the kids to bed?"

"He can, it's just easier if, uh…"

"You do it?"

"Yes. Easier on everyone."

"Of course." Stacie, her hands on her hips, squeezed the soft flesh under her French-manicured fingers. The flab-reminder only served to tweak her irritation into full blown exasperation. She sighed dramatically. "Come on kids! Katie! Brian, come on down! Your Mama's gotta jump in the shower!"

"Thank you, Stacie," Janie's long dark sheet of hair swung around the wall into the stairway as she watched her daughter and son carefully navigate the stairs to the waiting arms of their Auntie. "You've got'em?"

Stacie swung the pajama'd little girl onto her hip and took the boy's hand. "Just hurry. I've got clothes down here for you. And uh, make sure you shave, uh, you know, well, everything."

Stacie watched Janie's eyebrows shoot up, "Excuse me?"

"You know," Stacie shrugged, "just please take care of the essentials."

"I know I haven't been out in awhile, but what are you expecting to happen at this concert?"

"It's for the clothes."

"I know." Janie replied warily, "You've mentioned this twice to me now and you're making me self-conscious. I know I don't go out much but I'm not gonna be some kind of Yeti in a tank top." Janie thought, "And what exactly are you dressing me in?"

"Listen," Stacie avoided, making her direction very clear, "it's your husband who is making me late, which could prevent us from getting up close. So if I want half a chance at getting my ass backstage, I need the whole package - you, me - to be in top form." Stacie thought aloud, "I wish you were still nursing, we could have used the Big Guns."

Janie drew her brows down, throwing her bemused look down the stairs. After eight years of being both distant neighbors and tentative sister-in-laws, she had to admit she knew what Stacie was all about. And she had agreed to go. *It is her night.* Janie shook her head, turned on her heel and headed for the shower.

Chapter Two
Billy Smitts LIVE!

The music was pounding through the walls of the ladies room and as usual, there were more women in the little lavatory boite than really was necessary. *Well, if you could call these twenty year old cupcakes "women,"* Stacie grimaced as she glanced about. She was just about done with Janie's face – a couple of touchups before they went out to hit the dance floor again.

Without makeup, yeah, Janie was maybe worth a second glance. She was tall and lean, her hair was dark, long. In her daily uniform - the perpetual ponytail, jeans and sneakers - she usually looked like a fresh-faced kid, more like the babysitter than the mom of two little ones. But with the whole shebang all done up like this, Stacie thought as she swept a blush over Janie's cheekbones, the girl really could have been that beauty queen her husband had always purported she had been. *Mrs. Perfect Beauty Queen.*

Janie sighed, "I don't know why I let you put so much of this stuff on me, Stacie. It's gross."

"What's gross is all that sweat from dancing. This stuff feels nice," Stacie motioned with her lips to pucker, "Gloss and we're done."

"Alright," Janie bubbled her lips, like a kid attempting to be patient.

It annoyed Stacie, "God, it's not like you've never worn a lot of makeup, Janie."

"I don't think I wore this much," Janie frowned.

"Please." Stacie frowned right back, then puckered herself, running the brush over her own lips. "Done. Let's go."

Janie stood up straight and without a second glance headed for the door. It wasn't until there was a little more careful study that Stacie followed behind her. They opened the door to the pulsing rhythms of a true nineties punk anthem. The crowd was pogo-sticking and Janie tried enthusiastically to join them. "Need a sports bra for this!"

Stacie was not amused at her friend's guileless gusto, pulling her close and stopping her jumping, "Not attractive, Janie."

"Come on. Let's have fun!" Janie laughed.

"Just stay with me." Stacie took her arm and led her to the center of the dance floor, the beating heart of the male club-going population, the spot where the view was the absolute best all the way around. "Does anyone want to buy us a drink?" Stacie asked to the crowd around them, and quite a few pogo-stickers were happy to stop to oblige.

Janie never really talked about her pageant thing, Stacie mused, looking over at her friend enjoying herself on the dance floor. Not even as Janie had been trying to get herself out of that weird situation with her mom and some other guy – not her dad... *Stepdad, maybe? Someone like that* - back Junior year in college. It was how Janie met Scotty actually. Well, Frankie first, then Scotty.

Back then, Stacie's soon to be boyfriend, then ex-boyfriend, then boyfriend again, and then fiancé, then ex-fiancé, then father of their first child and finally, her husband Frank, had had an Art History class with Janie. He used to talk to her now and then when he could think of something to say.

The story went that one day Frank had cleverly thought of a topic, specifically about Janie's living arrangement plans for the next year. He came up with it during the Greek Revivalist part of the lecture; Janie had said she wasn't sure what she was going to do. She was having trouble coming up with tuition money on her own for Senior year. Well, Frankie just so happened to have a brother who was as a grad student interning in the Financial Aid department. Frankie'd be happy to walk her over to the office and maybe his brother could help her out.

Stacie always imagined that the little setup didn't quite go in the direction that her Frankie had hoped - he didn't get to be the Knight, helping the beautiful Damsel in Distress. He got to be the one who introduced the Damsel to the Knight.

In fact, Stacie always believed that she and Janie would probably have been better off switching husbands. Frankie was always at home, always around after work, always calling Stacie during the day, just to see how she and the boys were doing.

He was always just there.

And Scotty, well, he traveled and worked so much, you couldn't find him without a GPS. So considering Stacie's little penchant for nights out and her many attempts at 'extracurric's', being married to that other brother would probably have made it all a lot easier to pull off.

Not that Stacie didn't love Frankie, she did. In her heart of hearts, she held fast to the belief that really, she adored her husband. How couldn't she? He was great with the children and you couldn't ask for a more solid guy. He never nagged her about the kids or the house or money. He pitched in with the dishes and the laundry. He was kind and gentle. He was Dough-Boy adorable and he was always offering to help her with anything.

Everything.

It was sort of all of that overbearing, sickly sweet, loving, caring attentiveness that drove her absolutely, stone cold, certifiably crazy. She knew it shouldn't. But it most certainly did.

Stacie's grand scheme hadn't really included kids; she hadn't really planned on getting married. It all just sort of happened, one right after the other and not necessarily in what most people considered the right order. And quite frankly, Stacie was completely freaked how her life was turning out. Looking out over the crowd at these cupcakes wasn't helping her through the thought process either. Not that she and Janie were doing so bad, attention-wise. It's just that these young girls didn't have complications like she did, like Janie did. They had their whole lives ahead of them to screw up in anyway they wanted.

Stacie loved her husband, her children; she couldn't imagine life without them. But some days, she would just really, really like to. Oh, think about what she'd be doing right now if she were just free, *like these girls!* if she didn't have to constantly worry if what she was doing, and saying, and showing to her two sweet, adorable little boys.

This parenting stuff was such a huge, gigantic, overwhelming, frightening, horrible, burdensome, terrifying responsibility. The parenting magazines constantly talk about how mothers and fathers need to pounce upon those 'teachable moments' and 'squeeze every ounce of potential out of our children by maximizing high quality time at every possible waking second of the day.' And please, don't forget, Parents, 'One wrong move, one misplaced word can literally change the way a child sees himself, or the world around him and *oh my goodness, what are you doing right now?'* The bimonthly reminders mailed directly to her home with her last name misspelled on the back cover only served to remind Stacie about how crappy of a job she was doing as a mother. And the accompanying physical effects of all of that information made her feel like she had just downed a bag and a half of Tootsie Rolls. Like maybe it all seemed like an okay idea at the time, but the reality of motherhood left her bloated, heavy around the middle and feeling like she was ready to puke.

Stacie just felt like she could not relax, not in front of her kids, anyway. Not like now, just dancing, watching these men watching her, letting them hold her as she just moved to the music – *what would her husband say? But worse, what would her kids say?* Stacie was so damned afraid that maybe if those little kids saw her, really saw her, maybe they wouldn't like her, or that worse - someday, they'd blame her.

So she felt she really needed this night out. Stacie had been a very good girl going on what had to be at least six months. She had sort of been saving up the Naughty, hoping tonight would be her night. And dear sweet Janie, dressed and made up properly, would be just the thing she needed to set the reel on a big, big fish. Her plan was to send in a real live beauty queen for a quick introductory fluff and then the switch up for a bona-fide big-boobed blonde. The man could not resist that. Not even for an itty bitty cupcake.

What? A little bait and switch never hurt anyone.

Stacie could not be more pleased with how the night was going. She had lubed up Janie on a few gin and tonics, well, at least enough to make her stop self-consciously pulling up the neckline of the tank Stacie had just barely convinced her to wear. The men had been crowding around them for most of the concert. Janie was slightly looser with her strictly enforced boundary lines after a little Tanqueray and the guys breached the perimeter as soon as they felt that barbed wire wall tumble in the slightest.

Yeah, buddy, you think you're getting somewhere with former runner up to Miss California! Lure 'em in, Janie and I reap all the Mr. Getting Nowhere benefits.

Stacie's plan involved fully exploiting her sister-in-law's leggy good looks, drawing in the attention from as much and as many as she could get. *But of course*, Stacie's eyes narrowed, *we must keep our eyes upon the birthday girl's big prize.*

Perhaps a little twinge of guilt may have come over her - using her poor, socially-starved sister-in-law. *Martha Stewart under house arrest had more time away from home than Janie gets.* But it's not like she was setting Janie up or anything.

And Stacie did tons of stuff for her. *Like tonight, for example, what did I do before I got to her house? I picked up a gallon of milk on the way over.* Not that Stacie minded running to the grocery store or popping in Home Depot, it saved her from having to come home early and face a few hours by herself in the house, having to find some way to entertain her two boys at least until Daddy got there. *Oh for chrissakes, Janie needs some help and who's the only one there to give it to her? Me!*

And tonight, so what? Janie was unknowingly serving a purpose. No one is convincing me I'm wrong to do it. As long as these guys will stick around after the Window Dressing had made her own unavailability perfectly clear, Stacie would be grateful to Janie for any extra attention the girl would garner.

Here comes a little hottie right now, breaking off of the small Janie circle. The little random hottie smiled over at Stacie, dancing for the moment by herself. She gave him her best come-hither, beckoning him much closer to her than Janie would have allowed him. And he took full advantage of it.

But you know, Stacie looked back, catching the girl's eye, *if the damned girl could get over her little principles, we could probably have some real fun together.*

Janie danced up to Stacie and her new partner, sipping on the last vestiges of her fourth gin mixer, giggling into the straw about the gurgling noises that emanated from the air between the ice cubes. She was pretty drunk, "Good song."

"I think it's on his first Greatest Hits," Stacie nodded. "Do you know it?"

"Nope," Janie replied, swinging her slim hips away into the crowd again, but stopped halfway out, "Stace," she called, "You've got an elastic?"

"You're not putting your hair up!" Stacie admonished over the shoulder of the man who was now grabbing her ass.

"It's hot in here!"

"I don't care!"

"Fine," Janie made a face around the precious straw, her two hands wrapped firmly around the glass jumped as she shrugged her shoulders, sauntering away in time to the music.

See? Janie seemed to be enjoying herself. "I'm doing her a good," Stacie assured the little random, ass-grabbing hottie. "She's got a house and kids - it probably wouldn't matter where she was or who she was with, that poor girl can finally let off some steam that had been most likely building up for the past three decades." And as her dancing partner nodded and smiled at her, Stacie knew she was definitely doing her dear, repressed, sweet, sometimes sickeningly wonderful Janie a huge favor.

So it worked out for everyone that after the concert, in an impressive display of Stacie's manipulative expertise in timing, as well as in female asset presentation, of course, *he* would notice Janie.

Stacie watched him out of the corner of her eye, as did most of the other women at the bar. Except for a very woozy Janie - the bait oblivious to being lowered on the hook - who stood, with all of the breezy nonchalance of the happily intoxicated, up for the drinks Stacie had sent her up for at precisely the right moment. Billy Smitts had exited the small stage, toweling off his hard body, enveloped by a couple of bulky bodyguards.

Okay, Janie, I dressed you for this. Get us backstage, girlie.

He headed right for her.

Hook, line, sinker, Stacie smiled.

His chest was bare as he approached the bar next to this tall, dark-haired pretty and he conspicuously flipped his black t-shirt over his head. She smirked at him and he smirked back. "Hi," he said affably. It usually worked.

Janie just sort of gave him a quick nod of her head and busied herself looking for the bartender.

He waited; he was giving her about one more minute and then he would have to move on - a pretty like this? Snubbing him? At his own concert? *Clearly, that is just not going to happen.*

Recognition took a couple of seconds, but finally, Tanqueray-time caught up with Janie and she squinted over at the hazy, yet striking combination of blond, black and blue standing next to her, "Hey!" she realized, "That was a fun show," she leaned in, remarking with inebriated enthusiasm.

He grinned, "Thanks. Glad you liked it," turning himself to her, leaning against the bar.

She hadn't paid all that much attention to his singing, but his speaking voice was positively arresting. These deep tones rang out to her and she immediately thought that it was like something dark and intensely rich – chocolate, she thought. *His voice, it is the sound of chocolate. Ooh, a little gin and I'm a poet.*

Janie tucked her long hair behind her ear, she wasn't used to wearing it down, but Stacie had insisted. Oh, like her own mother used to. *Annoying.*

But of course, he took it as a good sign. Pulling a box of Marlboros from his back pocket, he dragged one from its box. "Can I buy you a drink?" Lighting up, he slipped the pack into his shirt pocket.

Janie was feeling no pain, "Nah, don't worry about it, I'm getting one for my friend. Well, she's my sister-in-law, and one for me. It's her birthday, Stacie's birthday. That's my sister-in-law," she hooked her thumb over her shoulder. He glanced politely but didn't really look. If he had, he might have seen Stacie trying to fend off her little random hottie in order to make her way towards him and Janie, now that she could see the ice had officially been broken. But Stacie was unfortunately completely unsuccessful. Billy's attention was on Janie, who continued on with her superfluous drunk explanation, "She went to college with me, so I could say we were 'friends.' You know, first. Although, we weren't really close." But she put up her hand, stopping herself, and shook her head, "So, to recap, I'm getting us both something to drink." She blew out a breath, laughing at herself.

He smiled, "I can buy one for each of you, I bet. What are you having?"

"Oh, all righty. She'll have a Cosmopolitan and I am having a water now. Five gin and tonics and I'd be having a little nap under the bar."

"Lightweight."

"Yeah, you think? But I am going to have one of these," Janie reached into his shirt pocket and grabbed a cigarette.

Without missing a beat, he lit it. "You sure you can handle it?"

"Yes, Sarcastro," she dragged and blew. "I am one of the highest-ranked social smokers in the West. Check the records."

He chuckled and rubbed his stubbled chin, "Can't without your name."

"Oh, oh, yeah, Janie." She held out her hand. "Jane Hadley."

"Billy, William Smitts. Pleasure." He shook her hand with mock formality.

"Who are your friends?"

"Who? These guys?"

"Yes, the two enormous men behind you." She bypassed Billy and held out her hand, "Hi, I'm Janie."

The bigger of the two men stepped forward, "Hello Janie, I'm Del, this is Bobby."

"Where are you two from?"

Billy interrupted, he had to take hold of his conversation again, "So what do you do, Miss Hadley?"

Janie whirled back around, "*Mrs.* Hadley." Billy's face betrayed a slight disappointment as she continued, "I run a daycare. Out of my house, private, really small. My kids…" It took her a minute to get the meaning of his expression - the Tanqueray again, "HA!" She guffawed right out loud, right in his face. "Oh, please! Like I'm a prospect to Billy - William Smitts!"

"Why not? A pretty girl, had a few too many, seems like it makes perfect sense to me."

"Come on, a club like this? It'd be like shooting sexy fish in a sexy barrel."

His smile refreshed, "I'm glad you started on water."

Her nose wrinkled, "Me too."

"All right then. Help me choose a sexy fish."

"Ooh, hey! Fun! I'm good at that! I can do that!" Janie spun around and leaned against the bar, "You've got a wide array to choose from. Like here." A short girl with curly brown hair strolled by, attempting to throw Billy a glance. "That cute one. Seems very nice, there's our sweet little guppy."

"Hmmm," he thought it over. "I think we can stop with the fish analogy, now."

"Shush, I've got a good one. How about that one there, she's a shark!" Janie pointed to a black-haired beauty smoldering around the room, a trail of smoke billowing behind her. "Huh?"

He quickly glanced at Janie sideways, amused, "Again, I say, 'hmmmmmmmm.'"

"And there goes a puffer fish," Jane noted a large Slavic blonde strutting by, carving a path through the crowd with her boobs. "Wow." Janie, watching the girl bobbing across their field of vision, cocked her head to the side, fascinated, "Those are like a cowpusher on a train."

Billy snorted with unexpected laughter; his drink almost ended up back in the glass. Del and Bobby heaved their massive forms with surprised and appreciative chuckles. Billy recovered, "So you heading home soon, back to Mr. Hadley?"

"Probably. Most likely jumping right into a warm tubbie, wash this smokiness off me. Although I should get back to my, my sister-in-law. It's her birthday. Stacie."

"You told me that." He dragged from his cigarette, "You have kids."

"Hey, yes, I do. Two, a girl and boy. How did you know?"

"No one who doesn't have children calls it a 'tubbie.'" He smiled. "Plus, if I wasn't so intuitive I would have just remembered that you mentioned it just a second ago."

"Ah, yes. Hey, don't you have a, no, wait, give me second, ummmmm, a son?"

"Nope."

"A daughter?"

"Yep."

"Aha!" Janie thought for a second and frowned at him. "There were only two to choose from."

"Yeah, s'okay," he smirked, "it's nice to know there are some out there who haven't memorized all of the intimate details of my life. Here." He pulled a battered black leather wallet out of his back pocket and displayed a cut-out picture of a darling little blonde. "Wanna see her? She's five."

"So sweet," Janie cooed. "I have a five year old girl! Wait, here." They exchanged wallets. "And he's three. They're gorgeous, huh? I do good work."

"I want a boy someday." His marvelous face twisted into a look of wistfulness, taking the harder edges off of him.

Janie looked around and the big blonde was heading this way. She leaned in to whisper, "Well, it looks like your fish is about to jump into the boat. And I've gotta go find my… well, you know." She winked and gave him the thumbs up.

"It's her birthday." Billy smiled.

"I told you that." Janie reached into his front shirt pocket to steal another cigarette. "One for the road." She grabbed Stacie's Cosmo and split.

He nodded. "Great talking to you."

Over her shoulder, "Yeah, you too. Thanks. Bye Del, bye Bobby. Nice to meet you."

They harmonized a "Buh-bye," and watched her walk away. Billy already had an arm around the blonde, but Del didn't miss the boss' slick little move. Del just looked at Bobby and shook his head.

Stacie pounced on Janie, she had been trying to get over to Billy and Janie at the bar but that random hottie had turned out to be a drunk, gross, pain in the ass, taking the groping and attention way past the point of 'creepy,' in fact, closer to 'slimy.' So, having missed out on the good action, Stacie was eager for the scoop, "So are we backstage, after-party, what is it?"

Janie, stunned, "Oh, um, nothing."

"What were you doing? You were just flirting with him for like fifteen minutes."

"Stacie, please. I'm a married woman, I don't flirt."

"Any form of male to female conversation is flirting, Janie." Stacie rolled her eyes.

"That is not true. Women and men can have normal conversations."

"Okay then, any form of male to female conversation in which the female laughs repeatedly and/or touches her hair automatically qualifies as flirting. At least, in the guy's mind, it does. And you touched your hair. YOU TOUCHED YOUR HAIR!"

"It was IN MY FACE! We were having a NORMAL conversation."

"Please. 'Normal conversation.' What the hell would a rock star/movie star," strong emphasis on the quotes and the slash, "and a daycare provider have to talk about in a 'normal conversation'?"

"Our kids." Janie shrugged a shoulder, "Well, his kid, my kids."

"Only you," Stacie shook her head. "Janie, you even got in good with the bodyguards."

"Oh, Del and Bobby," Janie nodded, "They seemed nice."

"Ugh. 'Nice?!' What, did you exchange recipes with them? Or give them tips on getting their whites really white?"

Janie thought, the alcohol prevented a lot of Stacie's sarcasm from really absorbing, "No. I didn't really get a chance to talk to them. He interrupted..."

"Didn't you mention it was my birthday?" Stacie interrupted, too.

"Of course I did! He bought you this drink." Janie handed over the garnet colored liquid, "Sparkly red booze!"

"Oh my Lord." Stacie shook her head at her own stupidity. "Four gin and tonics are apparently way too much." Stacie grabbed Janie's arm. "Okay, we are going back there and you are getting the two of us, or at least me, to a party at his hotel room."

"How do you know they are even having one?"

Stacie, fuming, "Do you ever leave your house? Read a magazine? Look at the papers in the grocery store? Of course Billy Smitts is having an after-party!"

"Well, we can't go back and talk to him now – he's leaving with that big blonde cow – girl, cowgirl. What was it I said earlier? It was funny."

"Oh crap, the blonde with the big boobs? Yeah, even you couldn't get around that… you don't put out. Hmmm…"

"Cow… something to do with a train…"

"Never send a very married woman to do another not so married woman's job." Stacie resigned, "Oh well, that totally sucks. No celebrity birthday bang for me."

"Cowpusher! That was it! See, her boobs, so big, like going through the crowd," Janie pantomimed, "Cowpusher, get it?"

"Let's go. I can at least go sleep with Frankie." She grabbed Janie's hand, "Come on."

Chapter Three
Hung Out To Dry Out

Janie awoke to her three year old's demonstration for his keenly observing big sister of how you could see almost all of Mama's eyeball if you just peeled back her eyelid by the eyelashes.

"Happy Birthday!" Little Brian hollered enthusiastically as soon as he saw the other eye spring open on its own.

"It's not Mama's birthday, Brian," Katie admonished.

"Today is my birthday," Brian then insisted.

Their little voices were almost loud enough to drown out the distinct creaking sound of Janie's swollen eyelids lowering over her blinking bloodshot eyes.

"Not yet, honey. The end of the summer. It'll be fun," she groaned as she lifted herself out of bed to the dancing steps of her two little darlings. Her head felt like it was about to split open into two alcohol-soaked halves.

"He thinks everyday is his birthday," Katie sighed. "Is it breakfast time yet?"

Janie nudged the sleeping form next to her, "Scotty, can you get it this morning?"

"Huh?" Scotty looked down to Katie and Brian waiting at the foot of their bed, their five and three year old eyes, peering hopefully, hungrily at them, "Seriously?"

"Please, just a half an hour? Get them some cereal."

"All right, but next time, you do the crime, you do the time." He scooted the kids out of the bedroom.

"Ugh, I know. Thank you." She gently laid herself back down on her pillows.

A moment passed before, from downstairs, Scotty hollered, "Janie! I'm going to take the kids to Denny's for breakfast!"

"We have food here." *Ouch.* "Better food." *Ow-ouch.*

"I know, but they'll cook it for us. Can I grab some of that cash I gave you from last night?"

"Wallet's in my bag on the kitchen counter by the door." *Ooooh, bad gin. Bad, bad gin.*

She was almost back to sleep when he yelled back up, "Not in there!"

"What?"

"Check your pants! Your wallet isn't in your bag."

Aw crap, she pulled her body out of bed. She found she still had on Stacie's white tank top, but somehow in the night, she had stumbled out of the unbelievably annoying thong and into her regular white boycuts. The only thing that she remembered clearly at that point was that there had been an audible sigh of relief, purportedly from her own voice box. Now, this morning, she was bracing herself against the laundry basket and pulling out Stacie's distressed leather pants – *leather in the laundry hamper? Yeah, I was seriously drunk* – with no wallet. *You're kidding me. Come on.* She sunk her full-cut white cotton-covered ass back on the bed. *No.*

She trudged down the stairs, belting her red flannel robe tightly around her waist. "Hold on, everybody."

"Hi Mama!" Katie beamed up the stairs at her. "We're going out for breakfast!"

Janie pulled it together, smiling for her lovely dark-haired daughter, "I know, honey, that's a special treat with Daddy. Let's go get you some money so that you guys can go, okay?"

"Okay!" Katie took her Mama's hand and led her to the kitchen.

Scott looked over at her, "You okay?"

"Yeah, can you hand me my bag?"

"Sure," he handed it to her. "Hey, uh, you looked really good last night, in Stacie's stuff."

"Thanks, maybe I could wear it again. Later, maybe," she rummaged through her bag.

"Oh, uh, I've got these reports to give on all of the current employees for the new crop of potential buyers for tomorrow and I was going to go in a little later and stay..." Scott looked sheepish.

"Crap."

"Well, sorry. It's sort of a big deal and I've been so..."

"No, not that, my wallet is gone." She dumped her bag on the counter. "Maybe it's with Stacie, in her car or something."

"Well, we'll head out and you can give her a call. I'll stop by the bank machine on the way."

"Okay."

"Hey, you know what's good for a hangover?"

"Shh. The kids don't need to hear that, repeating it in the neighborhood," Janie laughed into her hands. "What's good for it?"

"Chocolate. The caffeine and the sugar will help you out at least until you can get in the shower."

"I think all we have in the house is the bitter, the bittersweet kind, you know, for cooking."

"Maybe that will help."

"Ew."

"I don't know. Try it." To the kids. "Okay, you two! Denny's!"

"Thanks, okay bye, guys. Kisses!" A smooch from the smaller two and off they all went, slamming the heavy door behind them.

A phone call to Stacie gave her nothing. Stacie said she would check her car and call back but she was pretty sure it wasn't there. "So what are you gonna do?" Stacie warned.

"Well, I guess I've gotta call the bank and the credit card people. I've got their numbers right here as we speak."

"See there we go," Stacie dug, "even efficient when hung over."

"Ugh." And Janie hung up.

The morning was just not going well. She took a bite of the large hunk of cooking chocolate from her cupboard and immediately spit it out. Mr. Tanqueray himself was dancing in spiky boots behind her forehead on the very matter of her brain and it hurt like hell and she had been on hold with Wells Fargo for about a half an hour.

"Yes, Wells Fargo Customer Service, this is Cindy, how may I help you?" a southern drawl spilled like molasses from the telephone receiver.

"Hey! Hi Cindy. Um, my wallet has been stolen and my credit card and my ATM card were in it. I need to cancel my cards before they get any cash."

"When was it stolen?"

"I am assuming last night."

"Assuming?"

"It had to be last night."

"Okay." *Is it possible to hear a condescending sneer over the phone?* "Give me a moment to access your account. What is the number?"

"675," The doorbell clanged and Janie's head was about to open itself up and she could barely hear snotty Cindy on the telephone. "323… Dammit, I'm sorry, the door, Cindy, can you just hold on a second?"

"Yes," Cindy slowly hissed.

The phone to her ear, muted, Janie tried to open the front door. And the door wouldn't open. She began to swear. Over the past five years, she liked to believe that her swearing had *almost* come to a complete halt – resurfacing only in dire circumstances or really, in any instance when the children weren't around. *No one uses the front door.* The cursing was making her head throb worse than it already was. Finally wrenching it open, she spied a sleek, black Mercedes sedan in front of her house and a vaguely familiar face at her door.

"Hi," Billy Smitts said.

"Hi," Janie looked at him, complete incredulity, the phone still at her ear. Motorcycle boots attached to long lean denim legs, his hands deep in the pockets of an imposing black leather trench over a six foot frame, the obligatory piercings, the platinum blond hair over the thick black eyebrows – it was all just too much for a hung over Janie to bear. Her face crunched up in squinting pain. As his sharp cheekbones lifted in a devilish smile, she became desperately aware that she was wearing nothing but a frayed flannel robe over a white tank and underpants and there had to be a layer of mascara'd eyecrust an inch thick over her reddened pupils.

"Can I come in?"

"Um, sure. I guess so." Jane turned as Billy took hold of her door, covering her mouth, she breathed into her hand, *Oh dear God.* "You want coffee?" She laid down the receiver of her cordless phone.

"Love some. I need it. It'll help my head."

"Apparently a Hollywood hangover looks a lot prettier than mine. Kitchen, come on." She led him through the dining room into her small kitchen. "Sit," she commanded and he settled himself at the table. She poured him a mug of steaming coffee, "Cream and sugar?" like he was a neighbor popping in for a cup and some gossip.

"Please."

She handed him the "World's Greatest Dad" mug requisite in a house with children, and inquired so politely, "So, um, quick question for you. How do you know where I live?"

"I took your wallet."

"You took my wallet?"

"The pictures, remember? I decided I would like to meet you again so I just pocketed it." He smiled disarmingly.

Not enough so.

"You stole my wallet? Are you insane? I have a good mind to call someone and tell them this." She asked him, "Who do I call?!"

He shrugged.

"Hey! And don't you remember I'm married? That may not mean anything to you or the girls you usually see but it sure means something to me. Yeah, I'm married, buster. Don't most celebrities have stalkers not the other way around?"

"I'm sorry," he tried to conceal his laughter. "I wanted to tell you that I appreciated your conversation. Most girls only want to get a little piece of me…"

Janie interrupted, "Oh you poor, criminally insane movie star…"

"No," he laughed again. "Here is your wallet. I am sorry if I caused you any trouble. I'll go. Thanks again." He didn't make a move to actually leave, he just smiled; it was friendly and disturbingly contagious. Janie found herself unable to help but return it. *This is why he is a celebrity. Goddamned charming asshole.*

"Wait, have your coffee. Just don't get any weirder…" Janie looked ominous.

"Well, now, that's a tall order."

"I know I'm expecting a lot. I mean I guess I could be more tolerant but I'm not used to having an international movie star in my kitchen, especially not one who just confessed that he stole my wallet. An International Wallet-Stealing Movie Star."

"I was originally a singer. Don't forget singer."

"I was trying to," she sipped her coffee.

A good natured, "Oh wow, harsh." He pointed, "Don't you have someone waiting on the phone?"

"Crap! The bank!" Janie ran to pick up the phone, canceling the Mute as she rifled through her wallet's contents. "Cindy, sorry for the delay. Yes, no. I have my cards back, no need to cancel now."

"Are you sure?" Cindy's drawl diminished with her irritation.

"Umm, yes, I have my wallet back – it was stolen by a celebrity so that he could more accurately stalk me. I don't think he spent any money, hold it… Did you?"

"Nope."

"Good for you Scary Stalker Movie Star!" To the phone, "No, he didn't make any unauthorized purchases."

"Thank you ma'am and have a pleasant day."

Janie hung up. "I could have told that woman that anyone - you, even! - had taken that card and she wouldn't have cared."

"Good." Billy swigged his coffee. "As you have made it so clear that I am not welcomed here as a suitor, I have another thing I wanted to ask you."

"No, you cannot see my passport."

Billy laughed again. "No! You mentioned you ran a very private daycare, here in your home?"

"Yes. I do."

"Would you have an opening for the next couple of months? See, I am shooting in the area, hence the bunch of concert dates up here, and I need someone reliable to watch Ashley, my daughter."

"Don't you have people on staff to do that? A nanny?"

"Well, I did but she and I, uh… parted ways… decided it was best if she left."

"Oh crap. I am not sure I feel comfortable with this."

He placed his hand on Janie's. "I'm sort of in a bad position and your business comes highly commended…"

She pulled her hand away, "How do you know anything about my business?"

"Oh, I, uh, ran a background check on you."

"WHAT?!"

"I had the information, I knew what I needed from you and I know you can be trusted."

Janie stood up so quickly that her aching brain suffered at the hands of the Earth's gravitational pull, seeming to bumper-car bounce repeatedly against the inside of her cranium, "You did that without my permission! Who are you?! What are you?!" She couldn't believe this – *what with the unnervingly easy conversation and the charming bullshit smile and I just ate it up and this man was crazy and I let him in my house!!* "Oh my God, you are a fruitcake! You're an invasion of privacy, kleptomaniac, nanny-boinking fruitcake! I've spoken to you for five minutes and I can tell you NOW that this is not how I do business."

He stood up, "I know that…"

"Of course, you know that! You ran CORI forms on me!"

"It wasn't like it was a fascinating read – an hour or so I won't be getting back. For chrissakes, 'Miss Perfect' couldn't get a parking ticket or something?"

"THAT'S 'MISSUS' PERFECT!" she yelled. "And I'm so sorry my criminal records were boring. I mean, I know having an interesting rap sheet is an important stipulation when choosing a daycare provider!"

Stacie, a blonde vision in a pink sweat suit, popped the side door open and trotted in, stopping to take in the scene in front of her. A slow smile broke on her face, "Oh my God! Janie, are you telling me... last night... Did you... What is Billy Smitts doing here?" *Check out, Miss Morality!*

"He's just leaving, Stacie."

"Please, I need your help."

Stacie looked at Janie. "He needs your help?"

"Yes, I do," Billy saw an opportunity and swung into recruiting a sympathetic ear - *the Girlfriend Angle.* He turned to Stacie, his face full of sweet desperation, laying his hand on her forearm gently, "Stacie, I am in desperate need of quality childcare for a few months for my five year old daughter. She's been so lonely and she misses her nanny and she hasn't many friends her own age because she travels with me so much so I can have her near me. And I thought since Janie came so highly recommended..."

Janie rolled her eyes at Billy, "Did you rehearse that?" To Stacie, "Don't listen to him. He's being charming. It's his job. He's an actor. Don't fall for it. The psycho stole my wallet last night, stalked me to my house, and come to find out, ran a background check on me without my permission. No way, no way, Stacie."

Stacie had been so moved by this beautiful plea by the incredibly handsome movie star, who happened to be touching her, she looked as though she was about to cry. She turned to Janie, her own face mirroring the sweet desperation of the man beseeching her good will, "But his daughter... he said she's lonely. And your kids are so good." To an attentive Billy, putting her hand atop his on her arm, clutching him to her, "She really is amazing with them, gets them to do crafts and they sing and dance, and she does a Circle Time. She taught my Ben to read I swear to God."

Janie unclenched Stacie's hand from his, "Cut it out. Stop that." To Billy, pulling his hand off of Stacie's forearm, "I know what you're doing. Quit it. And stop listening to her."

The side screen opened again and Janie's Katie and Brian hopped through the doorway. Scotty's voice, uncertain came through the door, "Janie, whose car is parked out front? There are two humungous guys just sitting there..." Scott walked up the stairs and stopped at the door, pointing, "Why is Billy Smitts in our kitchen?"

Janie started in, "This psycho..."

Billy strode up to Scott with his hand out, interrupting Janie, "Hi, I'm Billy. Beautiful house, are these two yours?"

Scott, momentarily taken aback, recovered quickly and shook the man's hand. "Hey, Scott Hadley, yes, this is Katie..."

"I'm five!" Katie squealed.

"Hello, Katie, I have a girl your age. Her name is Ashley."

"Can she come over and play with me?"

"I hope so, but that is up to your daddy and mommy."

Scott turned to the little one at his leg, "And this is Brian."

Brian gave a soft "Hi."

And Billy squatted down to his level to shake hands, "How do you do, sir?"

Brian giggled and took the large, scarred, silver-ringed hand and shook it. "It's my birthday."

"It is? Well, Happy Birthday. Are you going to have cake?"

"Chocolate with strawberries and green grapes."

"Wow, that sounds good."

Stacie and Scotty were entranced. Janie looked at them all, her mouth open, her hands spread out before her in sheer exasperation, *What is going on here? Who are these people? What am I seeing?!*

"It's not his birthday!" Janie snapped out, disturbing the sweet reverie. "And you, Peter Pan, you have got to go. I will not be railroaded by some magic celebrity pixie dust!" She picked Billy up by his leather-clad shoulders, looked at him squarely in his deep blue eyes and said, "No."

"Five thousand for the month, eight for the second, incremental for the third. I drop off early, pick up after all the others are scheduled to leave. No one knows I'm up here for a couple of months, I ensure your privacy, you ensure mine, standard non-disclosure contract."

"I said, 'No.' Leave."

Scott and Stacie screamed, "DON'T! NO! JANIE, ARE YOU CRAZY?"

"Ten for the first month, twelve the second, incremental. I have you on reserve for concert dates for sleepovers."

"Get out!" Janie started at him.

Scott restrained her, speaking calmly, "Honey, please. Think about it. Mr. Smitts is offering you a very large sum of money to take care of his daughter for a limited period of time."

"'Mister Smitts'?" she spat. "This man has invaded my home, my privacy."

"Honey, really, he is just trying to do what is right by his daughter. You have to respect that, right?" Scotty leaned in, whispering excitedly, "And ten thousand dollars! For a month? We could buy a new car."

"We don't *need* a new car," Janie fumed. She could see it happening right in front of her, like some kind of nightmarishly Freudian car crash she was being forced to watch. There she was, sitting in that new car getting repeatedly rear-ended by this guy, this insane, pretty man in the driver's seat, flashing some cash around, spewing out all of that phony, charming crap. And what's worse, Janie's own husband and her best friend were sitting in his backseat, laughing. *It is for his daughter... but hey, wait just a second!* "Scotty, he hit on me last night!"

But Billy didn't let it drop, not once. "I was totally out of line, I apologize for that but you have to know that I didn't know she was married until she made it very, very clear."

Janie, her fists clenched in front of her, "Oh. My. God."

Scotty explained, "See, it was completely innocent, he didn't know you were married." Quietly in her ear, "Ten thousand dollars." Janie's Knight may have failed her but at least he could be chivalrous enough to reassure her about the other man's intentions.

Janie was disgusted. "You're selling me out." She looked at Billy, who smiled patiently. *Oh, I'd hit him right in that pretty smirk if I could.*

She exhaled loudly. *He is doing it for his daughter.*

I've done weird stuff for the sake of my kids, NOT THIS INSANE, but still, it's not like he has to live by regular people's rules.

No! You know what? He should have to!

She looked around the room, shaking her head.

Okay, Scotty wants me to take the ten thousand dollars. Okay, we'll see. "I want to meet Ashley. I will only take her if it is a good fit with my children. I don't want any weird influences of genetic kleptomania imposed on my kids. I only take in ones who will bond with our family."

Billy felt victory was at hand, as it almost always was. "Absolutely."

Stacie and Scotty stood by, bated breath, watching one Titan alternately surrendering to another.

"Bring her by later Monday morning. Around 9 am, the children will have settled in and then you won't have to deal with any parents. You can spend about an hour here with her and then you leave. You can pick her up later in the day. It won't be overwhelming to her that way and we can see how she can settle in with just us and the other children."

"Sounds good."

"We'll talk when you come to get her after the other parents leave. I'll give you my answer then."

"Okay, good. I'll bring the contracts then."

"No," she stopped him. "You'll bring yours her first real day, Tuesday. If I accept." *Rear-end that, Mr. Famous.* "I will have my contracts for Monday."

"Got it."

"Now, go. And try not to take any of my personal papers on your way out."

Billy Smitts smiled, waved and said goodbye. As soon as the door shut behind him, Stacie and Scotty screamed in victory, jumping up and down, hugging each other and laughing to Janie. "Ten thousand dollars! Ten Thousand Dollars! Billy Smitts' TEN THOUSAND DOLLARS!!"

Scotty ran to hug a thoroughly pissed Janie, "Gotta go to work, honey! That was AMAZING!" He walked off, marveling at the win, "Ten Thousand Dollars for a month! A month! Ten Thousand Dollars!"

Watching Stacie dancing about in her Pepto-Bismol colored outfit with her hands clasped together like an excited child, ironically made Janie nauseous. Her headache had come back with a vengeance.

Chapter Four
Tryouts

Monday morning, promptly at 9 am, the large black Mercedes sedan pulled over in front of the house. Janie watched warily from the side door as Bobby exited the front passenger seat and opened the door for Billy. He was unbuckling a pretty blonde child from her car seat. Janie recognized her from the picture.

That must be Ashley. She's beautiful.

Well, duh.

But her mother must have been blonde too. Sure as hell know Billy's cuffs and collar don't match.

She shook that thought out of her head. *Ew.*

He looked almost normal this morning, just in a white t-shirt and jeans with leather sandals.

Hmm, he has feet. Bet they're pretty too.

Annoying.

Janie saw him lean into the back of the car but she couldn't hear what he was saying. Out of an irritating curiosity, Janie peered into the back seat as best as she could. A long, lean, tanned leg was visible and she saw what looked like a twenty year old face come up to give Billy's a kiss. He took it on the cheek.

Ooh, harsh, blowing her off, whoever she was.

Billy spoke briefly to the two massive forms in the front seat, *wait, that's Bobby and what was it, oh, Del? - Yes.* Janie saw the driver sharply pull out and speed off.

This drop-off process was taking far too long, she stuck her head in on the other kids. Luckily Stacie, at Janie's instruction, had brought over some supplies this morning to engage Katie and Brian as well as Stacie and Frank's Benji and Marco, Joey Sweeney and Austin Sawyer in an activity. Janie often employed this technique to settle in a new child and felt that today such a project would help her have a little time to speak to Ashley and What's-His-Face once they finally got inside. Of course, the Welcoming Project usually wasn't on this scale. And despite the fact she was feeling guilty for not portraying her professional best, Janie smiled a little to herself.

"Good morning," she called from the door, opening it for the two of them.

Billy put Ashley down so she could walk up the stairs, "Good morning, Mrs. Hadley."

She could sense some sort of amused satisfaction from this introduction and she relished giving him what he thought was a moment of condescension. *Just wait, buddy.*

So instead she knelt down to the small girl, "Come in, Ashley. I'm Janie. The other kids are waiting to meet you and we have a special project to get started on."

Ashley smiled shyly, reaching out to touch Janie's long dark hair. Janie smiled back at her and Ashley, assured by the pretty lady with the friendly voice, ran ahead into the dining room.

Janie straightened up and squared herself to him, attempting to compensate for the three-inch height difference, crossing her arms. Billy could read these signals loud and clear, but it didn't seem to stem his amusement. In fact, he grinned right at her. She chose to ignore it, deciding to lull him into a feeling of secure superiority with polite professionalism, "This way, please." Billy followed her through the kitchen as Janie explained her procedure, "On our trial day, I usually like to start the children off with some pictures from home. It gives the child a chance to, not only start off with some familiar faces but, it will give her the opportunity to get to know the other children by working with them on a project."

They entered the dining room and the kids were quietly cutting Billy Smitts candids from about a hundred different gossip magazines, the National Enquirer, People, US Magazine, the Sun, the Weekly World news, as well as InStyle, Rolling Stone, YM and Cosmopolitan. They were then pasting the prints onto a huge life-sized poster of Billy Smitts that lay across the length of the table. "As we didn't have any family photos, we just decided to do a search game for pictures of Ashley's daddy." Janie smiled devilishly over at Billy, "There were a lot to find."

Billy's level of shock could have been measured on the Richter scale, except there was no rumbling, no sound coming from him, just a wide gaping hole where Janie smugly recalled some sort of smarmy grin had been.

"Look, Daddy! It's you!!" Ashley yelled happily, holding up a small picture on newsprint of her father outside of some questionable nightclub.

Janie turned shoulder to shoulder to him so that she could whisper very softly in his ear, "I let it happen once, but don't think you can get around me, especially in my own house, ever again. Got it?"

"Got it." And a small chuckle erupted from his chest. *The girl's got a set.*

But he quickly turned his attention to his daughter, "Can I help, Ashley?" And much to Janie's surprise, Billy sat down with the children and happily cut and pasted pictures onto the full-length poster version of himself for the full hour.

He had left and Ashley spent the better part of the afternoon playing well with Katie, Brian and the others. Janie was friendly to her, but not overly so. Children usually responded to honest affection instead of fast and forced adoration. Janie had always treated her kids with respect and expected the same from them.

She did enjoy their company, learning to appreciate each child's talents and quirks as they revealed themselves to her. When trying to explain her little business philosophy to prospective clients, she always said she wasn't there to lead the children, she was there to help them discover who they were and how they would like to be.

Still, despite her marked enthusiasm for the wee ones, she did realize that her usual limit of six kids, all under six years old, up until six pm at night, had to be more than just a coincidental relation to the sign of the devil. Very early in her daycare career, as Janie had tried to wing her way through the day, she had discovered that an unstructured day with a gaggle of preschoolers was a heartless, soulless enemy to be avoided at any and all costs.

It had all the elements of an errant hostage situation, including that trick when FBI agents came in and began playing ABBA until the perps would run out screaming, begging to be taken to prison, anywhere, as long as the onslaught of Swedish pop rock would stop. Well, replace the cops with kids, ABBA with "Row, Row, Row Your Boat," and switch out the perpetrators with a single daycare provider, and there you go – same results.

In order to save her sanity, Janie had quickly adapted a strictly adhered-to schedule of activities, clean up and

snack times, even time-limited free play was fit into the day
to try and keep a lid on squabbles, boredom and the ensuing
possible coup complete with blood.

Another key element of her success was that she never
let them figure out that the kids actually outnumbered her.
She was constantly doing, getting, answering, helping. It
was a lot of work, a lot of preparation, and a lot of energy
but it seemed to function well. And because she had a
limited amount of children, Janie was able to adjust her
program to fit into each child's individual interests.

Janie's neatly formatted, cleverly graphic'ed

WEEKLY PROGRAM
Benji: Cooking, Baking
Austin: Construction, Blocks, Fine Motor Skills
Katie: Music, Instruments, Dance
Marco: Role Playing, Action Figures
Brian: Birthdays, Birthdays, Birthdays
Joey: Dinosaurs

*Written in, between the bottom corner graphic of a
basketball and the center graphic of a set of blocks:*
Ashley: TBD???

The Swapping Days program made it fun - some days
they'd all cook with Benji, other days they would build
high block towers with Austin Sawyer, or her own little
Katie would want music; they'd draw and paint and make
mucky messes depending on who's 'Day' it happened to
be.

During the kids' free playtime, Janie safety-gated
herself into her kitchen as the kids shared, or more
accurately, didn't share the toys in the dining room, never
out from under her watchful gaze or away from range of

her trained ears. If necessary, Janie knew from experience that she could leap the safety gate in a single bound. She could name that scream in two notes - Frustration, Fun, Pain. It was all just part of the practice.

Actually, not so much practice any more, it was her whole life.

So, every day, Janie would sit at the small sanctuary of her kitchen table with the biggest, hottest, strongest cup of coffee she could possibly extract from the dark-roasted grounds, dutifully taking notes in each of the children's journals. These few moments of relative peace coincided with the end of what Janie considered to be the most telling time of the day, Circle Time. Janie learned more about the families and the children during those quiet, conversational thirty minutes than most parents would ever know, or most likely ever want to imagine.

"My daddy isn't sleeping in my mommy's bed."

"Oh really, Benji?"

"Yeah, he's sleeping on the couch. He gets to watch TV all night."

"I have a big TV."

"Do you, Ashley? You're very lucky."

"And we eat our dinner in front of it and we order our food out all the time."

"That's nice."

"Daddy can't make dinner. We have take out!"

"My uncle likes dinner, he eats a lot, he's as big as a tractor."

"Austin, a tractor? Really?"

"Yes, he told me."

"Wow."

Given an attentive audience, the kids didn't censor their language. It was one of the things that made Janie glad she did daycare. It is good to be with children, you always know what they think of you. They were, for the most part, straight, true - just demanding they be loved outright.

No questions, just love me.

Really, who wouldn't like to be like that?

It was most often easier to deal with the kids than with their parents. Reading their needs had been a practice in intricate translation of annoying subtext and irritating insinuation. Once or twice, as she sat trying to decipher what a mother or father was really trying to pull out of her as they hemmed and hawed about discipline styles and the Berber method and "Parents Magazine this month told me I should be…," Janie wanted to scream out loud, "What is the problem?! PLEASE FOR THE LOVE OF GOD, JUST SAY IT!"

Patience with kids? Pretty easy.

Patience with adults who should know better? Very, very hard work.

Not that all that the kids said was twenty-four karat gold either. The stuff that did spill out of the darlings' mouths with the graham cracker crumbs and the boxed grape juice could get a little questionable. Janie would occasionally have to hold in a giggle or bite her lips to keep from smiling. But she had made it her own practice to keep her mouth firmly shut. She knew that it would keep her as well as her business safe and let people know they could trust her. It worked against her occasionally, because most people who don't talk are usually surrounded by those that do.

Speaking of Stacie, Janie was getting a little annoyed with her sister-in-law. She was late to pick up Benji and Marco and Janie knew exactly why. Billy Smitts was supposed to show up for Ashley in about fifteen minutes, everyone else had left and Janie was going to sit down with him to discuss whether or not she felt Ashley was a good candidate for her daycare. *Stacie had all the transparency of a big bay window. Washed down with vinegar. Wiped off with newspaper.*

T-minus ten minutes and counting.

T-minus Five,

Four,

Three,

Two,

AH! Here pulls up the little red sports car with the two car seats jammed in the back. Stacie blocked the driveway, popped out with her sunglasses on and her blonde hair casually tousled and guess-who is pulling down the street. Billy Smitts' long black Mercedes sedan pulls in front of the Hadley home. Bobby opened the door for Billy and *what is that?* Another long, lean, tanned female leg is showing out of the back seat. *That can't be another one, can it?* Janie practically pushed through the screen to get a glimpse of the face. *Could it seriously be two in one day?* And wait, oh Stacie is waiting at her car door, trying to look busy while Billy is getting out of his car. This is embarrassing and *Oh my God, it is a new girl! Wow!* Janie stifled a shocked laugh in her hand.

Billy was still leaning over into his car and Janie called out to Stacie to save her further embarrassment. "Stacie!"

Stacie pretended not hear her.

Louder, "Stacie! Benji and Marco have been waiting."

Stacie, gritting her teeth, gestured towards Billy.

Janie shook her head 'no', silently laughing, "STACIE! BENJI AND MARCO ARE COMING OUT TO YOU NOW. I'VE GOT THEIR STUFF."

Stacie's heat vision scorched through her sunglasses, down the asphalt driveway and sliced right through Janie's heart. Luckily, the deadly wound cauterized quickly and Janie found she was fully able to smugly escort her two little nephews down the stairs and into their mother's arms. Stacie packed them begrudgingly into the car seats, got in the driver's seat and scowled at Janie, "Ruin my fun."

Janie smiled patiently, "Bye boys, see you tomorrow." To Stacie, "Go home to Frankie. I've got business."

"Hmm, business." The red sports car tooled off, but not before honking at Billy Smitts' ass hanging out of his open car door.

Janie took a deep breath, *to the sideshow we go,* "Hello, Mr. Smitts."

"Hello, Janie."

"Do your friends want to come in?"

"Huh? Oh uh, no."

"We're going to be a few minutes."

"They don't mind."

"Sure?"

"Yep."

Janie walked over to the open driver's window. "Hi Del, Hi Bobby. Coffee?"

They both looked at their boss through the windshield, who shrugged his finely muscled shoulders, "Oh, yes, ma'am."

"It's Janie. How do you take it?"

"Both black," Bobby replied.

"Mine with sugar please, two," Del leaned over.

"How about your passenger?"

A sweet young warble came from the back seat. "No thank you."

"Soda, juice, a water maybe?"

The trilling bird chirped again, "I have some back here."

"Okay." To the drivers, "Be right out."

Billy followed Janie through the side door into the house. "Where's my girl?" he asked quietly.

Janie, "She's in the living room, resting on the couch. She's with Katie and Brian."

Billy disappeared into the room and returned in a second to the kitchen, "She's asleep."

"We wore her out. Wait here, I'm going to get the coffees." She hefted the large pot of dark, almost pitch black liquid. "You're a fan, aren't you?"

"Big one."

"I'll get you some. I make it kind of strong though. So if you think you can handle it…" She filled up three mugs.

"Yes, Sarcastro. I am one of the highest ranked coffee drinkers in the West." He smiled at her.

She smirked, "Don't try and make nice with me. I have already decided that I do not like you, which is making my choice about today very difficult to swallow." She handed him a steaming cup. "Cream and sugar right there."

"So, you'll take Ashley?" he rapped his silver rings on the table.

"Hold up, be right back." Janie went out with the cups and in a flash, was back. She leapt back up the stairs and he noted her athletic stride appreciatively.

"You've had coffee all ready?"

"Yep, coffee makes me a better mother. Reflexes like a cat." She sat down, *let's get this over with.* "Okay, I may have given you a hard time this morning and although it wasn't exactly professional, I thought the message was pretty clear."

"Crystal."

"I don't know who you are really but you have proved to be able to charm people who are close to me to convince me to do something I didn't want to do. That means you're dangerous. I don't mean physically, well physically you're… uh, fine, not 'fine' but okay… I mean… forget it." She sighed. "What I mean is you are manipulative. You call it charm, I call it false. In my home, in this business, I need to know that the people coming in and out of this house are people who I can trust and who trust me. I take the care of these kids seriously and their physical safety and emotional well-being are my priorities, even if it means that I might piss off a client. And when it comes right down to it, my kids are here." Janie took a deep breath. "So, if it was simply a decision based on my experience with just you, I would say 'no.' The loudest 'no' you've probably ever heard. But Ashley, on the other hand, is a sweet and intelligent girl which makes me think better of you. Although only very, very slightly."

"Okay." He sounded very, very slightly amused.

Janie went on, "She is in need of a strong female in her life – she mildly challenged me today – no, it's fine - it means to me that she is growing up into a strong independent girl. But I would also read into it that it would seem that she is used to having her own way. I am assuming that she did have her way with the previous nanny or nannies." Janie thought for a second, "Oh, like father, like daughter."

"I was waiting for that, you know," he shook his head.

"Anyway, I will take her. I need to know more about her mom though, is she in the picture?"

Billy was serious for the first time since Janie had met him; he cracked his knuckles and sat up straight. Janie took notice. "Her mom, my ex-wife, is in Europe. Previously, she had limited custody of Ashley and now, only visitation due to a drug problem. Ashley's been only with me for about two years now."

"How many nannies in the two years?"

"Three."

Janie just shook her head, her shoulders dropped, "Oh, Billy, not good."

"Yes, I know." He didn't know why he was suddenly playing the role of the straight shooter, but it was something to experience. This woman was unsettling, not unpleasant, but he knew she was telling him the truth. She spoke to him and it didn't seem to matter to her what he thought at all. She was just compelled to say exact words so he could understand how she felt. *When in Rome, I guess.*

"Doing your best?"

"Yep."

"Just keep your hands off the help."

"Well, now that won't be a problem will it? You are a married woman. Am I clear?"

"Crystal," Janie repeated back to him. She pulled out some paperwork and a notebook. "These are her release forms, medical information form, a copy of my license and this is Ashley's journal. I write down her day's activities, health issues. You're welcome to call me to talk about any of the information in the journal but it mostly serves as daily update for you and a paper trail for me. So, if there are any meds you need me to give her, you write 'em in there with instructions, times, et cetera, okay? Probably your best way to communicate with me. See you tomorrow." She gave him a tight-lipped smile, took his mug, stood up and dumped it in the sink.

He took the hammer-subtle hint. He went and gathered up the sleeping Ashley and Janie helped him out to his car.

"Thank you, Janie," the two fellows in the front chorused as they handed over the empty mugs. "That was some strong coffee," Del grinned.

"Bye guys."

Billy turned to her but she was heading back up the driveway. Del's eyebrows shot up as he watched his boss run to her and catch her elbow.

Billy, "Thank you, Janie."

She shrugged him off, "You might want to save that."

"Well, I also wanted to say that Del will drop her off and pick her up. He'll also have some of my legal paperwork for you as well. Can you and he take care of that tomorrow night?"

"Absolutely."

"A pleasure doing business."

"Here's hoping." She shook his outstretched hand and he smiled right into her black eyes.

She had gotten in after her driveway conversation to the phone ringing and her little cherubs awakening from their slumber. "Hello?" she answered and kissed the two sleepy foreheads that filed into the kitchen.

"How'd it go today?" Scotty sounded hopeful.

"It was fine, Scott. His daughter is very sweet."

"So you accepted? He's going to have her at the house?"

She sighed, "Well, you know I have a soft spot for strays."

Scotty was beside himself, "Oh man, I'd kiss you if I were there!"

"Yeah, it'll be all right, I think. I still don't like him though. Although he's apparently a real stud."

"Janie, I don't think it would hurt you to be nice... a stud? Did you just say, he's a stud?"

"Yeah, he showed up here with a blonde this morning and a different one this evening. If I weren't a staunch feminist or even not, say, a woman, I'd be seriously impressed."

"Ah, to be single again."

"Ugh, if you want to live through that again."

"It wasn't that bad!"

"Oh Scotty! Yes, it was." Janie expressed.

"We got through it okay."

"That's because we were different, we were upfront about what we were looking for. I was so sick of trying to be something I wasn't. With you, it was just different - good different, but totally, completely different."

"Well, yeah, honestly, I can't even imagine what it would be like to be single anymore. Life is just easier with a real partner."

"You're not kidding." Janie thought, "So, are you going to be home maybe earlier tonight?"

"Oh, man, I forgot to tell you my good news! We are being... what is that noise? Is everything okay?"

"Oh, Katie, Brian, hold on..." Katie and Brian had begun a power struggle over a pirate ship. The very familiar sound of bickering stopped bothering Janie years ago, and she had learned through some serious trial and error that her kids usually could work it out better themselves, under some close supervision, of course. Parental involvement was best used as a last resort, when the grousing gained the potential to turn into some sort of Pee Wee Ultimate Fighting tournament.

The problem here, Janie had guessed, was that as their father's exposure to their normal sibling squabbling had been so limited, it really just bugged him. Janie got it; she had some seriously tough days too; those days when you were willing to poke out your eardrums with toothpicks to make the noise just stop. So when Daddy was around, Janie made it a practice to try and intervene early with the petty quarrels rather than to have Scotty's nerves suffer.

She muted the phone, "Katie, Brian... Daddy." She acted out zipping her mouth shut and tiptoeing, then she hooked her thumb towards the living room. Katie and Brian giggled at their mother's silly antics but understood their special secret code. "Thank you." She called after them as their exaggerated baby steps led them into the living room. Janie put the phone back to her ear, pushing the Talk button. "Sorry, what was that, Scotty?"

"Everything okay?"

"Just fine."

He dove in, pleased to share his business report without interruption, "Oh Janie, its great news! We're being courted by a huge publishing company and we are going out to dinner with them tonight. I'll be home probably after you're in bed."

"Oh, okay." Janie sighed, her shoulders drooping resignedly. *Must be supportive. I've got to be supportive.* "Well, good luck!"

"Thank you, maybe it'll be just what we need!" He effused, "Let's hope it's a victory for both of us today. I'll talk to you more about it in the morning. Love you."

"Love you." A weight pulled at her neck, tension knotting back there. *Oh, a hot shower.* "Bye."

"Bye, honey." Scotty hung up.

She ticked off on her fingers of one hand up one way and down the other:

After dinner,
and bedtime
and picking up
and the vacuuming
and the dishes
and the laundry

and the kids' paperwork
and set up for tomorrow,
a serious hot shower would be good.
She sighed.

Within moments of the chaotic comings and goings, the various names and faces that made up most of the living that went on daily in her house, the silliness and volatility brought on by this new and unusual influence, today, Janie noticed the complete and total silence it had all left behind. It stole over her quickly as she sat at the kitchen table, like the ocean tide stealing up to meet her toes, gliding in to drench her knees, chilling the small of her back, enveloping her shoulders, suffocating her with its depth and its unfathomable strength. Her head was below the surface and the dull roar in her ears was the ocean's version of silence – churning disquiet, inexplicable sound, pressure. Her home was just a deep and encompassing silence, filled with what seemed like everything in the world and absolutely nothing.

Slowly, billowing slowly out from underneath her, an eerie presence that had been exposed by the stillness, its dark, murky tentacles stretching, feeling its way up her body, Janie felt something grab at her heart. She didn't panic, she wouldn't panic, she won't panic. She forced her breathing to calm, and pushed her lungs against the odd, stifling sensation. She could fight it, it rattled her a little, but she could fight it back.

Janie's mind raced as she sought to understand what that all was, where it had come from. Zeroing in on a particular memory, like flipping through a photo album and stopping on something that caught her eye, that pressure seemed so familiar to her. A physical strain of overwhelming, almost panic – like the odd, heavy pressing feeling of the flat edge of the cardboard moving boxes against her thirteen year old chest, the contents shifting and stabbing through the thin brown flimsy paper. She was taking them down the stairs to her mother's car, the weight of her father's eyes watching her as she had tried to smile and say goodbye. 'I'll see you this June,' her throat was scorching and…

STOP.

NOW.

The children, the kids.

It's just too quiet, she assured herself.

She wouldn't admit it, but fear rallied her tired body; she hurried to the living room to her children, took up her two babies on her lap, kissed their cheeks, tickled their bellies and induced their sweet laughter, chasing the pregnant silence, the empty fear and the disquieting fatigue of stupid, useless memories away.

"Come on sugarplums, let's go make dinner."

Chapter Five
Stacie's 199Sometime

"He's going to be such a great father," Janie, her chin had been on her hand, her big black eyes all moony, sighing over her Early Childhood Ed textbook.

"And you, such a great mom," Scotty had returned over his Business Stats spreadsheets. He had put his hand over Janie's, squeezed and had returned it to let his fingers continue flying nimbly over his calculator keys.

"Yeah, okay." Stacie, her incredibly over-plucked eyebrows had been raised dramatically, two penciled-in V formations flying from her forehead in search of better climate. She had looked from one to the other as a young Scotty and Janie had gazed admiringly into each other's eyes. *How did we seem to always get to this conversation? I was fricking talking about the Beta frat bash next week.* "Talk to you guys later." Stacie had had to leave the living room of the tiny two-bedroom campus apartment and find solace in Frankie's tidy little room.

Frank had looked up at her from his Economics textbook as he lounged on his little plaid flannel hospital-cornered twin bed, "What's wrong?" he had laughed at the grimace on her face.

"Oh, the Mutual Admiration Society was getting to me." She had sighed, "Do they ever go drinking? Party? Do anything but plan what brand of minivan they're going to buy in six point two years?"

"No, not really." Frankie had grinned at her; she slid up next to him, laying in the cramped space on the dormitory issue bed.

"I mean, what about now? Don't they just ever drop the whole married act and deal with now? College? Best time of our lives is supposed to be now! Jesus. Now. Now is fun."

Frank had nuzzled her neck, "Now is fun."

Stacie had been too irritated by Mister And Soon-To-Be Missus Perfect to be convinced of Frank's concurrence, as well as to comprehend her own contribution to the Irony Continuum as she had brushed him off, "Oh, not now Frank." She had lain there, mulling, while he had finished reading his assigned chapters.

Truth be told, whenever she had looked at Scotty and Janie, Stacie had thought she had never seen two people more perfect for one another. She'd only known them for a few months but from the interaction she first witnessed between the two of them, they both seemed to be facing in the same direction with clear plans for the future and what their lives were going to be like, where they would live and how many children they had planned on having. They even spent time together planning their wedding, which according to schedule, would be held shortly after Scotty finished his graduate program.

It seemed that was how they spent most of their time actually – planning, plotting out their future. Scotty and Janie rarely went out, "saving for stuff for the house," Scotty would proudly declare. "We'll have her school loan paid off and then we can put the rest toward renovating Janie's Dad's house."

Renovations? Saving? Loans Paid Off? What the hell?

Cheap Booze, Possibly Dangerous Sex, and Overdue Credit Card Bills - now THAT was what college was supposed to be about.

Still, Stacie had been in awe of two people who seemed so grown up, when all she cared about right now was what night 25 cent beers were available at which of the local bars in walking distance, for an easy stumble home. Two people, so young. So mature. *That's gotta be what marriage is about – being forward-thinking, serious adults. I mean, the girl had her own house.*

"Serious?!" Frankie had laughed, "Well, Scotty, yes. Janie, definitely no! Have you met the girl?"

"Yes! And she's always either got her head in some child psych book or she's in some type of business conference with her husband to be."

"Ah, that's just around Scotty. He's Mr. Serious. Always has been, I mean, since we were kids. He knew he was going to school here when he was like twelve. But Janie, she's really funny. Talk to her sometime." Frankie had chuckled, "Get her to tell you some of the pageant stories, oh my God. Like the spray glue and the duct tape story - the way she told it, I sprayed Mountain Dew and vodka out of my nose, which you know what? It's painful."

"Wait, pageant stories?" Stacie had stopped, "That girl, out there? Was in pageants? Like beauty pageants?"

"Yeah, but not anymore, she quit 'em. She used to do lots of shit like that, I guess. Actually that's how she and Scotty met. She and I had a class together and her dad left her the house and her mom…"

Actually, Stacie didn't really get a chance to get to know Janie at all back then. A couple weeks later, Stacie started dating some cute frat boy that she had hooked up with during last winter break. Although, she was starting to realize that she had not much more in common with him than the fact that they both really got hot for his nicely defined abdominal muscles.

Janie did catch up with her one day as she sat for lunch alone in the Southern campus cafeteria, Stacie had watched the tall "beauty queen" trying to catch her eye and she had tried to look like she was busy studying. *Oh, who am I kidding?* She had looked up from her books and saw the girl heading her way. Watching her stride across the crowded café, *she's nothing special*, Stacie had thought, her eyes narrowing.

"Hi Stacie."

"Hi Janie," Stacie had answered coolly.

"How are you doing?"

"Fine. Great. Fine. How are you?" Stacie had straightened her spine and looked down at her books then pointedly back up at the tall girl standing across from her.

"Oh good, busy. Mid-terms. Last ones though, that's something to say, I guess." Janie had smiled. "Um, I wanted to tell you, I've been sorry that you haven't been around the apartment lately."

"Really?" Stacie's annoyed glare had softened. Girls usually didn't want her around, *threatened by a blonde with a cute bod,* Stacie had always confirmed with herself. It was weird to hear another female her own age say something like that; girls usually lose the universal camaraderie of girlhood some time around thirteen.

"Yeah, it was nice, you know, to have another girl around. It's hard sometimes, living with the Obsessive Compulsion Brothers by myself."

This had made Stacie laugh out loud, which only served to encourage Janie's humor.

"I've got The Scheduler with his trusty Day Calendar and Captain Meticulous, never without his Hand Sanitizer and Portable Vac. They could be a super hero team." Stacie had giggled even a little more, *Frankie was ridiculously clean, he trimmed his fingernails and toenails every single day, then dutifully vacuuming them off of the carpet in his room.* Janie had kept going, "Ridding the world of spare time and clutter, one poor misguided freshman at a time," Janie had smiled, "They could have costumes and masks, the whole nine."

People were coming towards Stacie asking if she needed the Heimlich. It had taken her a minute to get the image of the two brothers standing heroically in capes and tights out of her head. She finally had settled down, the remainder of the laughs punching their way out of her aching stomach. Janie was still smiling at her.

"Plus," Janie had added, "I think Frankie misses you."

Stacie had stiffened, "Oh." *So, here's the motive.*

"He just seemed happy when you were around. I haven't really seen him like that with anyone else. Sort of more relaxed, if you can call it that, and more silly and fun. It was nice to see. Frank's a nice guy."

"Yes, well, 'nice guys,' you know what they say," Stacie had frowned, feeling almost guilty. "So, did he send you as a messenger or something?"

"No, not at all," Janie had shaken her head, "I, uh, - I must be getting my very own compulsion - I just like to help out people I care about, you know? They are going to be my family and, it all comes around, right?"

"I haven't seen it." Stacie had sighed, dismissively looking down and opening her books again.

"Well, maybe I'll see you again." Janie had tried to sound positive. "Good luck with your mid-terms, Stace." Janie had turned to go.

"Yeah, thanks, you too." Stacie had shot off, but stole one final glance. Janie had given her a small wave as she walked out of the cafeteria. *Wow,* the thought came over Stacie even as she had fought to ignore it, *she really could be somewhat of a pretty girl.*

For an Amazon.

Chapter Six
Hunger Strike

Scotty woke Janie extra early the next morning. "Hey, sleepyhead. Janie. Wake up."

Janie opened an eye, "Hi. I missed you. How'd it go last night?"

Scotty was already dressed and excited for his day. He sat down next to her. "Amazing. They want to begin due diligence almost immediately. I just can't believe this windfall, Janie. First you and the Smitts deal and now me and Houghton Mifflin. Incredible. The bad news is that this is gonna take up so much more time."

"More time? More time how?" Janie asked suspiciously.

"Well, travel time and meetings and stuff."

"So, does this mean you won't be around here too much?"

"It won't be a huge change, probably just a few more weekends away and nights out." Scott slapped her thigh and stood up. "Nothing you can't handle. You're a pro! You've always got stuff under control here."

"No, that's fine. I just miss you. The kids miss you."

"I miss you guys, too. But we're sacrificing for us, right? We're doing the right thing for us and the kids' futures. Think about it, this deal goes on and we'll have the kids' college paid for, we can pay off our entire mortgage. We'll be set."

"I know. I just think about, you know, what are we missing right now?"

"Ah, can't be anything too important, honey." He smiled at her reassuringly, "Plus, it's not like I'm really gone, you always know where I am."

Del was dutiful in arriving for drop off and pick up of Ashley at the appointed time. He came in at around six pm in his own car and handed Janie a stack of paper almost three inches thick. "Standard Non-disclosure."

"Wow." She looked up at Del, "You know I have to read through this right?"

"Billy said you would."

"Oh ho, he thinks he's on to me, huh?"

"He gets on to most people pretty fast."

"Most of the women in a five mile radius, I'm sure." Del giggled.

Janie smiled up at the big man, "In all seriousness, knowing people, figuring 'em out, that's gotta be all part of the business... businesses... show business, right?"

"As far as I've seen, it's helped him out a lot with whatever he's working on. He's good at it too. He pays attention to what people say, how they say it, and he gets what he wants."

"I guess that makes sense, although honestly, I wouldn't have figured it. I always assumed celebrities would always just be too enthralled by the sound of their own voices, blah, blah, blah." She absentmindedly mimed a hand puppet.

Del giggled again.

"Coffee, Del?"

"I was hoping."

Janie looked at the massive stack in her hand. "Let's make it dinner. You and the kids eat and I'll read, okay?"

"That would be wonderful."

"It's a piece of cake getting dinner ready with you here."

Del smiled up at her, "Smells good."

He seemed to be a pretty pleasant guy. The children talked around him as he sat at the table. They were making plans for Brian's ever-favorite topic - birthdays. Their plans were complete with themes, cakes, hats, games, *you name whatever a couple of five year old girls and a three year old boy could come up with and, there you go.* Del didn't even seem to mind when they commandeered his newspaper for folding pirate hats. She laughed at the sight of him sitting good-naturedly with a paper triangle over his massive bald head.

Cooking was one of the two of Janie's more Zen activities during the day, the other being the backend of all of this preparation - dishwashing. As disdainful as many people could be about both activities, more pointedly the latter than the former, Janie could at least appreciate the time it gave her to kind of think and plan for the next projects, work out what still needed to be done for the night or what paperwork needed to be done, all with the most crucial element of keeping her insanely busy.

But usually, the moments of relatively peaceful frenzy chopping vegetables, checking the timing of the courses, and monitoring temperature were punctuated by interruptions of very immediate needs – juice boxes, shoelace help, answers to the ever pressing question of "Why can't I have a cookie before dinner? Oatmeal and raisins are good for you." To have another body there, occupying the children's attention for the span of the prep time was like a small and gracious little heaven. In fact, the only interruption she had was a call from Frank, asking her about Benji and Marco's lunch. He didn't want to feed them the same for dinner.

When she was first married, Janie used to really enjoy company in her home. But she and Scotty rarely had their own dinners together anymore, never mind a couple of friends or a client, or even Frank and Stacie. But back in the old days – *"old days,"* Janie laughed, *six years ago,* - she and Scotty ran a pretty good dinner party. On the party duty roster, Janie was listed under "Food" and "Dry Observational Humor Which Not Everyone Appreciated." And small talk eluded her a little. So, alone in a room with people she didn't know all that well, without liquid fortification, she could be caught with her verbal pants down, with not much more than a "Uh, so, what's new?" or a "Hey, nice shirt," to save her.

But Scotty used to be really good at that part. At a dinner, he could handle the "Where are you from? What do you do? Did you hear about..." type of things that had always given her some trouble. But nowadays, unless she had an actual topic or question to address, she had learned that it was a hell of a lot easier to talk to new people if she herself just shut up and listened, taking her conversational cues from them. *Without backup, you've gotta work with what you've got.*

Also, to be totally honest, Janie kind of assumed that no one really had any interest in her little profession, except for maybe when they may have had a need for it. In social conversations, Janie had a little inkling from the look on their face, their posture, the glaze that would come over their eyes that the person who had just asked her about the children and how she was doing with the daycare was really just being polite, serenely waiting until her lips would *just please stop moving so that they could launch into their own diatribe about their exciting and fascinating hey-you-know-what-Janie?-I-actually-get-to-leave-my-house life.*

After a while, she stopped answering the questions with anything more than a smiling "Going fine, and you?" And then she would listen. She would try and really listen, see what they were all about.

Watching Del sitting quietly amongst the children's chattering, Janie concluded he was probably a good listener, like she tried really hard to be. So, maybe even if Scotty had been there, Del might not be given much to small talk either. Janie figured that she and Del, as they were now pretty much working together, would probably get along fine. *And plus, even if they didn't,* she grinned to herself, *no one ever cared too much about conversation after they taste my food.*

Emeril? Ha! Rachel? Oh honey, nice try! Old School Julia? Hell yeah.

But, okay, Billy Smitts - the subject had been annoying her and she had been trying to put it off, but the appeal of faulting that guy was just way too strong *– an asshole like that - good at listening to people? Pfft.* Janie shook her head.

But Del had just said it.

You know what? I bet he's not actually listening to anyone, he's probably just figuring out how to use them. Or get some sort of information. Hell, it has to be easy if all you need to do is steal their social security numbers and run illegal credit and/or criminal record checks.

Just... it seemed so unlikely.

Billy seemed to be such... such an actor - so full of shit, so oddly felonious and clearly, ultimately self-serving. Pretty much like every other celebrity who had ever pawned themselves on MTV, or VH-1 or E!.

But there it was, on a big ugly billboard pasted right in front of her, Del's large, somehow amiable but yet still somehow intimidating face, his vast hand extended into a friendly wave and just above the fingers, in story-high letters, "BILLY SMITTS PAYS ATTENTION."

Could he really be something ... ugh... like me, in that way? The conversations she had had with him, when she felt like being civil and he felt like being a human being, were, admittedly, surprisingly easy. That was new. For her, anyway. For him, that's probably just part of his whole persona – annoying, celebrity, charming bullshit.

Still, the improbable thought kept picking at her, popping into her head as she read through the paperwork, forcing her to mull over that irritating disclosure throughout the rest of their dinner.

And maybe, it gave her something to think about after everyone had left.

"Where have you been?" Billy grilled Del as he came out of Ashley's room.

Del put his fingers to his lips, "She's asleep." He pulled Ashley's notebook out of his jacket pocket, "Janie asked me to give this to you. She put in the picture Ashley drew of you today. And she's copying the non-disclosure because you failed to include one for her to have in her files."

"Shit, Del. Is that where you have been this whole time? I've been home from the set since 7:30, by myself, all alone in the house. You could have called! Had I known, I could've sent Bobby to make copies." He shook his head, "Call me next time you're late, Del. I was starting to worry about you two." He sighed and looked at the big man, "You hungry? I mean, should we order something for you?"

"Nope."

"Did you eat?"

"Yes."

"She fed you and Ashley?"

"Yes. I can pick up Ashley everyday if you want me to."

"What, what did she make you?" Billy sheepishly asked.

"Roasted garlic chicken that opened up from this huge breaded crust – I've never seen anything like that before but it was amazing. And then there was fettuccine with some kind of pesto sauce and broccoli with parmesan cheese."

"Oh, wow." Billy looked thoughtful.

"Oh and salad." Del smiled in remembrance as his boss stood next to him, hugging his shoulders in sweet physical agony. "With this homemade raspberry dressing."

Billy salivated, "Did she have dessert?"

"Uh-huh." Del was enjoying dinner the second time around. "She and the kids made chocolate-covered strawberries today so we ate those. That little kid, uh, Benji, apparently he loves to cook. They were so good! Dark chocolate and milk chocolate with white chocolate drizzled over them. Oh! And that coffee, man she makes good coffee!" Del eyed Billy, coyly. "What did you have?"

"Craft services. Carrots, water. Woohoo." Billy said sullenly.

Del gave Billy a very self-satisfied smile.

"Oh man." Billy responded to Del, hurt. "That's just cruel, man. Cruel."

Chapter Seven
Getting to Know You

So it was out of sheer animal lust that Billy decided he must endear himself to the cagey Janie. The lust didn't fall under the sexual category - *although not that the girl wasn't somewhat appealing, if you were into that whole no-makeup, boring clothes thing* - but Billy's truly last unfulfilled salacious desire existed for the fact that he had a deep and continual longing, for food. Real food. Food you could smell and bite and taste and engorge yourself on, afterwards to gently fall into a satisfied slumber – like a big old male lion who'd just gorged himself on a morbidly obese zebra. Billy wanted zebra so bad. He hadn't eaten real food since 1995.

Last year, he had briefly employed a nutritionist to oversee his food intake and all those dietary freaks were those strict vegetarians, *veg-ohs... vegas... vegans, whatever.* Plus this ultrafit guy started sleeping with Ashley's nanny while Billy himself was doing her. And just as far as celebrity household hierarchy goes, to keep your job, you just don't fuck with the alpha male of the house.

The problem with Janie was, he couldn't endear himself to her in his usual manner. She didn't fall for the compliments no matter how earnest, the engaging smiles, the sweet looks. He had this one trick where he would look down, then quickly, the baby blues would come up from under his eyebrows, he'd cock his head slightly, flash a smile and then, the finishing touch on the person's forearm. Precisely executed, it had never, ever failed him. It had gotten him movie roles, music deals and - Christ! He had gotten laid with that look so many times he couldn't even keep count. And yet, this girl, this Janie, he got nothing. She just looked at the hand on her arm and then back up at his face with some sort of knowing smirk. It was maddening as hell and it made him laugh right out loud.

Billy had to be honest with her. And for an actor, there is really nothing harder to pull off than sincerity. But that was all she seemed to respond to, and even that was just a little. Still, he had been trying really hard for awhile, working on her territory, and still he wasn't getting any closer to getting the food from her directly.

So he employed his other dastardly plan - the leftover smuggling ring he had Del, Bobby and Ashley working, was closing in on zebra.

"Don't try to get around me, she says!" wolfing down a slice of medium rare roast beef that had been accompanied by an asparagus and twice-baked potato plate Del had brought back with him. "HA!"

"Well actually, boss," Del began, "she told me to tell you to cut out the middleman and just stay at her house for dinner tomorrow night."

The lion's jaws full, "She knows?" licking his chops.

Del replied, "Yeah, and she said that trying to use me and Bobby was bad enough, but playing Ashley into this, was just plain shameful."

Billy, "Goddamn it."

Janie had been on to him for about a week. Ashley had ratted him out during a Circle Time when she described how Daddy was getting fat from all the food Janie was giving him. *He's hungry again today; could they help Janie make those strawberries one more time? Although, could they make some extra just for her? Daddy liked those so much he wouldn't share.*

Chapter Eight
Ass Magnets

Billy had gotten off the closed set early that day so he decided he would pop over to Janie's house for the whole afternoon. He should have gone for a workout or a run or something - the director was getting a little pissed at him being so puffy - but he just didn't feel like it. He wanted to see more how Ashley spent her time during the day; also Janie had told him that although she knew he wanted his presence to be kept private, he, as a parent, was always welcome to spend time at her house with the children. So, that open invitation plus the request to dinner tonight made it an easy decision to make.

Janie was surprised to see Del dropping off Billy in her driveway. She ran to the door, "I'm not letting you in," she called out. "You are a despicable person."

"How any more so than you thought before?" he laughed.

"You have to promise me that if I feed you, you will not take food away from your five year old daughter any more."

"I didn't take the food from her," he rolled his eyes.

"But you do admit you took food not intended for you."

"Nope. Won't admit anything."

She smiled, "Then I will not admit you."

"You can't disinvite me into your house. You can't even do that to a vampire. Besides I dressed up for the occasion." He was dressed directly from the set wardrobe, his piercings out, clothed in a beautiful grey tropical wool suit.

"Are you supposed to be a vampire?" she called out from her door. "Because I definitely have garlic."

"No, I am playing the evil, Irish pirate drug lord intent on funding the IRA bombings until England gets its ass out of Ireland. I even get to say, 'Argh!' once or twice."

"Are you always the bad guy?" As he stepped around her driveway, kicking his duffel bag of street clothes to the length of its tether and then reeling it back in.

"Yes, mostly. It's the whole singer/rock star thing; we make so much more interesting bad guys than heroes. Plus, for me, the bad guy thing is so much easier than trying to be the earnest and hardworking and honest type. Just doesn't seem to ring true."

"That makes complete sense." She held the door open, "The kids are having free playtime. You hungry?"

His stomach was aching, he desperately wanted in. He sniffed the wafting scent of baking coming from the door behind Janie. *This is what Hansel and Gretel went through.* But he relented, no cute comebacks, no witty lines, he finally gave himself over to the last place he really ever intended to go - honesty. "Yes."

"Okay then, we've got a promise from you?"

"All right, I promise." He said as he ran in the door, afraid she'd close it if he had given her the time. "Argh, ye vixen!"

She quickly made him a Dagwood-worthy sandwich - leftover ham, bacon, thick slices of American cheese, pickles, plum tomatoes and spinach, spiced mayonnaise and brown mustard on wheat bread she had baked with the kids that morning.

"This is too much. Fresh baked bread? You, my dear, are trying to impress me. And oh my God, there's bacon!" he melted.

She laughed, "I didn't know you were coming this early."

It was the first time he had heard her laugh since the night they had met. He smiled, "You lie. You must have sensed it, like Spidey-senses, knowing when evil is afoot. Only instead of fighting crime, you feed your enemies a continual supply of food until they are fat, bloated and comatose."

"Sorry," she shrugged.

"Oh, don't be," he chomped, asking with his mouth full, "So what is on the agenda for the remainder of the day?"

"I have notes for the journals and making you lunch has thrown off my schedule a bit. Do you think you could occupy the kids for a few minutes while I finish up?"

"I owe you don't I? Mmmmmm. Too good." And he inhaled his last bite. "Could I change first?"

"But you look so handsome," she protested, immediately regretting it. *Oh, stupid girl. See? You just shouldn't talk!* Sarcasm swooped in for a weak attempt to save her, "Plus it would be so practical, playing with the kids, in a suit."

He looked at her quickly, what she had just said didn't escape him. She read it on his face. "Oh, please, you wouldn't be half as famous if you weren't so pretty."

He looked surprisingly shy for a millisecond, but then grinned devilishly, "Be right back."

He returned in a t-shirt and jeans, his knuckles covered in his large silver rings, the silver barrel rod through his left eyebrow, his feet bare. "I forgot my shoes."

"I always wondered, do those hurt?" She poked at his eyebrow piercing.

"Yes, when you do that." He rubbed his forehead. "Actually that one wasn't bad. This one hurt like hell," lifting his t-shirt to reveal a stunningly rippled chest and a silver ring embedded in his left nipple.

She reached out involuntarily but then withdrew her hand. "Ouch."

"And those didn't hurt half as much as..." he caught her gaze and purposefully dragged it to his crotch.

"What?!" It dawned on her what he was trying to convey. "Oh my GOD!"

He burst into laughter, "I'm kidding. The thought of that gives me the willies."

"Willies don't cover it." She shuddered. "All right, go to the kids. All this friendliness is making me nauseous." He smiled at her and *again, with the contagious!* she couldn't help but return it.

"Yeah, I just figured you got laid last night."

"You are continuing to operate under the notion that I like you," she called after him, "And it is just not true."

Billy stepped out of the room and waited upstairs as the parents of the Sawyer and Sweeney kids came in for pick up, taking the opportunity for a quick smoke and maybe a look around. He opened her window, lighting up. It only took him a moment poking around in Janie's room until he found the buried treasure. "Argh, let's see what the girl's really like." He chuckled evilly, white boycuts, cotton bras, *bo-ring*, tank tops, *okay, sort of hot.* He rummaged through most of the deep drawer coming up with not much interesting booty, he sighed. *Poor, repressed little Ja... hold on! What is this?!* His fingers had hooked into a sweet, little red lace teddy. He shook it out in front of him, nodding with approval. *Good for you, dearie.* He dropped it back in the drawer.

Eavesdropping, he wondered how Janie dealt with those parents all the time. They talked on and on to her about their kids for what seemed like forever. But Janie was pretty patient and offered a suggestion or two to their endless questions of the right way to deal with this issue and that.

He heard Janie laugh again and Billy decided he liked the sound of it. *The girl just needs a good time.* Bored with eavesdropping, he wandered slowly around her bedroom, looking at the pictures that scattered the room. Most of them were of Janie and Katie and Brian. Janie, Katie and Brian at the beach, the park, Disneyland, Sea World. *Where is Scott in these pictures?* He must have been behind the camera. *Or maybe he wasn't there at all?* Billy thought about it, of all the times he had been at the house, Scott was never around. And Del and Bobby and hell, Ashley hadn't mentioned him. *Absent daddy.* One thing he could congratulate himself that he never had been. *One up on you there, Scotty. That girl's so strong. Maybe it put him off of her or something. Some guys can't take it. Oh well.*

Billy went to the door again and heard Stacie's voice and decided to keep looking around. *Wait a second,* the pic here on the bookshelf, *holy shit, who is that bird?*

Stacie knew something was up but couldn't put her finger on exactly what it was. "I could call a sitter and you could come out with me tonight once the kids are in bed. Just down to the bar, no big deal, okay?"

"No, um, Scott is supposed to come home earlier tonight and I was hoping to spend some time with him."

"Oh, okay. You sure? It might make your 'spending time with him' a little more fun?"

"Nope that's okay, thanks Stacie. You gonna go?"

"Uh-huh. Frank is working and I'm bored with him."

"You're awful, Stacie."

"Hey, no judging. We're not all celibate nuns married to the Saint Scotty." Stacie meandered around. "Are you sure you won't come out?"

"No thanks Stacie." Janie gave her nephews a kiss each. "See you tomorrow guys okay?"

"Bye Janie," Marco and Benji chorused.

"Your loss, honey." Stacie tossed over her shoulder on her way out. "Or maybe not."

Billy's footsteps were on the stairs, "True? Am I intruding on a night with Scotty? I can easily just grab a couple of plates of dinner and go."

"No, I assumed that since you stayed up there, I didn't want to rat you out."

"Well, thanks. But seriously, Ashley and I can head out…"

"Nah, don't bother. Scotty won't be home until after midnight. He called earlier to say he had to go out with the buyers."

"Well, that sucks, doesn't it?"

"Par for the course," she shrugged. "I'm not complaining. If this deal goes through, Scotty thinks we'll be set for awhile. He's been working so hard for this for so long." Janie turned her head. "Still, it would have been fun to go out. I don't get out too much. Too busy and it's just easier on me and the kids if I am just here."

Billy nodded, "I get it." His empathy was sincere, but with his little discovery in hand, he absolutely couldn't help but turn impish. "Hey, I found something upstairs that I want to know about."

"Oh dear lord, what is it?"

"Thi-is." He took the picture from behind his back.

"Oh no, that should be put away." She reached for the frame and he held on to it for dear life.

"You were a pageant queen? Oh, ho, you speak to me of being false - although, I can pretty much tell these..." he pointed to the photo, "...are not false - and you were in the Miss California pageant? Oh my word, woman, a pageant girl? How much more insincere can you get?"

"Ugh, my mom made me do them."

"Yes, that is what all daycare ladies who are trying to hide their true pageant passion tell themselves and anyone who will listen."

He was teasing her. It was good-natured and she felt no reason to rebuke him. *It was a little funny.* "I know! I have a dark past!" She said with mock horror. The children were drawn in to the sounds of silly talk and soon Katie, Ashley and Brian were involved in Billy's desperate game of keep away from Janie. The giggles were getting higher and louder just as a timer dinged in the kitchen.

"Dinner's ready!" Janie yelled and Billy shoved them all out of his way to beat them to the table.

Ashley in Katie's room and Brian finally quiet, Billy and Janie collapsed upon opposite sides of the couch, feet up, facing each other.

"I don't know how you do this everyday." The dark resonance of his voice rumbled through the cushions of the couch. She could feel it under her as she watched his fingers unknotting the masterpiece of his heavy, dark brows.

"Ah, this is nothing," Janie scoffed as he chuckled in disbelief, "but I have to admit, that this is usually how you will find me about this time every single day."

"There you go. You complain about not leaving the house but you didn't tell me that leaving is a physical impossibility."

"Exactly. Although, I believe it isn't so much a problem of my physical stamina but a flagrant misuse of something I think is called, an ass magnet, that has been embedded in these actual couch cushions. I'm thinking of contacting the manufacturer."

"He should be sued."

"Agreed."

"I mean, Christ, I don't even know when you would have time to like, go to the bathroom."

Janie laughed, "Oh, I've been caught with my pants down many a time."

Billy chuckled, "I can imagine."

"Ah," she yawned as she spoke, "Not a pretty picture."

"Not for the pageant portfolio?"

"Hush up, pretty boy," she said, exhausted, closing her black lashes over her eyes. She pulled out her ponytail elastic and ran her hands into her hair to massage where heaviness had put pressure on her scalp. "Ponytail headache."

"I remember those."

"You had long hair?"

"Grew it out for a role. Had it in the later nineties for about a year or so."

"Tee-hee."

"Did you just say 'tee-hee'?"

"Yeah, I just can't picture it," she yawned again. "You'll have to show me a picture sometime."

"It's gotta be on a website somewhere. We can look right now. It'll be good for a laugh."

"You don't find that weird?'

"What?"

"That you have websites with pictures of you readily available? That people have, just dedicated to you? It'd freak me out."

"Part of the job."

"Jobs," Janie yawned.

He laughed, "Yeah, jobs. It's what everyone wants, isn't it? Being recognized for your work?"

"It goes beyond recognition, Billy."

"I will admit, it isn't easy. Thus the easy access to the lovely cutouts you pasted on my daughter's project."

Janie laughed, "My point exactly. How do you deal with all of that? I could never deal with any of it."

Billy continued. "You have to realize that those PR firms plant a lot of that stuff out there."

"'Plant?'"

"Yep, okay, a celebrity pays his agency an exorbitant fee to keep him current and visible. To PR, that doesn't necessarily mean in a good way or in a bad, just visible. That's what makes their client hot, that's what gets their client jobs, that's what makes their clients money. So PR use the tabloids to boost visibility. They plant pictures, or leak information as to what their client is up to, where they are, who they are with and the papers go out and do their job."

"Its sort of a back-alley part of the business, isn't it?"

"Exactly, and a very powerful one, too. But you have to consider, that contractually they are supposed to both protect and market the image. But the protection part doesn't necessarily make the client money."

"Ah."

"So, in light of all of that, and despite all that you may see and what you might think, I am generally a very, very discreet man." Now it was Janie's turn to chuckle in disbelief. He continued, "I'm serious! And I'm actually pretty lucky. I've got Del – he's great about this stuff. I know that in and around LA, New York, I realize I'm fair game to anyone with a camera. But I'm away working, it's not so bad. And I know what precautions to take."

"Precautions?"

"Yeah, like, okay, I rent a house instead of staying in a hotel, cuts down on foot traffic and visibility. As long as I'm not out in public with some little bird, it's usually pretty safe; no one really needs to hear about it. It would take something unusual to surface to draw them up – like if I was out and about gallivanting about this little town all night with some chickie, they'd swarm into town like angry bees, droning over and over," he affected a buzzing sound to his voice, "'IS BILLY HEADED FOR THE ALTAR?'" which made Janie laugh a little, "Stuff like that. It's bad and then again, its business, the business is recognition."

"I understand the whole recognition thing, Billy. But I get acknowledgment from the kids and their parents and it doesn't involve half-naked pictures of me splashed on the internet or grocery store newspapers."

"See, in my opinion, it would be so much better if it did."

Janie laughed, "Yeah, I am sure that would draw in lots of business from the parents."

"Think of it, a whole new level of parental involvement – from the dads, anyway. Or maybe the moms. Nowadays, we just don't know."

She smiled drowsily, "No more talking now. Sleepy."

His eyes closed, "You could do a 'Ladies of Daycare' pin-up calendar." They sprung open again. "Wait, how do I know there isn't one out there all ready? I mean, I find out today you were Miss California..."

"Runner up."

"Yeah, sure. Next I'll learn you were in some sort of weird cooking fetish movie." He thought it over, "And I might look for that."

She chuckled softly. "Quiet. Sleep now."

"Come on, calendar, movie distribution, we'd make millions." He shut his eyes.

"Sshhh."

The house was completely quiet when Scotty walked in. The downstairs lights had been off except for in the living room so he strolled in to shut them out and head on up to bed. But on the big couch, on opposite ends, were his wife and the famous singer/actor Billy Smitts sound asleep. He wasn't exactly sure how to take this. He cocked his head to one side and then the other, opening and closing his mouth as though words out loud would sort this out, but none would come. *I mean, it looked innocent enough –* there were no blankets involved, their feet weren't even touching in the middle of the couch, and he often found Janie sound asleep here, if not in one of the kids' rooms, after he came home late at night.

Billy must have stayed late or something for Ashley. *Oh, Janie said she was inviting him for dinner!* Janie was so good with her clients. She must have finally realized that being nice to this guy was a smart plan, just like he had told her, especially considering how much he was planning on paying them. *I'll just wake him up then.* But then Scotty stopped again. *How do I wake up a movie star, or singer or whatever... just walk over there and tap him on the shoulder?* "Billy." He tapped. "Billy, wake up."

Snorting, Billy awoke and recognized Scotty through a haze of eyecrust. "Hey, my man. So sorry. No harm, no foul about the couch thing. The kids wore us out."

"Yeah, It's Janie, no worries," Scotty smiled at him.

Billy had snapped his phone open and called Del, "All set." He snapped it shut.

"That's pretty cool service there."

"Oh yeah, Del. He's good to have around." Billy stretched his arms over his head; the muscles tested the will of the seams of his shirt. "Oh man! Sorry, I'll go get Ashley."

"Billy, don't worry, she can sleep over, no problem."

"That would probably be better for her, rather than me rousing her up, plopping her in the car and getting her into bed again. Thanks." Billy yawned. "You sure?"

"Absolutely."

Billy stood up and the pageant picture clattered to the floor. Scotty picked it up. Billy laughed, "I was giving Janie a hard time about that. I didn't know she was ever into any of that stuff."

Scotty looked at the picture. "Her mom drove her into it. She was happy to give it all up after we met."

"Happy to give it up?"

"Yeah, she hated it."

"Really?"

"Her mom had these crazy ideas of TV and commercials and whatnot. She told her that she, Janie, shouldn't waste herself behind a husband and kids, like she did. I think her mom kind of wanted to live through her daughter. The irony of it was, all Janie wanted was her own home and her own family so that she could give her own kids what they wanted, rather than what she decided for them." Scotty thought, "It's why she's so good with them. She tries to understand them for who they are, rather than for what people want them to be. They gravitate to that, to her."

"Hmm, the kids do like her a lot."

"I think I was just the lucky guy who wanted to give all those things to her. I helped her get out of all that stuff her mom put her in."

"Lucky she had you then."

Scotty chuckled, "We're lucky all around."

Billy, "Well, I'll be off. Tell Janie I'll pick Ashley regular time tomorrow and thank her again for a great, great dinner."

"It was good?"

"Amazing."

"Hmm, good." Scotty rocked on his heels. "Well, goodnight, Billy. Please don't mind if I don't show you out. Ti-red." He started up the stairs.

"Um, what about your Miss California there?" He pointed to Janie, asleep on the couch.

"She's fine. She's a great sleeper, can sleep anywhere." He shook his head. "Plus…" He elbowed Billy knowingly, "…huge bed, all to myself, are you kidding?"

Billy just looked at him for a minute, like Scotty was in fact kidding him. When Scotty didn't turn around, go wake up his wife and take her up the stairs, he just faked a laughing smile. It was his most charming, hiding a barely imperceptible "You jackass," behind it.

"Well goodnight."

And Billy stood there and watched Scotty climb the stairs, turn into his room and shut out the light. He shook his head, searched the living room for a blanket, covered the girl and shut out the light.

Chapter Nine
Routine

Billy had been standing in the doorway from the kitchen to the dining room for what had to be about three straight minutes, watching Janie before he dared say a word. Ashley had spotted him almost immediately, but he put his finger to his lips, motioning for her to keep dancing with the rest of the kids. The smile he gave to his daughter stuck to his face. He tried to bite it back but it just kept broadening with each whirl of Janie's dark hair, each flail of her arms. She kicked and wiggled with ridiculous abandon to both the music and the hiccupping giggles of the children dancing around her. He really didn't want to say anything, he didn't want to disturb this perfect moment of absolute silliness but he was afraid that in any second now, he would burst into the uncontrollable laughter, right along with the kids. At this point, the best thing to do would be to just say, "So that's how you stay so skinny."

Janie jumped to the sound of his voice, leaping around to face him. She merely gave him a look and said disparagingly, "Oh. It's just you," to continue her unabashed boogie to Laura Berkner's latest and greatest. Janie spun and picked up each one of the kids for a turn as she waltzed, polkaed and mamboed around the room. And Billy cocking his head to watch her suddenly got caught in a thought, he couldn't help but sort of notice, *he was a man*

for chrissakes, and it was in healthy appreciation.
Healthy... observation. That she, Janie, she could kind of...
shake it... The song ended and Janie finally picked up the
remainder of the conversation with him, "You should see
my Playground Workout, the monkey bars are a killer."

"My trainers would want to see it, I'm sure. It would be
all the rage in Hollywood. You wouldn't be able to get near
a park in Los Angeles for under a thousand an hour, I bet."

"Well, actually, you've stumbled upon the last vestiges
of what used to be called, 'My Talent.'"

He laughed. "Dancing, huh? I think it was a good thing
you gave up pageants."

She shook her head, but a reluctant smile slowly forced
its way out.

Over the past couple of weeks, Billy had slowly been
becoming a fixture in her house. The food had driven him
there, but the laughter, the great smells, the noise of the
kids and finally, the company of the surprisingly funny
Janie made him want to stay. He picked up Ashley more
and more nights of the week. During his day, he found
himself taking mental notes of reasons to tease or argue
with Janie, just so he could linger a little longer. But it was
hard on him too. She didn't like when he slipped easily into
what she called 'celebrity mode,' attempting a well-worn
line on her. Janie would roll her eyes or shake her head and
say, "You have got a bad habit, there, sir. Who falls for
your line of crap?"

"Twenty years of practice and so far, everybody.
Except you." He would crack up at her indignance and then
sort of silently rebuke himself for trying too hard.

"Okay then, what went on with the whole pageant
thing?" Billy asked her across the very raucous dinner
table.

Janie groaned, "No, this is a dumb conversation."

"I genuinely want to know." Billy went on. "Scotty mentioned that you were in commercials and stuff."

"Yeah. My mom made me do it."

"Stage Mommy?"

"Uh-huh." Janie took a bite of her dinner. "Is that what started you off?"

"Sort of, but my mom wasn't pleased about me becoming anything but a classical pianist."

Janie snorted, "Oh, my, how far you've come from that!"

"Did you just snort?" Billy laughed and the kids giggled. "You are trying to change the subject, Miss California."

"I was runner UP!"

"Yeah so, spill."

"Stage Mommy had me in pageants since I was about thirteen. Not a great time for me and I kind of went along with it because I didn't think of anything else to do."

"You were thirteen. I can't even tell you what I was thinking about then."

"I know what you were thinking about then."

Billy looked down at his plate, cutting his meat. "Not in front of the children, dearie."

Janie laughed, "Anyway, I was in a whole bunch of pageants around, well, first here and then LA. My mom tried to hook me up with a children's agent. It… it didn't go well, so I sort of decided then I hated it and would stop doing it as soon as I could. She told me I could stop when I graduated college; it was sort of a hostage-tuition situation. I think she thought she would change my mind. She didn't."

"Hmmm," Billy thought.

"Hmm, what?"

"What was with the agent?"

She looked across the table at him and then decided to busy herself with Brian's plate. "What do you mean?"

"Pivotal moment you just mentioned. In acting, we would call that the 'causal moment,' or the reason why you are what you are."

"Not really, Billy." The corner of her lip turned down.

Boundary, impassible, he changed his line. "So you found Scotty, got married, had some kids and now run a daycare out of your home."

"Yep," Janie said. "It seemed logical. I wanted to be home with my kids, we needed money. I happen to like the little ones…"

"Couldn't think of a better way to spend the day. They are good to be with." Billy agreed.

He watched her eyes alight. "They are!" Janie was enthusiastic, *someone got that, finally*. "It's great to spend time with them. To listen to their little thoughts. They'll tell you all of them if you are interested. And most of the time, you learn the truth." She looked across at him again. "They also don't have any agendas, you know? All that they want is more cookies, or chocolate milk or attention. They won't try to take anything from you; they just want you to be near them."

"Very, very true, Mrs. Hadley." He smiled in what he hoped was a reassuring way. She was exposing a little more of herself than he thought she realized and he didn't want her to feel she couldn't do it again.

"Thanks," he shouldered the sleeping Ashley and grabbed her little backpack.

"No problem. She's a good girl, Billy, you should be proud."

"I am."

"I'll take Del's plate to the car and you can give it to him when you get home."

"Thanks." They walked down the driveway. Billy put Ashley in her seat and got behind the wheel.

"Don't eat it. I will ask Del tomorrow morning if he got it."

"Don't trust me in the least, do you?"

"No."

Billy laughed, "Good night, Janie."

"See you tomorrow."

And he drove away. Janie looked up at her big silent house, rubbed the back of her neck and headed inside.

So would begin the routine. True to his word, Scotty was rarely around. Traveling back and forth to Boston would keep him away for days at a time. It didn't change Janie's life too much. But she was beginning to feel as though her usual smattering of loneliness was pressing itself into a permanent stain on her life. That stifling feeling had been slowly constricting itself around her. The silence had been sneaking in on her at odd times; like late at night, when she would put herself to bed.

When they had first been married and Scotty would have to go away, Janie remembered climbing over on to his side of the bed, laying her head on his pillows, legs curled up, her hand under her head, mimicking how he slept. It gave her some odd sort of comfort, like it kept another presence in the house. She couldn't remember the last time she had done that.

At least, for now, Janie could occupy some of her thoughts, making adjustments to these two new people in her life. It seemed to be working out okay. And it had become really nice to be able to actually have a grown-up conversation with someone, *well sort of grown-up.* Billy was not half as psycho as his original behavior had led her to believe. His daughter was a telling sign that underneath all the crap he spewed out he could have actually been a pretty decent person, *you know, if he was normal.*

But, all that celebrity living, he's probably pretty well past redemption now, she smiled to herself, *but then again, aren't we all?*

Billy was funny at least and he seemed to handle Janie's biting tongue and odd jokes with a good amount of humility and equal sarcasm. *That can make up for a multitude of things, I suppose.* She wondered what he was driving home to tonight. She imagined a bevy of young actresses waiting for him, all in the throes of passion just at the sound of that sinfully chocolate voice. She laughed at the ridiculous thought, equally ridiculous in the fact that she realized there had just left a man who could have actually had that happen.

Janie's prediction wasn't too far off, except for the actual amount - just one, still a hot little number, an "under five" twenty-two year old from the set, that he had told to come by later. She could barely wait until he put his daughter to bed. He made her pass the time in the kitchen. After Ashley was gently tucked in, he led the sweet little blonde actress into his inner sanctum. He made the bird sing a couple of times, finished up his part of the action, then watched as the girl silently got up, dressed and left.

Oh, thank you. He turned over and lay in bed, his magnificent body naked under the sheets. *What a great night – the food, the kids were so good, that crazy story about Janie – and why is her husband never there? Regardless of any business - that food, that funny, that ass - if that were my wife, you wouldn't catch me staying away from that for very long. Especially if I could get it into that red, lacey thing she has in her drawer. Hmmmmmm.*

Oh, and that blonde, that was a nice little nightcap to a great evening.

Everyday should be like this.

Chapter Ten
Janie's 198Something

THINGS THAT MAKE ME HAPPY

What makes a thirteen year old girl happy?

Thirteen was that magic age where you are so desperate to love someone or something, you'll still even eagerly take a parent's love. Fourteen is the boundary limit on that.

Fourteen is the age when whatever your parents want is stupid and boring. Thirteen is when you still want their approval so much that you will do whatever they want even if it is stupid and boring.

Thirteen is the age where you will do anything to get them to talk to you. Fourteen is the age when you notice that your parents don't speak at the dinner table and you don't want them to talk to you, so the three of you sit in silence, night after night.

Fourteen is the age that your mother tells you that your weekends will be spent in Los Angeles - no more playing with ponies - now you should be preparing for your "grown-up life outside of this house. You'll be able to have everything you've ever wanted, Janie." Thirteen is the age when all you ever wanted was in your house.

Fourteen is the age when you notice your father's eyebrows knotting together, his eyes glistening, as your mom talks about all the things you and she will need to do, and where you will stay. Fourteen is the age you begin to notice that Dad isn't involved in any of those plans anymore.

Thirteen is the age when you had first gone to Los Angeles, excited to go to such a glamorous place that you never realized you only saw the inside of a few office buildings where they made you sit, turn, walk and dance on cue and you never questioned why. You just smiled at your mother and she beamed back at you from behind the cameras.

Thirteen was the age where nothing could have made Janie happier than that smile.

Except maybe, if that smile could have been given to her father, too.

THINGS THAT MAKE ME HAPPY
Horses
Ballet class
Babysitter's Club Books
Dad, at the barn
Mom and Girl's Nights Together
S.O.V.S.

She couldn't reveal the name of her S.O.V.S. - SomeOne Very Special - someone else might read it and God, Janie would be so embarrassed, she wouldn't be able to show her face in seventh grade again. They'd have to move.

To LA maybe. Mom seemed to love it there and she had seemed to make friends where they had stayed. Her mom didn't have any friends around home.

I wonder if Daddy would like LA, too.

Fourteen was the age you realized that you and your mom were moving to LA and Daddy wasn't coming with them. And there was another man waiting to meet you and your mom at the new apartment. A man who hugged your mother so tightly he lifted her out of her shoes, who would then turn and press you to him, just as hard, like you knew him. Like you belonged to him.

Thirteen was the age when you looked at your mother and saw that she was so beautiful that you would have done anything to be, to look, to stand, to act like her. That Daddy was handsome and funny and he could cook anything and he liked to spend time with her even when she was dirty. He'd lean over the railing to joke with her when she was cleaning out stalls at the barn. And when they would come home and Janie would run so fast to shower so her mom didn't get mad at her dad because he was ruining Janie's hair or the paint she had just applied to the girl's fingernails at that useless barn. Janie would run downstairs after cleaning and scrubbing as fast as she could, put on pretty clothes and brush her hair. Dad would look at them proudly, calling the two of them "His Beauties."

Fourteen was the age when her mother took that all away.

Fourteen is the age when you start to hate your mother.

Chapter Eleven
Brian's Hero

"I'll be offstage at around midnight but I think it would be better if Ashley just stayed overnight, okay?" Billy looked up from over his mug.

"Uh-huh, got to see a man about a bird?" At the sink sorting dishes, Janie smirked out of the corner of her mouth.

"Uh-huh," he laughed, she was using his language and she was starting to know him pretty well.

"Stay away from the married ones just for me, okay?"

"I will run a thorough check previous to copulation."

"Why would that not surprise me?" She laughed at him, "Do you have one of those little scanner thingies that gives you a big printout on the funny file-y paper with the holes on the sides?"

"Huh?"

"Aw man, one of my lead balloons, joke totally didn't work."

"Maybe if you knew the name of the kind of paper or knew what type of scanner thing you were mentioning, that would have tightened the whole thing up really nicely."

"Yes, it needed tightening. It's always good in the head." She thought a minute, turning to him, "Billy, I've wanted to ask you for awhile now."

"What is it, dearie?"

"What happened with your wife? I mean, what was it like? Were you a good husband?"

Billy puffed himself up a bit. "I was actually."

"I think I can see it. I mean, apart from a sense of entitlement to and from everything and everyone around you…"

He held up his index finger, "I like it, I want it, I have it."

"Having a major sincerity defect…"

He held up a second finger, "Um? Celebrity."

"The sleeping around…"

His count remained the same. "Covered that with one and two."

"And generally just being a major pain in the ass, you seem to be okay. I mean, you're a good dad, you are nice to look at…"

"'Pretty' is the word you used, I think."

"I won't outlive that, will I?"

"I always have to go with what I know are my strengths."

"What happened? Why aren't you married anymore?" She hesitated, "Is it because of the birds?"

"Actually no. I was a very good boy, believe it or not." He took a deep breath. "Okay, the story. Let's see, Sheila and I got together about a year before we were married. My career was basically in the crapper at the time. It was… you know VH1 did a 'Behind The Music' on this right? I could just show you that and this would be a lot easier on everyone."

"From you."

"Alright, you're right, I can't get around you."

"You're getting it, Handsome."

He smiled. "Okay, it's sort of a funny story. But then again," he chuckled ruefully, "not really. It was how I met Del, actually."

"Really?"

"Uh-hmm, it was before I started getting movie roles – that was actually a genius thought on the part of Sheila – and my music wasn't doing all that well. I don't know, I just was kinda pulling stuff out of my ass and I knew it was crap. I was running low on cash and unfortunately spending a bit too much of it on coke."

"I didn't know that."

"Yeah, I was a bit of a 'head. I got started on it late nights in the studio, but then started hitting it at parties and shows." He disclaimed, "But not around the house. Or the baby. Ever. I wouldn't allow it." Rubbing his knuckles, he looked up at Janie, as if for her approval.

"Well, okay, that's a good thing," she encouraged, "Go on."

"Okay," Billy crouched down into the story, hands expressing it as he went along, "One night, I was at this really rank club down in LA and I was supposed to go on and the band before us went over set time and I was coming down off pretty hard. I just wanted to go in the backroom and have another snort before I went on, I felt like I really needed it. I was being a complete dick to the manager and this bartender and the bartender called over this enormous bouncer. Of course, as high as I was, I thought I could take him. Huge, huge guy. And the big, bad bouncer didn't say one word to me. Didn't say a thing. Just sort of stared down at me. And there I am, high as a fricking kite and it's like I got my string cut, and I'm plummeting fast and all I'm wanting is two seconds to blow a little snow. I'm yelling and screaming and making a complete ass of myself. So here I go, I got up all in this gigantic dude's face, he's literally like five inches taller than me and I'm swearing at him, telling him who I was. You know, like that made a difference. And then I lay my hand on his enormous forearm – which is a big bouncer no-no, by the way - and what happens? The bouncer, a Mr. Delbert Marks to you and me, proceeded to punch me right in the face, broke my nose wide open. Blood everywhere."

"Oh my God. Is that what made you stop? Was it because of Del?" Janie sat down across from Billy.

"No, actually. But I did come back about six months later to hire him, but wait," he put up a hand, "it gets better." He readjusted himself for the dramatic retelling, "So I back off, retreat to the bathroom, trailing these big, disgusting clumps of blood, pouring, what had to be, crushed bone, cartilage, snot, whatever, all down my face, in my hands, all over my chest. It was awful."

"Ew, gross."

"Oh, I know."

The two of them sitting there, it was like no one else was alive; there was just a storyteller and an audience, one's reactions and emotions completely enthralling the other. She was just listening to him, focused. It was pretty unusual. It wasn't like people didn't listen to him, *Christ, he was Billy Smitts, right?* Del listened to him, ah, but he paid Del. And Ashley, she was good, but she was, um, five and he was her daddy. The girls he went around with sorta listened. Well, he usually had their undivided attention but it wasn't necessarily because he was a fascinating conversationalist, *you know?* Billy had a rap, no doubt about it. If he had to he could probably come up with some firm Completed Pass Stats proving he had closed many a deal with some conversational finesse, but Janie was just into his story. His story. His memories. The way he was telling it. This right here, this was why he wrote songs. He hadn't done it in, *whew, forever.* But that was always how he had always truly connected, when someone heard his stuff at the beginning, before it was taken and shaped and sleekly packaged into a commercial 3:12, when he was just fooling around, playing with some words and they would form together and it would be like he was talking about a memory and it would just come out in phrases, like it was supposed to be told that way. It was the only time he figured anyone really listened to what he was saying. He couldn't remember the last time he had felt connected like this to another person, right in front of him. It fed him. It fed him a little bit.

Billy eagerly continued, "And my head feels like it is about to explode and I'm standing there at this completely disgusting sink in the men's bathroom, and you know that you never touch the sink in a men's bathroom, right?"

"Why?" Janie looked confused, and Billy smirked, cocking his head at her, "Never mind, I don't want to know." She waved it off.

"So, I'm standing there and I've got the coke in a little box in my hand and do you know what I am thinking?"

"What? What are you thinking?"

"Now, how the…" for the benefit of the kids, he whispered, "…fuck…" and then returned to normal conversational tone, "…am I supposed to snort this now?"

"No way," Janie slapped the table, "You're kidding me."

"I am totally serious! I remember the actual thought in my head." He straightened up, "I wouldn't go on stage and they threw me out, and when I started seriously considering finding someone on the street to help me inject it, I kind of just stopped myself. Time to stop."

"What did you do?"

Billy, his hands clasped between his knees, "Right then, I dumped fifteen hundred dollars worth of a sweet grade cocaine into a sewer drain, walked myself to the Emergency Room where they patched up my face and sent me home in a cab. And I've been clean ever since."

"Oh my God, Billy, that is incredible."

Satisfied in his story's reception, "Wouldn't have been on VH1 if it wasn't a good story." He paused, "Well, actually, yes it would have."

Janie laughed, which made him feel even better. "Ooh, did they do a dramatization? Like did they Johnny Rotten-up some poor actor and film him, real shaky and gritty, in black and white? That would have been cool. Who would have played Del?"

"Wait! There's more story!"

"But seriously, how did they do it? Did you interview or was the story all second hand accounts? Because you never really know if what they report is really…"

"Janie?" Billy interrupted, "Can I finish? I'm getting to your question part."

"Oh yes, sorry."

Billy frowned at her, "Well, now I've lost momentum."

I've so got him here. Janie could barely contain herself, "Should we wait a half an hour and you can try again?"

Billy's head unhinged from his neck and his eyes popped open, "Janie Hadley. I am stunned. And… and quite frankly, appalled." However mocking his look of horror was, there was real surprise at her ballsiness. Again, it shocked and delighted him. "You are a *mother. With children.*"

"Oh come on, I couldn't let that one go. You set it up so beautifully for me," she giggled, "I had to make up for my bad one earlier." Janie tried to stop the flow of chuckles, putting her hand over her mouth, they slipped between her fingers.

He watched her, a look of amused patience on his face, chin in hand, as her giggles slowed, came back, slowed, came back again, and finally, ran dry, "Are you okay now?" pretending to be so serious, "Can we go on?" when really, he could have let her go on for another hour.

"Yes." She settled herself down and answered sincerely. "I'm sorry, I really want to hear the rest. I would like to know."

He grinned over at her, but squinted, trying to look suspicious.

She responded with an earnest interest, "Please."

He continued, but now, Billy was a little more serious, a little more discomfited. Janie watched as his brows worked up and down, his hands tucked between his knees, *in his eyes a trace of, I think it's, 'regret'? maybe. Something.*

Billy went on with his story, "Anyway, that was it for me. The unfortunate part of it was that it wasn't for my wife. She used to come out to all of these parties with me when I had really started using it and she had all these pain in the ass women friends who did coke to stay skinny. And then, after Sheila had Ashley she felt really bad about her weight and started on it, a lot. It got to be where I didn't want her around the baby at all because she was just continually stoned or she was coming down and that can get bad. She didn't want me to help, she didn't want help." He reached up to scratch his lip. "And then, I started working on movies, and ironically, it was at her suggestion, and a couple of times, I had to go away for a few weeks and I didn't want Ashley to stay at the apartment with just her mom. So, that was pretty much it."

"That totally sucks, Billy." She stood up, her lip curled down, shaking her head.

"Yes, yes, it does." He looked up at her. He was surprised at Janie's hurt expression, and then, as he was starting to know her too, he wasn't, really. "The funny thing was, despite everything - the problems with coke, the money running out, all of that crap - is I actually liked being married. You know, the basics of it. And although VH1 would never tell you this, I was pretty good at it."

"I bet you were. Riling up the kids, eating all the food, passing out on the couch while someone else does the dishes – I've seen all that in action." Janie went over to the sink again. "Isn't your story kind of like the James Bond story, something about his wife splitting and then he goes out and has all the women he wants?"

"James Bond's wife was killed."

"Oh, well that's a little more romantic."

"You are weird if you find that somehow romantic."

"Sad, trying-to-fill-in-the-holes romantic. Yeah, weird, sorry."

"Hey, I'd make a good Bond."

"Except you're not English and you're never the good guy."

"True on both counts." He stood up, drained his cup around Janie, as she began washing dishes. In his best British accent, he said, "All right, Mrs. Hadley. Must run. Saying 'Cheerio' to the progeny, then, popping off."

"See, you could be a good guy – that sounded like the Avengers, uh, Mr. Steed!"

"And you, Mrs. Peel. I did rather like you in leather." He bid a hasty exit.

"You'd better get out."

"After what you just said to me, dearie? That little joke you just made? Yeah, watch out." He smiled back at her as he slipped through the side door. "Call the cell, emergency."

Janie had been asleep for about two hours when she heard a noise downstairs. For a second, she thought it could have been Scotty, but when she looked out the window there was a strange car in the driveway. Well, not exactly in the driveway, more like across the driveway.

She put her ear to the stairway and heard giggling coming from downstairs, it sounded, *possibly familiar?* But with no weapon at hand she felt a little scared about just trotting down with a big wave and a hello for the intruder.

She walked quietly to Katie's room; both Katie and Ashley were sound asleep. Janie gently closed their door. She tiptoed to Brian's room and pulled down a Louisville Slugger off of his memorabilia shelf of his first Giants game. She closed his door tightly behind her. Feeling the heft of the bat in her hands, she slowly placed one foot on each stair, steadying herself, ready to land the death blow.

Stopping in the middle of the staircase, she heard even more giggling and the low murmur of a male voice. It didn't sound exactly right, but... *what if that were Billy down there, drunk, and for some reason he decided to bring a bird here to my roost? Oh my God, that unbelievable prick! Would it frigging surprise me one little bit, honestly?! Going back to that whole entitlement thing and the "watch out" and that "I like it, I want it, I have it" crap he was trying to be so cute with earlier today. You want cute, huh? I'll show you cute, Billy Smitts.* She swung the great bat in her hands, ready to land the death blow. *Only he would do something this ridiculously intrusive and immat...*

"Stacie?" Janie recognized the form on her couch but it wasn't the usual male one she was getting to know so well. "Stacie, what is going on here?" Stacie was disentangling herself from the drunk man underneath her. But he wasn't letting her up without a fight.

"Oh hi, Janie. Sorry I woke you. Sorry we woke you."

"Woke me? Did you hope you'd get this done and have the place picked up before I woke up?" Stacie smiled and shrugged, Janie was furious, "What the hell are you doing here?"

"Come on, baby… come on," the guy on his back whined.

Janie walked to the edge of the couch, shouldering the bat, "Um, excuse me. I'm trying to talk to my friend here; do you think you could let her up?"

"Hey, you are totally hot."

Stacie let her head drop to the side, heaving a dramatic sigh, "That is my sister-in-law."

Janie just ignored her, "What's your name?"

"Billy."

Stacie snorted, "See? I've got my very own Billy, too."

"You have got to be kidding me." Janie glared down at her, "Okay, Billy, now, can I have her please?"

"Gladly," he smeared the words, "Can I watch?" He laughed, flopping around gleefully on her couch.

Janie rolled her eyes, shaking her head. She assessed Stacie's stability, dropped the bat and hauled her inebriated body to an upright and standing position. Janie led her around the loveseat to the stairway. "Stacie, help me get him into a cab please and then, I will get you into one. You two have to get out of here."

"What?" GrossDrunkBilly yelled.

"I'm sorry, Janie. We just obviously couldn't go to my place," she leaned in to stage whisper, "'cuz of Frankie and the kids." Even her wink is slurred, "And this guy…"

"Billy, Billy Sanderson!" came a GrossDrunk yell from the couch.

"…guy's place is being fumigated. We had nowhere to go."

"So you thought it would be fun to come to my house?" Janie, fiercely, "I am alone, Scotty is away for the week in Boston, and it's just me and the children. Stacie, come on!"

"I don't know, I thought it would be okay. You know, like a double-date. I figured he would be here."

"He who would be here?!"

"Billy."

"Billy Sanderson!" came from the couch again.

"What?"

"Don't fight ladies, Billy's right here!" GrossDrunkBilly Sanderson sat up on the couch.

"He is always here, lately."

"This guy?!"

"No! The pretty one! Billy Smitts. Your Billy!"

Janie grimaced, "He's not my Billy, Stacie. I am taking care of his daughter."

GrossDrunkBilly Sanderson picked up the baseball bat at his feet, "Gotta fight these girls off with a stick."

Posturing herself, Stacie placed her hands on her hips, leaning forward to emphasize her important point, but not enough to send her overboard – it took her a try or two to get the balance right. "Ashley's here a lot, Janie. And so is her daddy. And do you know who is not? Scott."

"Stacie, you are not in any position to start making accusations about someone else's marriage."

"Who's marriage?" GrossDrunkBilly hooted and stood up, barely, out of indignance. "Who's married? No one told me about married."

"Stacie is married, Billy, I think it is time for you to…" Janie started.

"She's married? Well that ain't right. Stacie, you married?" He yelled and stumbled back but caught himself, the two women noticed, with the bat.

"Aw, crap." Janie spat through her gritted teeth. Stacie clung to Janie's arm, the fear that was coursing throughout her was almost outrunning the alcohol.

"Whatcha doing running around with Billy Sanderson when you're married, Stacie?!" GrossDrunk-BaseballBatSwingingBilly ranted on. "My wife used to do that too. Now, she's my ex-wife. The whore. You're a whore, Stacie."

"No one is a whore, Billy." Janie tried to remain calm but the bat kept swinging and he was stumbling closer to them. "Let's get you going home, okay? Let's just give me my bat, that's my bat from the Giants, you know."

"I like the Giants." Billy Sanderson said. "I wanted to be a baseball player." He hung his head.

"Did you?" Janie said. Aside to Stacie, "Phone, now."

Stacie slunk to the phone table, picked it up, holding it behind her leg, trying to hide it. "Who am I calling?"

"Wait," the GrossDrunkHead came up, "Watchutwo doing?"

"Were you a good player, Billy?"

"Billy? Is that who I should call?"

GrossDrunkConfusedBilly, "You calling me?"

"Yes." Janie agreed with Bill Sanderson. To Stacie, "No."

"What?"

"Put that phone down."

"Stacie! Dial!" Janie, urgently.

"Who?" Stacie whined.

Janie looked right at her, "Are you kidding me?" *Dear God, how does this happen?*

"Hey! Hey! You're calling the cops."

A light dawned on Stacie, "Oh! The cops!"

"He gets it?" Janie, exasperated.

"NO! No cops! I told you to put the fucking phone down, whore."

Janie had had it, "Can you just stop with the whore thing, Billy?" She spat. *Somehow this is my fault, 'soft spot for strays,' this is where it gets me.*

"NO!" GrossDrunkEnragedBilly screamed to Janie, startling her into realizing that the man with the bat was really the one in control here. Billy Sanderson yowled at Stacie angrily, "And you, put the fucking phone down!! I hear a cop car and I'm fucking... uh, I don't... I don't know... but NO FUCKING COPS!!" He smashed the bat across the mantel over the fireplace, the framed photos, in pieces, scattered across the room.

Okay, I let myself get upset. Can't do that. Calm, stay calm. Janie took a deep breath, making her voice as quiet, as low as when she needed to reason with a two year old in the midst of what would have to be considered the Mother of all Tantrums, only complete with weapons and swearing, "Hey, now. Okay. No need to get excited. Okay, no cops. But how about we... how about we... uh" *Come on, Janie, think! Wait!* "Oooh, who should we call then?" letting her voice get a little singsong-y.

The soothing tone had an immediate effect, placating him, emphasizing the tranquilizing effects of the obviously large quantity of alcohol he had ingested. "Huh?" GrossDrunkNowConfusedBilly asked.

"Well, we've uh, got the phone, so why don't we, umm," her voice trailed up and then sunk back down, lifting back up again, talking to him as though she was trying to entice a couple of three year olds out of an argument. *Okay, Dr. Spock - keys to dealing with a tantrum, remain calm, inflect a soothing tone, use distraction.* "Let's give someone a ring, good idea? We could call someone and talk about baseball again…"

"I've got a better idea." GrossDrunkBilly suggested softly, "Lets call that one's husband, tell'im what a whore his wife is."

"Okay, yeah, good plan." Janie was covering the octaves.

Stacie, who had been using Janie as a human shield, phone at the ready, as confused and soothed as the drunk man swaying to and fro in front of them, now popped up, "Oh no, we are not calling Frankie."

"Sure Stacie. Come on, let's talk all about the whoring," Janie, over her shoulder. "Speed dial 5."

"No, wait gimme the phone. I wanna tell him."

"She's got it, Billy. She'll confess it all. Every last horribly, morally wrong…"

Stacie protested, "Hey…"

GrossDrunkSuggestingBilly interrupted, "Whore - ish…" slowly swinging the bat for good measure.

"Yes, every last 'whorish' detail. I promise." Janie agreed.

"No, no I won't, I can't, Janie. Poor Frankie."

"Just speed dial five, Stacie."

"That's not my number."

Oh. My. God. Janie, gritting her teeth again, hissed, "Dial!" She now turned her attention to the disgusting baseball bat swinging man named Billy in her living room, "That's a mighty good swing you've got there, Billy. You said you like baseball? A Giants fan?" She could do it. Small talk could come to her rescue. It was the only way she could distract this guy away from Stacie and the telephone, which now could be their only lifeline. *Think, Janie. Just simple conversation. Something he can get a hold of. You can do it.* "How about those Giants? What do you think about this season? Did you think you could have played for the Giants?" To Stacie behind her, again, "Please, Stacie, just dial speed dial five."

"Who am I calling here, Janie? Can't do the cops, a siren and this guy could freak. Scotty?"

Janie shook her head, "Scotty's in Boston."

"Who am I calling here, Janie?" Stacie whispered.

"Oh. *My. Billy.* Were you any good, *Billy*? Did you play ball when you were a kid, *Billy*? What position did you play, *Billy*?"

Billy Smitts was on fire. His voice was coming from the deep recesses of his muscled body and he had the crowd in his silver-ringed, black-nailed hands. He had scanned the audience during the performance. *Many, many beautiful young birds out there tonight. Eager, pretty young birds.* He grabbed his black Gibson Nighthawk, flinging it over his shoulder; the audience was going crazy as he began to play the bridge of the song.

Okay, but really, was it worth it? I mean, hell, what the fuck am I doing with these girls? That "I like it, I want it, I have it" crap he had pulled on Janie, trying to be cute, trying to make her laugh. You know, anything to get her to laugh. Today, he'd gotten so high off of that conversation with her – *ironic, really.* He couldn't talk to anyone like that, *it was just fun.*

He had to concentrate on the notes in this part... right...
here. The chord changes could get tricky.

*Okay – but I mean, what I said to Janie today, really,
about how I live my life, all of that was bullshit, right? Just
a joke between the two of us. I don't have anything to
prove. Nothing. These girls, they're fun, too. I mean, it's
not like I can go over Janie's house to just hang out after a
show. Right? Right. This late? No. She'd kick my ass.* He
grinned absentmindedly, the crowd responded. *So I mean,
really, what other options do I have? Just go home? Be
alone? Fuck that. Yeah, so these girls can be fun, just in a
different way. Some little pretties who know what they are
getting into when they come back to see me, now that's
nothing but fun. Right?*

Fuck yeah, he decided. *Right? Absolutely.*

He ducked backstage.

"Del, get me a drink!"

So, Billy was in his room, working his favorite position
on this dark-haired, tight-assed honey he had picked out for
the night when his cell phone began to ring the 'Janie' tone
on the nightstand. 'Long Tall Sally' sang out and his head
lifted from the depths. "Crap!" Despite heavy protests, he
struggled out of Dark Honey's leglock and grabbed for the
phone.

She pouted behind him, "You have to answer that
now?"

She grabbed for his vitals and he pushed her away.
"Hold up, it's my daycare lady."

"You have to answer a call from your daycare lady in
the middle of sex?"

"My daughter is at her house, pretty bird. Now let me
answer it." Snapping the phone open, "What's up?"

The voice was very quiet and it took him a second to place it - he had listened to the same voice muffled from the downstairs, as he had taken refuge so often in Janie's room, "We need someone here to help us. Now."

"Stacie, are the kids okay?"

"Yes, they're fine. Janie and I are in trouble. At the house. I brought a very drunk man him here, and now he's swinging a bat. Please, Billy." He could hear Janie talking in the background, her voice loud and steady. And then he heard the smashing of glass. "Please come, he is yelling and he's started breaking stuff and he won't leave. Janie keeps trying but he won't go. Billy, she needs you."

Billy snapped the phone, grabbed his clothes and leapt across the bed. Dark Honey watched him go.

A fucking Mercedes and I can't get it there fast enough. Christ! Billy's hands spun the wheel as Del sat anxiously next to him. Not only was Del worried about Janie and the kids but never having passengered with Billy before, this insane driving was making him very tense.

Billy strategized out loud, "We go in the side door. But be calm, Del. No sudden moves until we know what we've got, okay?"

"Right," Del agreed as he clung to the door handle, the g-forces misused his large frame in the passenger seat. "I could have driven Mr. Smitts."

"If we have to beat the shit out of him, so be it. But not in front of the kids or the girls."

"Got it," cringing as he was thrown against the door. Del desperately hoped his death grip on the handle wouldn't pop it open and spill him onto the street.

"And we can call the cops once he's out of the house. But the number one priority is to get him out of the house."

"Absolutely," Del sighed as Billy screeched to a halt in front of Janie's house. Finally on safe ground, big knees wobbling, Del knew he was ready to kick some ass.

Janie was inching towards the belligerent Gross-DrunkOnlyOccasionallyRaisingTheBatBilly Sanderson as she spoke to him about the Giants last season. He was both responding to the baseball talk and passing out on his feet. If she could get close enough, she might be able to…

And then Billy Smitts walked in. If he had been a peacock, his feathers would have breached the first floor. Testosterone must be some sort of caffeinated substance because suddenly, Billy Sanderson was a wide awake drunk, and one very pissed at the arrival of what seemed to be the Alpha Male. "Who are you? You're Stacie's husband. She's a whore, you know. Whores all of them!" And the bat started swinging again.

"Whoa there. Hey, Billy, back down a little bit." Janie attempted to soothe.

"Why are you telling me to back down?" OurFriendBilly came down a notch.

"Not you, him."

"You said 'Billy.'"

"His name is Billy, too."

Stacie shrugged a shoulder, "I wanted my own Billy. But this one, no good."

"See?" GrossDrunkBaseballBatSwinging Billy Sanderson screamed. "WHORE!"

"Okay, let's try to resolve the confusion. Maybe you should call me William." OurFriendBilly said.

"I don't think it's really an issue, Billy." Janie hissed.

"BILLY SANDERSON! I COULD HAVE BEEN GREAT IF IT WASN'T FOR YOU WHORES!"

"You see what I mean?"

"Okay, William, can you please let Del come in?"

"Oh well, okay, Mrs. Hadley." And OurFriend Billy dramatically stepped aside.

"Okay, Billy Sanderson, could you please give our friend, Del, the bat? He'd much appreciate it."

Del walked slowly up to the GrossDrunkInAwe-OfDel'sSheerMassBilly and took the bat from his hands. "Thank you," Del said politely.

"It's a Giants bat. I love the Giants," Billy Sanderson pointed out.

Del put his hand on the defeated man's shoulder and started leading him through the living room. One who had seemed so threatening moments before now was crumpled like a child whose toys had been taken away for bad behavior.

"I've got to pee. Can I pee before I go?"

"No!" Janie said, holding her head, breathing deeply.

"You okay?" OurFriendBilly asked.

"I'm fine, *William*," Janie glared. "Of all the jackass things…"

"But I gotta go! Pleeeeaaaasssse?" GrossDrunk-HoldingHisCrotchBilly whined.

"Jackass?!" OurFriendBilly protested, "I came here to help you. You called me and needed help and I am here!"

"Uh-oh, Mom and Dad are fighting," Stacie sighed to Del.

"Will you shut up?" Janie glared.

"Please can I go? Come onnnnnn!"

"Did you just tell me to shut up?" OurFriendBilly flung his hands in front of him, incredulously.

"Oh, for the love of God, I was talking to Stacie, Billy! Wait! I'm sorry to confuse you, 'WILLIAM!'"

Stacie, petulant, "I wasn't talking to you, Janie. I was talking to, uh…"

"Del," Del provided.

"Yes, thank you. Del."

"You are unbelievable, woman." Billy shook his head in frustration.

"Thank you," Stacie smiled.

"Not you," Billy glared. "Her," pointing at Janie.

"I'm unbelievable?!"

"Yes, you!"

"I've gotta pee!"

"Just go!" Janie and Billy yelled at the Gross-DrunkWhiningBilly. Janie pointed absentmindedly, "Upstairs to the left. Then you are out!"

As that GrossDrunkBilly fell up the stairs, Janie whirled upon OurFriendBilly, "You do realize that you were nitpicking over your names when that man was ready to beat the shit out of all of us with a baseball bat!"

"I wasn't nitpicking! Jesus Christ, I came here from *actus resus in delictatum* with a delicious dark-haired beauty…"

"I thought you liked blondes," Stacie pouted.

"Well, tonight I wanted something different!" OurFriendBilly yelled. "Point being, I think I deserve some thanks. You did call for my help."

It hit Janie.

I did.

And here he is.

She sighed. She softened. She had to. "You are right, Billy. I did call for your help." Janie resigned, "I'm sorry. Thank you. And thank you, Del."

Del shrugged it off, but observed quietly, "He's been up there too long, Janie."

"I will go get him," OurFriendBilly said. "He probably passed out in the toilet."

Billy trotted up the stairs and walked directly to the bathroom. The light was on and the door was open but there was no sign of Billy Sanderson. He looked around and instinct told him to stop and listen, a rustling sound met his ears at the exact moment he saw that Brian's door was open.

The hackles rose up on the back of his neck and he broke into a run down the hallway. Billy thundered into the little three year old's room to stop dead at the end of the Bob the Builder bunk beds. An insane rage scalded the blood of his body as for the fraction of the second before he attacked, he watched Billy Sanderson standing over Brian's bed, his pants unzipped and his hands working inside of them, touching himself just over Brian's sleeping face.

The unknowing prey, Billy Sanderson smiled conspiratorially at his attacker, "Gotta get'em off somehow, huh?"

A roar escaped his throat. Billy's every muscle burned, hot blood rushing to his temples, pounding the skin on his forehead. He lifted the man by his shirt and threw him, battering into the hallway. Janie heard Billy's huge footsteps in the hallway and flew up the stairs, screaming, "BILLY!!!!" She reached him as he was straddling the frightened Billy Sanderson, punching the man's flesh within itself, his silver rings indenting the skin, blood collecting in their grooves.

The police had arrived and Del was speaking with them, Billy Sanderson's badly torn face in the back seat of the cruiser. They had asked Mr. Sanderson if he wanted to press counter-charges against Billy Smitts who had assaulted him in the house. Upon hearing the name of the famous singer/actor, he exclaimed, "Hell no! Holy shit, that was the Billy Smitts?! Fucking Billy Smitts! WOW!" It wasn't until later that he had thought, if he had a brain in his drunken head, he probably could have made a million dollars that night in PR cover up alone.

But actually, that was pretty far from the truth. Del had already called four of the Public Relations personnel on set and OurFriend's famous name never showed up in the town police report. The miracle of payola in a small town, as far as the movie's PR camp knew, the press never heard a thing.

Over the following weeks, Billy Sanderson would try and tell the story to anyone who would listen, but no one ever really believed him. Well, that wasn't entirely true. One night, at the bar, some random guy wanted to actually hear the story. But for Billy Sanderson that particularly promising storytelling experience ended up completely sucking, *with teeth.* The guy didn't care about how that whore, Stacie, who came around here still, had lured him to this other hot girl's house. The two girls were totally into him and then got all weirded out when Billy Smitts, who had to be the hot girl's boyfriend or something, got there and freaked out on him. That dude musta been jealous or something because, as Billy Sanderson told it, Billy Smitts and he had gotten into a huge fistfight.

The random guy bought him more drinks and he kept asking him over and over again, what was the name of the other girl, the hot one? But Billy Sanderson just couldn't remember. The random guy paid for Billy Sanderson's bar tab, handed him a few extra bills with a card with a number on it. He asked Billy Sanderson, as a favor, to keep a

lookout for that girl - Stacie, it was? - that came in from
time to time. See if you can get the name from her.

Billy Sanderson just told him, that yeah, that stupid
whore, he'd talk to her again. Stacie had some serious shit
to answer to. The random guy had just replied, don't do
anything stupid, just get the name and call him; there might
be something else in it for him.

See? Totally sucked. With teeth, man.

Meanwhile, those who could remember the story
without the help of a Reality-To-Booze Translator, were
still dealing with the immediate aftermath. Janie called
Stacie a cab and poured her finally repentant form into the
backseat when it arrived. "Janie, I am so sorry. I will
understand if you never want to see me again. I can't
believe I would ever have done something so stupid, to
endanger you like that and the children. Please Janie,
you're like my sister, I don't have anyone else like you,
please don't hate me."

Janie sighed, "I don't hate you, Stacie."

"You won't kick my kids out of your daycare?"

Billy just shook his head, and had to walk away.

"No," Janie replied quietly. "Just go home, okay? Bye."

"I will. Bye." Stacie's forlorn face, peering from the
cab window, dragged itself down the street and around the
corner.

Billy was waiting for her, smoking a cigarette at the
kitchen door. Janie walked up to him and wordlessly took
the butt from his mouth, dragged deeply, handed it back,
blew out the smoke and went inside. Billy took the final
drag and flicked it onto the street, following her into the
house.

Del was sitting quietly with the children in the living room. The noise had awoken them but Del and Stacie had shielded them from the violence.

Janie kissed the three cheeks and suggested, "Let's get our sleeping bags and camp out down here tonight." The children cheered and ran to go get their bags. Janie turned to Del and Billy, "You guys don't have to stay. Go home, get into a nice bed, okay? You boys have done too much tonight."

Billy looked a little sheepish, "Well, I'd, uh, prefer to stay. You know, to make sure its safe." He looked down. "I mean, my daughter is here, too.

Del looked up at Billy, "Yeah, me too. Janie. I'll stay."

Janie smiled at the two of them, "Okay then. Pick a spot." Del grabbed the large recliner and Janie handed him a blanket from the cedar chest. Within moments, Del was fast asleep, his big chest heaving in silent snoring. Ashley and her daddy picked the loveseat. She hunkered down in her Dora The Explorer sleeping bag and Janie handed Billy a blanket. She smiled down at him, "Thank you," she mouthed at him.

He bowed his head, not taking his blue eyes from hers, "You're welcome," he mouthed back.

Katie on one side and Brian on the other, Janie parked on the couch. She snuggled her two little ones against her and said to them, "We have two heroes in the house tonight, you know."

"We do?" they asked.

"Yes, two amazing heroes who came to help us when we needed them most."

"Who? Who? Who?" Ashley joined in the chant.

"Well, first Del. He saved us all tonight." The children cheered but Janie quieted them down. "And second is a special hero, a hero for Brian, who took care of a little boy and came to us, as swift and sure, as soon as we called upon him and knew just what to do when things looked their worst."

"Who, Mama? Who is it?"

"Ashley's daddy. He was the bravest hero who saved our little Brian from a devilish and evil deed doer."

"HOORAY!" The children cheered, "Hooray for Ashley's daddy! Brian's hero!"

"My hero, my hero, my hero!" Brian jumped up and down on the cushions and Billy sat across from Janie, in quiet awe of everything he was beginning to see that she was.

Chapter Twelve
200Sometime

Stacie had found Janie in the bathroom upstairs with Katie and Benji. "Oh Janie," Stacie had grimaced.

The first three months of Janie's second pregnancy had turned out to be much more miserable than her first trimester ordeal with Katie. The smell of anything and just about everything had set off waves of nausea and no amount of Saltines or ginger ale seemed to do the trick. "Oh sorry, Stacie. Only sixteen more days until the first trimester is over," Janie had groaned into the toilet bowl. Her little daughter, two years old, was patting her back as she had heaved into the porcelain. "I had to haul poor Benji and Katie in here with me, I brought some toys. I figured I'd be awhile."

"Well, let me take them outta here." Stacie had ew'ed.

"Thank you." Her voice had been raw from the bile in her throat, she had sounded so tired, "Just let me clean up a little bit. I'll just be a minute more."

Stacie had closed the door behind her, leading her three year old son and her two year old niece down the stairs to the kitchen. The sound of vomiting had been an unwanted follower.

A few minutes later, a very pale Janie had appeared in the kitchen. "Hey. Thanks. Tried to brush my teeth but the toothpaste…" she had stuck out her tongue.

"Spare me please." Stacie had directed, "Why is this so bad? Have you called the doctor?"

"Yeah, he said the same thing as last time. Ride it out. Sip water, eat when you can, try and keep the vitamins down and this should be all over soon. I just need to wait it out. After this is over, the rest should be a cakewalk."

"Can Scotty help you? I mean, with this? He's working from home now isn't he? With this new company?"

"Oh no, they just opened up offices, actually. He's been so busy."

"More than usual?"

"Well, it is a new company."

"I suppose."

"He should be home soon."

"Well then he can get dinner for the kids at least."

"Oh, no big, I'll get it."

"Janie, you're sick."

"It's just morning sickness. I'll open the window, hold my nose, put a cloth over my face or something."

"Janie, he can help out. I mean, he does know you're pregnant…"

"Of course, he does."

"Well, then like last time…"

"Um, Scotty didn't really know I got all that sick last time."

"What?" Stacie had been confused.

"I didn't want to bother him with it," Janie had admitted, sort of sheepishly, "He was working so hard to get ready for the baby. He had this goal, you know, of having a great savings account all ready for when Katie was born so he put in a lot of extra time and so, he sort of just, he sort of missed it." Janie had shrugged, "I mean, really, how much fun is it to hear about puking every day?"

"Huh," Stacie had mused, the confession had confounded her. *These two always seemed to be so together on everything. The Planners must not have scheduled for first trimester complications.* "Yeah, I'm hearing it first hand and am not too pleased about it."

Janie had let out a weak laugh. Stacie had then realized it was the first time in weeks she had heard that sound coming from the tall girl with the dark circles under her eyes - the one who usually was making her burst into surprised laughter.

It had been hard for Stacie to understand, she never had a bit of morning sickness. The only troublesome time in her first *and only pregnancy* or so she thought, was the last few weeks and of course, the delivery – not fun. Even though Janie had still been taking care of her son, it had been getting to be an exercise in enduring tolerance to come over here everyday and see the girl so sick - tolerance Stacie really didn't usually have to spare. *I mean, it's just a little draining to deal with day after day.* She had felt guilty for a minute, looking at the woman slumped in the chair, smiling weakly up at her. Maybe she should have stayed, cooked something for Janie and the kids, given her a little break. *But it was enough to deal with Frankie and Benji, who needed this?*

"Well, maybe you should say something to Scott, Janie, two more weeks is gonna do a number on you."

"I'll make it. Thanks." Janie had sighed. "Have a good night, Stacie. Again, I'm really sorry about today."

"Yeah," Stacie's eyes had narrowed. "See you in a couple." *Thank God, it's Friday.*

Chapter Thirteen
Closer

Janie was up making coffee when she heard stirring in
the living room. Heavy footsteps indicated it wasn't one of
the kids, but she didn't bother to turn and look, she knew
who it was. Billy walked in, his clothes rumpled, his hair in
all of the same upright angles at it had been last night on
stage. So for the night sleeping on the loveseat, basically
upright as his daughter hogged the remainder of the
cushions, he looked no worse for wear. His hands,
however, were a mess. He walked in next to his comrade in
arms, and placed a big mottled one on her opposite
shoulder, flicking his thumb over the nape of her neck,
"Coffee?"

"Yep." She removed herself from his grasp and grabbed
him a mug.

"Thanks."

"Lemme see your hands, first."

Billy put his coffee aside and stood facing her. She took
his hands and pulled him to the sink, where the early
morning sun shone through the window. "I need the light."

Her eyes down-turned to his palms, her dark lashes
covering their black color, Janie looked sleepy, but fresh
and somehow sweet this morning as she turned his swollen
hands over in her own. He took the opportunity to watch
her searching face closely. She usually had that sarcastic

smirk somewhere hidden in her expression, ready to appear at a second's notice. But this morning, Billy couldn't find it anywhere. *Huh. The wall is down, isn't it?* He imagined that this was what she looked like as a child, *maybe what she looked like before that agent got to her.*

Janie slowly removed the large rings, one by one from his fingers. Billy tried not to cringe or pull away, but once or twice he couldn't help it. "Toughen up there, Smitts," she said quietly to him. "Don't be a pussy." He laughed softly and decided to concentrate instead on her hands. They were soft and small, her nails clipped close, like a kid's, her long fingers almost disappeared under and around his large, rough, scarred ones. The swelling beneath the rings and his own blood had crusted the silver to his skin. She ran the warm water and held his hands underneath, gently rubbing his fingers to pick away at the blood between them. Her hands were sure, precise, insistent. Black and blue rings appeared in the place of the silver, just below the crimson knuckles of three fingers on each hand. She changed the water to cool, grabbed a dish towel and gently patted each hand dry, handed him his coffee cup and grinned, "Better for now. I'll wash these rings up for you before you go."

"Thanks." He took his cup and she watched him as he left the room. They were each different in their disappointment at the mention of his leaving, but both were confused by that same disappointment.

Del should have put it together, the call, the timing, the pretense, but he was late picking up his boss from the set which meant he would be behind picking up Ashley, which meant that their dinner would be cold. If he could just get Ian Dormande, Billy's personal PR guy - his overly tanned, metrosexual, personal public relations slimeball - off the phone he could concentrate on the road and get their hungry asses to Janie's. Ian was yammering on about the junket they would have to do next summer for this movie and Del didn't know why this was such an issue right now. But he couldn't seem to get Ian to shut up about it, "Ian, it's not like we have to book flights right now."

"I just want to be prepared," Ian had replied pleasantly.

"What? The Enquirer up your ass?" Del smirked.

"Ha. No, just being proactive for my favorite client."

"Uh-huh."

"So, Del, is there anything going on right now, you know, with Billy? I mean, is everything going okay?"

"Just fine, Ian. Why? What have you heard?"

"No, nothing, just checking to be sure there's nothing I need to take care of."

Del was irritated, but he rarely wasn't when speaking to Ian. He just didn't like the guy and each weekly call he attempted to end as early as possible. *But who likes PR people anyway? They were the worst of the all of the weasels in the business. With one hand they are handling you as though you were a precious gem and with the other they were selling your balls to the highest bidder.* "No nothing, Ian."

"Okay."

"We done?"

"Yes. Bye Del, give Billy and little Ashley my best."

"Yep, bye."

"Oh huh, how is Ashley? Is she with a new nanny now? How's that working out? Better than the last few?"

Del froze inside, managing a quick "Ian, I've got to go. Mr. Smitts is waiting. Bye," before he hung up. *Shit.*

Stacie had been in the same room with him for at least five minutes - FIVE MINUTES – before he even noticed she was there. It would be another fifteen minutes before that fact actually pissed her off. But she was just so entranced by watching him talk to Janie that his complete disregard of her didn't really register.

It did hit her that she was watching the rock star/movie star Billy Smitts, a man whose whole persona on stage or on screen just oozed sexual confidence, acting like a thirteen year old boy trying to pull some pigtails. But what really floored her was watching Janie.

To her, he wasn't even Billy Smitts anymore, he was just... I don't know, I guess... to her, he was just some guy. Some guy she made fun of and ordered around her kitchen and laughed with like Stacie had never seen her laugh, like Janie usually made other people laugh. In her thought process, Stacie didn't know what else to call this situation but 'flirting.' But it wasn't. 'Courting?' like animal shows, or old-fashioned aunts would call it? No. Billy and Janie, that whole dynamic was just stripped of all of that initial artifice, the I'm-Special pretension, and the Notice-Me posing of real flirtation – and that was the stuff Stacie loved. *Loved.* Those were the things Stacie thought the interaction between a man and a woman always should be. That inexplicable thrill of acceptance, that desire to be found desirable, *was there are bigger high than that?* She sought it out for whenever she was dealing with a man, any man, really. *This, this whole thing with these two?* Stacie didn't know what the hell to call it.

And his face, *look at his smile*, it crinkled the corners of his eyes, extending into perpetual expectation of a laugh and the wattage didn't dim, not for a second, not until those five minutes of freedom ended when he finally glanced in Stacie's direction and realized he wasn't alone with Janie after all. To witness that moment was like watching a thread of lightening snake across the darkness and the light still seared on your retinas long after it had actually disappeared, withdrawn back into the clouds. It made Stacie feel a little sad - sad that she had interrupted the freedom of this interaction and sad that she wasn't a part of it.

Stacie had called from the refrigerator, "You're out of milk, why didn't you call me?"

"Huh?" Janie, on the floor, had raised her head from changing Marco. "Oh, Billy called during his lunch break and he said he'd grab it on the way here."

"Oh. I see."

"Yeah, it's been good. He's really let you off the hook lately. He's grabbed bread and peanut butter for me a couple of times too and just the other night, I was talking to him and I just mentioned I had to finally fix the swing set and he offered to pop into Home Depot for me."

"I don't need to be let off the hook, Janie." Stacie had sauntered in, "So he calls you a lot?"

"Who? Billy? No, not really," Janie had thought, "Wipes please." Stacie had grabbed the plastic container and handed it to her. "He calls to talk to Ashley during his breaks and he chitchats then sometimes."

"So you talk to him everyday?"

"I guess."

"But you said you talked to him the other night," Stacie had noted.

"He had a question about something I wrote in Ashley's journal."

"Uh-huh. And then he went to the hardware store for you?"

"Yeah, for cement." Janie had finished up the messiest part of the job, "Dipe, please." Stacie had handed her a Size Four.

"Do you think he's really going to do this stuff for you?"

"Huh?"

"Well, I mean, it's not exactly like he can just go to the corner store, or something."

"What?"

"Him. He can't just pop into Home Depot."

"Oh," Janie had frowned, thinking, "He probably could. You know, just run in without being recognized."

"Yes, because this town is just bursting with bleach blond men with piercings."

Janie had chuckled, "I didn't really think about that." Janie had handed the clean little boy up to his mama, scooting by her to dump the dirty diaper and wash her hands at the kitchen sink.

"He's probably got some poor kid who's trying to break into the Biz doing your errands for you," Stacie had said from the dining room, holding Marco.

"Oh, that's just wrong," Janie had laughed, soaping up.

Billy had heard her laughing and called from the side door, "Hey! Right where I left you last night." He had been struggling to open the screen door with two gallons of milk in his arms. "It's like I never left."

"Hey," Janie had called over her shoulder, shook out her hands and had gone to him, "Give me."

"You're the boss," he had handed them over.

"Smart man," Janie had grinned, "Thanks."

"Hey, no problem, anytime."

"How'd it go today?" Janie had asked from the fridge.

"Just dandy, thank you, dearie." He had thought for a minute, "But I did have a little trouble with the hands,"

Billy had looked down at his mottled knuckles, "I had to hold up a gun in a shot, like shoulder level, and we had to do about fifty takes. They got sore."

She had pulled out that little half-frown of hers, beckoning him to the sink where she took his hands in her own and inspected them closely.

"Where are the kids?"

She had answered him absentmindedly, "They're working on a coloring castle in the living room." She glanced up at him, startling him as he watched the progress of her delicate fingers over his scabbed ones. "Want me to get…"

"No, not yet," Billy had interrupted, "I mean, they're busy, don't bug them yet."

"Everything looks fine, there's no swelling, really. I don't even think I need to clean them today," she had finished her examination, dropping his hands. "But you might want to try Advil tomorrow if it still bugs you. I've got some for now if you need it." She had reached up in her cabinet.

"No, feels fine now." He had crossed his arms in front of him, patting his biceps, fidgeting. He had bent over and peeked in the oven. "What ya making?"

"For dinner?" She had looked over at him in lighthearted exasperation. "Oh my God, you're like a goldfish."

"A what?"

"A goldfish."

"What the hell are you talking about?" he had laughed.

"Goldfish will eat and eat and eat until they

A.) Run out of food

B.) Die or

C.) Explode. That's you. You eat from the second you walk in here until you go – many times leaving with your mouth full and three plates in your hand. You're going to explode. There will be little bits and pieces of you all over my driveway and I'm not cleaning that up."

"You could get something for those on eBay, I bet." He had teased but then he drew his brows down, "You know those plates you make to bring home are not all for me," Billy had protested. "Usually," he then admitted, which had made Janie laugh right out loud. He had grinned. "Good thing I've been fully committed to the Playground Workout. You complained about the monkey bars but man, the seesaw, that's the killer."

She then had laughed again. "Hey, Stacie and I were just talking…" Janie pointed to the dining room where Stacie emerged, having spent about five whole minutes being uncharacteristically quiet, witnessing the entirety of the conversation.

Stacie raised an eyebrow at Billy.

She caught the cameo appearance of a frown on his face, for about a half a second, but Billy was a master, he caught himself and compensated for his slip, projecting a beautiful smile. But it wasn't the one he had just given to Janie, this smile was lifted from the pages of Rolling Stone, of Instyle, of Esquire, and Stacie was reminded that this man in front of her was, in fact, Billy Smitts. This man was someone else entirely.

She smiled graciously, "Sorry, I was running late today." Stacie was so on to him.

And he could kind of tell. "No problem, nice to see you again, Stacie."

Janie looked first at one then the other, "I'm gonna check on the kids. You two play nice." Janie took Marco from his mom and cut between them to the living room.

"I'm actually on my way out."

"I've got to go, too."

"Don't let me chase you out."

"I'm probably parked in your way."

"Yes," Stacie decided, "you should probably go."

"Oh, well, sure, yeah. I should. Absolutely."

"Well, I'm sure you have plans."

"Of course I have plans. I have lots of plans. Tonight."
This girl was attempting to engage him in some sort of
battle, and Billy felt the need to defend his territory, but
over what he couldn't quite get and what territory it was, he
wasn't exactly sure.

"Benji, Marco, we're going!" Stacie hollered into the
living room, "Janie, can you help me to the car?"

"Yep!"

Stacie spoke to Billy, "You seem to be nice company
for her. You stay."

He shrugged, "Yeah, whatever."

Janie breezed in the room with Benji on one hand and
Marco on the other, "Billy, can you go in with the kids?
I'm just helping Stacie out."

"Absolutely."

"You and Ashley want to stay and eat?"

"Yeah, whatever." He answered Janie while looking at
Stacie. This time the frown that appeared lingered for a
money shot.

Janie cocked her head at him, kind of smirking, "You
okay?"

But he couldn't do that, not with her. He gave up,
nodding to Janie, "That would be great. Thanks."

Stacie winked.

His eyes narrowed.

In the Great Contest of Coolness, Stacie may have just
pulled down the back of Achilles' sock.

Janie, "Okay. Be right in."

"Bye Stacie," Billy multi-million dollar smiled.

"Bye Billy." Stacie smiled right back; Crest Whitestrips had done their job, reflecting the magic right back at him.

Janie was buckling in Marco across from Stacie buckling in Benji, both jammed against the bucket seats in full incline.

"Big change there, Janie," Stacie remarked offhandedly.

"What's a big change?"

"You two, since the whole, you know, night, with me and the, uh, well you know." Stacie, although sheepish about that subject of the night with Billy Sanderson, still went on. She needed to know if Janie knew, she needed to know if this was deliberate. She needed to know if Janie was perhaps following in the path of Stacie's Dark Side. It would be terrifying and yet, ridiculously wonderful if she was. "You and Billy seem to have a lot of fun together."

Janie looked surprised, "Not particularly." But Stacie had made her think. Janie shrugged, "I think regardless of where that man is, he's going to find a way to have a good time."

"With you."

Janie laughed, shaking her head, "No. That's just who he is. And right now, he just happens to be here."

"Huh." Stacie watched her face closely. "Well," she kept looking, stalling, waiting, "Okay, well. Alright. See you tomorrow."

"Okay. Bye boys." Janie leaned across, steadying herself on the center console and kissed the two boys' faces. She reclined the seat into its upright and locked position and closed the red door. "Bye Stacie. Tell Frank I looked up that potty training book for Marco. I'll send him the link.'"

"He called you for that?"

"Yeah, no big. You know, Frank calls."

"Frank calls," Stacie sighed, nodding. "I'll tell him," Stacie got in her car and pulled out, almost clipping the black Mercedes pulled across the majority of the entryway. Stacie looked back as she shifted from reverse to drive, watching Janie wave and close the screen door behind her. *That poor girl,* Stacie sighed, *she has no frigging clue what she's doing.*

Two weeks had passed since the attack; Billy had had to cancel four concert dates until the swelling in his hands had abated. Janie had kept careful progress on his healing; day by day, inspecting the bruises and cuts as the damage of that night slowly disappeared. Billy started dreaming about her hands at night, the quiet ritual she put him through as he came to pick up Ashley. Except in his dream, Janie was rarely wearing a shirt. And she would occasionally place his warm, wet hands on her breasts. When he woke to the obvious consequences of that situation, it made him laugh, *stupid.* But when he started to really think about it - forcing Del off the set earlier each day, calling Janie just to ask if he should buy Tylenol or Advil when he wasn't really planning on buying either, waving away the set doctor and occasionally punching a door to *uh, well, damn it, test his strength* - he started to laugh harder. *Don't be such a dumbass, Smitts.* He shook it off.

But then, there was one particular afternoon - when it happened, it didn't make any sense at all to him, not a particle of sense. At first, it was what had become the usual, he was glad to be at Janie's house after a long day at work.

It had become rote and he liked every part of it, looking forward to the practices of the evening on the drive over and sometimes, even in the hours before. Then, suddenly, on that particular day, bubbling forth from this usual satisfaction came this raw and eager joy. It was so totally unexpected and completely and immediately wanted. And he had to find a way to make more of it.

And then as quickly as he felt it, as he recognized this cumulus cloud of emotion as something new and totally inimitable, it was gone, replaced by more familiar, yet equally baffling feelings of abandonment, anger, frustration, disgust and resentment *for her absolute prick of a husband.* It was a confusing, stirring, stimulating, irritating, ultimately fucking stupid afternoon. *It didn't make any sense at all.*

He had arrived to find that the side screen door was locked, so Billy followed the sound of the kids to the backyard. *They must be having fun.* He listened, first there was laughter and then shrieking and then, *wait for it, yes,* definite parental admonishment. *Maybe too much fun,* he grinned. By the time he made it in the gate, Billy had figured out that he would absolutely be spotting Brian sitting forlornly on the stairs to the back porch. "What's going on, little man?"

Brian frowned, "Time out."

Billy frowned back, settling himself down next to the three year old boy. "What you in for?"

"I threw a frog at the girls," he replied, the corner of his lip curling downward.

Just like his mother's does, Billy mused, "Hmmm, been there. That's some hard time."

"Yeah."

"Hey you!" Janie called from the small circle around the swing set she had safety-gated herself into. "Daddy!"

Billy's eyebrows shot up, *HA!*

Janie corrected herself, "Ashley's Daddy – sorry!" She shook her head, "No fraternizing in the penalty box!"

Billy stood up, "Find me when you get out, okay?" He held out his silver-ringed fist.

Brian knocked his knuckles against Billy's, his cheek resting heavily on his other hand.

"One more minute, Brian," Janie called over Billy's shoulder as he sauntered over to her, a little swagger in his step, a little glint in his eye. The girls stopped him halfway, rushing in for a couple of screaming, giggling hugs, and once satisfied, skipping away as quickly as they came. Billy stood up to continue his little strut over to where Janie was entrenched in hard construction, mixing cement for the swing set's leg holes.

"Hey, you. We almost needed you to sing at a frog funeral."

"I heard something about that." He glanced back at Brian who was busy doing time, pushing the weight of his little head first from one fist and then onto the other. Billy turned back to Janie, *man, am I going to tease her about this,* "I also heard you call me, 'Daddy,'" he said wickedly, "and I think I liked it."

She stopped what she was doing and smiled at him, it was wide and genuine, those black eyes of hers were almost playful. It was kind of giving him a twinge. She shook her head, "Couldn't let that one go, could you?"

"Are you kidding?"

She chuckled softly, "I am glad you're here early."

It was definitely giving him a twinge. "That's good," he grinned, flicking his eyebrows. *What is this about?* He was completely taken aback at her reaction to seeing him. It made him warm; it seemed to fill him with oxygen.

"Yes," Janie replied, "The other kids have left and Scotty and I are going out tonight and it would be so great to be able to have a little extra time, you know, just to look halfway decent. It's hard to get ready with so many little pumpkins running about."

And the weight of what she meant hit Billy.

And strangely hit him hard.

"Oh, so you're going out?" *You won't be here?* "I mean, Scotty has time. That's great." *Just great. Now I have to go make plans. I don't wanna make plans. I wanna stay at home... I mean, in toni... you know, here where I always... what the fuck?*

"Yes, I am so looking forward to it. I mean, I have just been so lonely lately..."

How lonely could you be? I've been here. "Uh-huh."

"...and Scott's been so busy and it's like we never see each other."

You don't ever see each other. "Uh-huh."

"I mean before it was bad but at least he wouldn't be traveling this much and I'd see him late at night or in the mornings and we could, you know, act like we were married." She laughed nervously. "Brian!" She shouted over Billy's shoulder again, "You're done. Come here, please."

'Act like you were married'-ugh, Billy snorted.

Brian trotted down to his mom. Janie leaned over the gate, "Say 'Sorry,' please."

"Sorry, Mama."

You know, I was a better, more attentive husband jacked up on coke than your Scotty ever dreamed of being. Billy crossed his arms in front of him.

"Kiss, please." Brian tilted his head back as his mother planted a quick smooch. "Now, say 'sorry' to the girls, and you're a free man." Brian scooted off to pay his penance to Ashley and Katie.

Billy's eyebrows were drawn down. *And I bet... no! Not 'bet,' I guarantee, GUARANTEE I'm better in b...* "Well, uh, do you need any help? I could, you know, take care of this and the kids could just run around and you could, uh, go get ready or something." *What am I saying? Am I a frigging idiot?*

"Billy," Janie looked over at him, totally surprised, completely grateful, "really?"

"Yeah, sure, sure thing. I can finish this up." *NO, NO, NO.* But he couldn't say 'no' to that look on her face, the way she just said his name. *What the hell?!* "Go, go'head."

"I can't tell you how nice that is. Billy, it really... you really are sweet. Thank you. Thank you." She impulsively grabbed his hand, leapt over the gate, and then ran up the stairs. "Katie, Brian, be good for Ashley's daddy! I'm right upstairs."

Billy watched her go, more pissed off than he had been in weeks. And damn it if he didn't want to know the reason why.

Scott came in through the gate to find Billy pouring cement over the bottom of the legs of the swing set. "Hey! Here's our hero!"

Billy's ire rose to his full height as he stood. "Hey Scotty, long time no see." *Prick.* "How's business?" *Absent daddy. Notice the kids haven't even realized you were here yet?*

"Amazing. We are in the middle of due diligence now with Houghton Mifflin and I think it is going really well."

Scotty seemed genuinely pleased with himself. "But I am so looking forward to just going out and relaxing. Just me and my wife."

I don't like you. Why would she like you?

"Where is she? Upstairs?"

"Yes, getting ready. I figured I could let her get stuff done without the kids bugging her." *How about that? Would you have done that? I don't think so.*

"You really have been our knight on the white horse lately. Janie told me all about what you did for Brian." Scott's voice cracked a little. "I can't believe we were so lucky to have you and Dev…"

"Del. It's Del. Delbert, but he doesn't like that."

"Well, to have you and Del come in and… you know, thank you. We, as a family, we thank you."

The words coming out of this man's mouth were just making the whole situation worse and worse. Billy's anger was spiraling down into the blackness of his fingernails and he wanted to fuck up his knuckles again in this man's face. He didn't like the experiences that he had shared in this house coming out of this guy's mouth. Scotty was taking something away from Billy, excluding him from this world, by even saying, 'thank you.' "Well, anyone would have done the same."

"But to think, of someone, you know, like you…"

Okay, is he giving me attitude, a chance to punch him?

"Like me, how?"

"I just mean, such a big celebrity in my house, helping us out, so much."

Dammit. No. He had to get out of here, before he did something. Something stupid. "Yeah, well okay. You're here, so I'm going to go now. Bye." Billy followed Janie's exiting strategy and leapt over the gate himself, he strode over to pick up Ashley from the sandbox. The little girl was startled by the sudden and abrupt end to her playtime, without warnings, or goodbyes especially, and she began to cry. Billy held her on his arm and stalked to the gate.

Janie, upstairs applying hot rollers to her long hair, heard the protesting Ashley and rushed to the window. She watched as Billy moved quickly to the car, buckled the little sobbing girl in, and once inside, Del took off, speeding down the street.

Scotty was bringing Katie and Brian upstairs. Janie met him at the top. "What did you say to him?"

"Huh? Say to Billy? Nothing." He handed one child and then the other over to her. "I said thanks and he said he had to go," Scott shrugged. "Can you hurry up in there, please? I need to get changed."

Billy had given this bird her third orgasm and he was still mad as hell. Something about it, besides the obvious, wasn't satisfying his need to punch that bitch-ass husband of Janie's who, technically, had done nothing but be sincere and nice to him. *I mean that absentee bastard has the balls to thank me on behalf of his family?! Asshole. Okay, so they were his family, but couldn't anyone else get the fact that he isn't ever there? He doesn't function as part of the family. Am I the only frigging normal one who thinks there is something wrong with that?*

He wasn't there to save his wife and his son from a lunatic pervert who had been allowed into his home during one of his many, many absences.

And Janie, making excuses for him, happy to see him, out with him tonight when she had plans with... well, she and I usually... I mean, I just assumed... fuck, I don't know...

Billy tried to explain this aggravating situation to his companion for the evening. She was sympathetic but not as annoyed about the circumstances as he thought she should be.

The girl looked at her nails and simply said, "It sounds to me like that woman is pretty stupid."

"Yes, thank you!" *SHE gets it.*

"I mean, it sounds like she could have you anytime but she insists on going back to that guy who is never there."

Wait. "No, she couldn't 'have me anytime.' That was not my point. My point…"

"She could have Billy Smitts, THE Billy Smitts and she chooses this slob who won't even stick around to help her with her kids. I mean, how stupid is that?"

"I never said she could have me…"

"Well, it sounds like she is just making one big stupid mistake turning you out for the night," she purred, "that I have definitely benefited from. I should go thank her."

"'Thank her?' For what?"

"Not wanting you."

It was ugly as he dismissed the girl from his company. Apparently, three orgasms weren't enough. *ARGH! THESE WOMEN! What the fuck do they want?*

Freud may have used sex as symbol, interpreting that one thought as Janie attempting to gain control over the uncontrollable aspects of her life. Freud's all about control. Control, and sex, ironically enough. Jung might have inferred something a little more subtle, like Janie was developing a marital-type relationship that may have caused her subconscious to equate Billy's fulfillment of some of the "husband" role to ALL aspects of the, ahem, marital duties. But Stacie, of course, after Janie confessed this errant vision to her almost two weeks after this night, would think something very different.

Janie had been a little mentally absent from the evening out with her husband but thankfully Scotty didn't seem to notice. He was chitchatting through the details of the due diligence process and was so enthusiastic it made her smile. But inside of her nods and grins, she was worried about Billy. He had seemed so happy when he arrived and the kids were all around him and then him leaving in a huff like that was just, well, *not him.*

Scotty and she were having a beautiful evening out and Janie decided she would figure out Billy later. Scotty had been so sweet to arrange the babysitting with Mrs. Sawyer across the street so they could stay out as long as they wanted. But it wasn't long before Scotty wanted to get home, Janie was anxious to as well. So they slid into his car and made their way to the silent Hadley house.

They kissed in the kitchen against the sink; they stumbled through the dining room and up the stairs. She was taking off his shirt, his pants; Scotty's hands were fumbling against her breasts, his mouth on her neck. They made their way to the bed. They made incredible, intense love, each hungry for something familiar they hadn't had in much too long.

But it was at that last crucial moment, as Janie was working the man beneath her, that the body transformed into a masterpiece of muscle and flesh working hard against her. She ran a finger gently through the nipple ring as the silver-ringed hands she had spent so long watching heal gripped her slim hips. And she held that incredible movie star face in her hand as his mouth met her breasts.

Oh shit. She lay back in the bed, catching her breath, as her husband kissed her goodnight and rolled over to sleep. *That son of a bitch Billy Smitts - you've got to be kidding me.*

Scotty woke her early the next morning. "Hey Sleepy." Janie awoke, startled by his voice. "Hey." She sat up abruptly.

"Wanted to wake you before I was off."

"Oh yeah, good. I'm glad you did."

"Last night was fun."

"Uh, yeah." Janie blinked rapidly, "It was. Yes, with you. It was nice for us to spend some time."

"I had a great idea."

"Oh? What is it?"

"Well, I know we haven't had much family time lately and I was thinking about making it up by taking a trip for Brian's birthday. You'll be done with Billy…"

"Huh?" her heart jumped a little.

"He's only got you under contract for a little while longer. So you'd be freed up a little and I'll have a day or so, and I thought that we could, you know, all of us, as a family, take a little trip. And I was thinking we should go down to Sea World."

"That would be a great idea," Janie, enthusiastically. "We had so much fun last year when we went for Brian's birthday. I bet he'd so enjoy that."

"You went last year?" Scotty's face betrayed a slight disappointment.

"Oh, yes, we did. Remember? You couldn't make it, so Stacie and Frankie and the boys drove down with me?" Looking at his face, Janie felt the guilt returning, with a couple of friends – meet 'Shame' and this is 'Remorse.'

She had to make this better. "But, you know, Katie and Brian had such a good time, I am sure they'd absolutely adore going again."

"Okay, good. We'll make the plan." Scotty smiled down at her, tying his tie. "We should also maybe have another night for you and me, in a couple of weeks. I think I'll have another night free and I could arrange my schedule so we could go out again."

"I'd love that, Scotty." Janie felt better. "I would really love that."

"Great." He seemed bolstered by the success of this idea. "Another date with your husband. I'll mark you on my calendar in ink - no meetings, no changes, no excuses. How about that?"

"Cool. I'm in ink." She smiled.

"Ink." He nodded reassuringly. "Gotta go. Have a good day, Janie. After last night," he winked at her, "I know I will." He leaned in to kiss her. She reached for him, the insane-irrational-fantasy penitence making her almost overly eager.

"Huh," he grinned, "I must have made a good impression too."

Janie laughed nervously, "Have a good day."

"Love you."

"Love you too."

Scotty left the room; Janie heaved out a huge breath, holding her face in her hands.

Billy had been the biggest bitch. Del was about to throttle him.

Everything sucked.

The coffee, the food, the stupid audience, the freaking weather, his shooting schedule - there was no pleasing him.

It had been a slow build to completely unbearable but Del had figured out what was wrong from the second Janie had first stopped him from coming in her door. Billy's face had looked like Janie had just kicked him in the balls; he dropped his ass into the back seat next to his daughter's booster. He had barely spoken on the way home, except for a word or two to Ashley. And as soon as she was in bed, he had pulled out a guitar and started picking over some Ray & Dave Davies' chords.

It was a bad sign.

And over the course of the following days, as the furrows in his brow grew deeper, Billy walked around the rented house with his guitar strapped to him like some sort of bow and arrow quiver - the saddest, angriest of Robin Hood's Merry Men, Robin PissedOffFellow. And the song selection moved from the Kinks to the Rolling Stones, played out real slow, with pauses - long, thoughtful, deliberate pauses, in between. The prolonged anticipation of the obviously familiar following chord was the key to making the music truly excruciating.

Oh, if Keith Richards ever heard what he was doing to his songs, he would throttle Billy with his wretched, cold, corpse-like, nicotine-stained hands.

And Billy did this

All.

Day.

Long.

Thank God, he hadn't moved his piano up here for the duration. Oh thank God.

And then that morning, Billy had laid into the little production assistant when he had asked if he needed him to run any quick errands for him, the kid was heading to the store and he'd be happy to pick up some mi… Billy just barked that he didn't need anyone – anything - and no one was gonna need the kid to do anything anymore for anyone.

The poor kid thought he was fired.

Del had to go talk to the producer, who ended up being pissed because one of his assistants was no where to be found and then Del had to go pick up the kid and oh Christ, it was a mess.

Del just prayed that Janie would let him back into her house sooner rather than later.

Before we got into the Beatles.

Janie analyzed any possible meaning that the O-thought may have had, except for the one that Stacie would have assumed was the most logical. "Did it make it better?"

"No," Janie said. Stacie didn't look convinced. "NO! Why did I bring it up?" Janie had been so distracted by this ridiculous, ludicrous thought that she shouldn't have been operating any heavy machinery for the past few days. And what was worse, she was letting it affect her relationship - business relationship - with Billy. She hurried him and Ashley out of the house at night, waiting at the door with Ashley's belongings and barely allowing him to step inside. She knew he and Del and Bobby were most likely starving to death on crappy take-out but sent plates home for Ashley every night, ensuring each day at Circle Time that Ashley ate it.

Billy didn't seem to take offense. He still seemed mad from the other night with Scotty, *which I will now never figure out what the hell is going on.* He barely looked in her direction as she greeted him right at the door.

Janie couldn't bear it anymore.

"So, most women have these types of harmless fantasies, don't they? With rock stars and movie stars? Or both, in say, my case, right?"

"Yes, but the fact is this is a movie star and/or rock star whom you know, well not technically Biblically, but at least intimately. I mean, he saved your son."

"I know! That has to be why this is hurting me so much. I want to know if he's okay; I just can't get over this stupid image, this thought, this millisecond of insanity. And Jesus, it's not like I would ever, ever, EVER, you know, act on it."

"Okay," Stacie said slowly. "Speaking as a friend, a casual observer, and not the wife of your husband's brother I must ask - um, why?"

"Stacie, come on, I am married. And have been for years, to a great guy. He is a great guy, really."

"Uh-huh." Stacie wasn't satisfied with the answer again.

"You know, Scotty and I have shared history, we have the same goals, and we know what we want out of our life together. Scotty is my partner. I just don't think anything would make me jeopardize that."

"Again, casual observation: I think you are just missing out on an opportunity of a lifetime. Or trying to convince yourself that you are not. "

"Well, I'm not." Janie sighed. "I'm just being stupid and I am missing out on my friend."

Janie rang the cell. Billy and Del were driving to the set for a night shoot. "Long Tall Sally" played out and Billy looked at it, panicked. He shoved it in Del's face. Del looked confused.

Billy whispered, "Answer it."

"What?"

Billy, whispered again, urgently, "Answer it!"

Del looked at the phone, "She can't hear you Mr. Smitts."

"Just… come on!"

Del answered. "Hello."

"Hello Del! What's new?"

"Hi Janie. Not much, just out and about with uh," Billy's eyes grew large as he shook his head, "…Bobby."

"How is Bobby? I haven't seen him in awhile."

"He is just fine. He's been out…" Del looked back at Billy, "…with a bad back actually."

"Does he need anything? I've got a heating pad if you guys need it."

"No, it should be fine. You're sweet to offer."

"You know me, Del. Just sticking my nose in."

"Well, you're just lucky it's a pretty nose," Del chuckled with Janie, stopping when he glanced back at his boss' pathetically anxious expression in the mirror. "But no, thank you."

"Well, tell him I hope he feels better."

"I will, Janie."

"Billy is shooting tonight, I take it?"

"Yes. Do you want me to have him call you?"

"No, it's okay. Just tell him that you and he and Ashley are welcome to stay for dinner tomorrow night if you guys don't have plans."

"I know I would love to come."

Janie laughed. "You are always welcome, Del. Tell Bobby to come by."

"Okay then. G'night." Del hung up and looked back at his boss in the rearview window. "She wants you to stay for dinner tomorrow."

Billy sat back, "She's not mad at me?"

"Didn't seem so."

"Then, what the hell's been going on?" Billy thought out loud. "It's that Scotty, he's been telling her not to hang out with me."

Del insinuated gently, "You mean, her husband?"

"Husband," Billy scoffed. "Yeah. Him." He looked down at his hands.

"Well, I am sure as hell glad she called." Del grinned, "I'm starving."

It took a minute, but Billy did smile.

Janie opened the door and for a brief moment Billy panicked, thinking that she was shuttling Ashley out to him again and he wasn't welcome back into the house. But he saw that she was smiling at him and was telling him to hurry up.

"Come on, the kids made something for you!"

Billy leapt up the steps, feeling light like he hadn't eaten for days, which was essentially true. He stepped into the kitchen and saw his beaming daughter, a happy Katie and a very proud Brian standing next to Ashley's Welcoming Project. Except, all over the full-sized poster of Billy Smitts with the cut-out newspaper pictures, were the words, "Our Hero!" Next to a picture of Ashley was pasted, "My Daddy!"; next to a picture of Janie, Brian and Katie was "Our Friend Billy!"

Billy laughed out loud and knelt to give his daughter a kiss and Katie and Brian a big hug. He turned to Janie and after a second's hesitation, put one hand in his pocket and with the other, waved, "That's very cool. Thanks."

She just nodded.

"And you guys!" He shook up Brian's hair, "I've been so busy with work, I've missed you all."

"Just like Daddy!" Katie exclaimed, then explaining patiently, "He's busy all the time. He misses us too."

"Yes, who wouldn't miss you, Katie?" Billy leaned down to say and she giggled and poked his pierced eyebrow. Ashley giggled at his exaggerated pained expression.

"Okay, come on, I need your help." Janie gently kicked the back of his knee. He clowned falling for the kids, which sent them giggling further. "Gotta go, the big boss Mama calls, scoot." The kids ran to the living room, their giggles trailing behind them.

"Take the roast out of the oven and I will put the potatoes in to melt the parmesan."

"Got it."

"All right then, put it on the counter and go get yourself a beer."

"Uh-huh," he opened the fridge to find chocolate strawberries resting on the bottom shelf. "Mrs. Hadley, you're trying to seduce me. Aren't you?"

Janie jumped, a chill went up her spine. "What?"

Pulling out the tray of delectable treats, "You're buttering me up for something."

"I am trying to say sorry I've been weird..."

"...keeping me from here."

"You could tell?"

"Did I do anything wrong?"

"No, absolutely not. I don't really have any excuse. It's just Scott has been gone for like almost a week."

"Uh-huh," Billy had known all about it.

"Yeah, and I think I've been alone too much." Janie's hands were in her back pockets. "I... the kids and I missed you. You've been such a good friend. Thus the strawberries."

"Del will need a plate of dinner if it's okay. But let's keep the strawberries between you and me. Or maybe just me."

Dinner was over. "Do you wanna stay, watch TV or something?" Janie ventured.

"Um, I actually can't. I have a night shoot tonight. Is it okay if Ashley stays though?"

"Absolutely," Janie replied. "Hey, you're just trying to get out of doing the dishes!"

"You need a dishwasher, dearie."

"Dare to dream," Janie chuckled. "I wouldn't know what to do with myself, all that extra time."

"Anything you wanted, Janie." His arms crossed, he kicked playfully at her shin, "And hey, when I am out of here and you get paid, you can buy whatever you want."

"Oh, yeah, I suppose. Sort of forgot about that."

"Only about a month more."

"Yeah, a month. Time…"

"Exactly."

"Okay, well, goodnight."

"Okay. See ya tomorrow." He went in to kiss Ashley, took Del's plate and his poster headed out the side door. "Thanks for this." He held up the poster.

"Trying to make up for…"

"I know." He looked in her eyes. He knew it was as close to giving her a hug as he could get. But when her dark gaze caught and held his, it felt closer. "Goodnight, Janie."

"Goodnight, Billy," she said quietly. Janie watched the door for a second after it closed and she sighed, *back to normal.*

Bobby had collected some information on Scott Hadley's dealings in Boston but it was exactly the information Janie had provided him with.

"No girls? I mean, not even a pro or two?"

"No, Mr. Smitts."

"Well, Christ, I mean, is he gay?"

"I wasn't able to observe any of that behavior, sir." Bobby replied.

"You're reaching, Mr. Smitts," Del remarked over his newspaper. "And I'm not exactly sure for what. Or to what end. What were you expecting to find?"

"I don't know," he said, petulant. "It's not like I was hoping for bad news for Janie or anything. It's just, I don't know." He decided, "I like to know what's going on with the people I work with."

"Uh-huh," Del snorted, turning back to page five.

"I do," Billy protested to the newsprint. "And I am happy that Janie's situation isn't what I thought it could have tragically been..." *The girl's right. I just can't get around her.*

The next morning, after witnessing Billy's debriefing of Bobby from his little mission to Boston, Del decided to warn Billy that Ian was acting a little suspicious back in LA, that somehow he may have heard about the whole night with that Billy Sanderson.

"Yeah, well, we can deal with that," Billy replied, as he was sitting in the makeup chair.

"I just didn't want him blindsiding you. He could try and get in contact with the guy and then there's a hell of a story for your Bad Boy angle. But then he asked about Janie..."

"What?!" Billy sat bolt upright.

"Well, not directly, he doesn't know anything, he just asked about the new 'nanny.'"

"She's not a nanny, Del."

"I know that."

"Janie and me, there isn't anything... what he's trying to imply... nothing like that, she's my friend, it isn't like that. At all."

Del put his hands up, "I understand, boss."

"Is it okay? I mean, you're sure he didn't say anything else?"

"Yeah, that's it. Just thought you should know."

"Okay, Del, thanks."

Del watched him for a minute, Mr. Smitts in the chair, chewing at his thumbnail. Del wanted to say something, more than what he had tried to imply here and there to his boss. *Janie,* Del sighed, *she wasn't anything like any girl Mr. Smitts had ever known before. She was well, normal? ...no, definitely not normal, but she was a real girl - woman, a real woman, as real as they come.* And Del was afraid that when it came right down to it, somehow all that reality was going to rock Mr. Billy Smitts. The Hollywood Man had been away from it for too long, wasn't used to it, and Del just knew that there was a rude awakening waiting for Billy when he would be forced to stop trying to play house with Janie.

And he would be, one way or another.

Within a week, Billy and Janie had returned to the pre-nocturnal-fantasy-coitus routine. Billy was over practically every night. And after they would bathe the kids and wrangle them into bed, Billy and Janie would sit on the couches, face to face and drink coffee and stay up watching a movie or TV or talking about nonsensical crap.

"Why is it, that you are technically the smaller of the two of us, that you get the bigger couch? You talk about my sense of entitlement!"

"I own the couches."

"No, I could go buy a bigger couch than that and bring it here and plop it in this room and you would still take the larger one."

"It's my house."

"Okay then, I buy two very comfortable couches, place them in the house that I am currently renting, which means, that at least for the time being, technically, it is mine. I then pick you up, take you to my house and which one are you taking?"

She smirked, "The bigger one."

"So you will admit it."

"No see, I am serving a purpose in your life. I am reminding you that you don't always get everything you want."

"Don't try to make it into a moral issue."

"Well then, I think it may be simply to prevent you from being too comfortable."

"Too comfortable?"

"Yes. You big celebrities are too soft, almost as soft as this big comfy couch. You need to be forced out into the real world, like on that too short loveseat, where you'll just have to make do, like everyone else, toughen you up."

On one or two of those nights, Scotty would walk in on them, both sound asleep on opposite sides of the room and he'd just leave them there. After night after night on spread-eagled across the metal bar under the lumpy office pullout, he'd grin at the thought of the whole bed - the soft cotton sheets, that clean laundry smell, all those feathery pillows to himself for another night.

In a few more weeks, Billy was scheduled to return to LA, the lease was just about up on the house and the shoot had all but wrapped. He had a scattering of makeups but he could easily do them back in the city. Tonight was his only last solid obligation, his last concert date to fulfill. He didn't let Janie know he could have left tonight if he needed to. Despite the fact he knew he had no real reason to stay, he just wasn't absolutely sure he wanted to go.

Ashley was settled at Janie's house for the night. Janie and Billy had a concert night routine and she handed him the cup of coffee that was waiting for him as he walked in the door. It was dark, hot, sweet and strong like warm chocolate. It slid down his throat gratefully. Del never could replicate it at the house; he kept trying everything Janie told him to do, even bought the same brand. He just couldn't do it. Del sat in the dining room, reading the paper with his own steaming mug, waiting for the boss to give him the signal. The kids were streaming in and out of the rooms, and Janie was washing dishes when Billy noticed, "Hey, you've got something on your face."

"What is it?" Her hands in the dishwater, she rubbed her cheek against her shoulder.

"Nope, you didn't get it." He stood up and turned her shoulders toward him. "It's brown, chocolate or something."

"You better hope it's chocolate," she laughed.

"It's on your neck too. Hold up." He tilted her chin up, and pulled away the long dark hairs where they had stuck to her skin. He grabbed a dish towel and dipped it into the sudsy water next to her hands. He pushed her chin away from him, holding it in the cup of his big hand, revealing the dirt attempting to climb the high peaks of her cheekbones. Her neck exposed so, he noticed the soft, gentle beating of her pulse just below her fine skin. He moved his hand around to the back of her neck, getting a handful of her dark, rich hair, to support the weight as he pushed back her chin to clean the mud off of her throat. He gently stroked the warm, wet cloth against her skin, clearing away the particles of dirt as the soap bubbles popped on her neck. He watched as the slow, quiet beating quickened. A lump rose in his throat. Del was watching them and Janie had cleared her throat and pushed his hands away, "Got it, got it all, Billy?"

"Yes," he said quietly.

"Well, break a leg."

He bent to kiss Ashley and signaled to Del that it was time to go.

The phone rang in the bedroom, late that night; Janie had fallen asleep on top of the covers still dressed in her daily uniform – t-shirt and jeans. She awoke and slid across the bed to grab it, "Hello?"

"Hey sweetie. Wanted to call and say 'goodnight.'"

"Oh, Scotty. I'm glad you did."

"Well, I figured since I can't be out of here for another couple of hours, I might as well just sleep on the pull-out couch here. Also, I wanted to talk about our plans, for tomorrow night?"

"Oh yeah, I bought a new dress online; it came yesterday, so just in time! Lucky me! And we have reservations at eight o'clock. So I can get the kids over to Mrs. Sawyer's house as soon as everyone else has cleared out..."

"Is there anyway we could, uh, make the reservations for earlier?"

Her heart stopped for a second, *no big, just a second,* "Um, yeah, I guess I could call."

"It's just that I might have to, uh, leave right after dinner. Well, not right after dinner, but probably out on a Red Eye."

"Oh. I thought…" her voice trailed off.

"Yeah, but Boston called and they need someone to come in and present to the Suits our profit margins for the last five years. And you know we've barely been making a profit over the last two years." He heaved a big sigh, "The quarterlies don't look great. I am really nervous about this, Janie. It could put us under, the whole deal, if they don't like what they see and at this point I am kind of forced to jump through whatever hoop they lay out for us."

"Um, yeah. I get it. I just was hoping, you know, since you 'inked' me…" She was trying so hard to sound casual. *He was stressed out, and God knows he doesn't need me added on to his problems.*

"I know, Janie. They just need me."

But she couldn't help it, she was hanging on here but the thread was thinning. "Well, me too, Scotty." *No, Janie, don't.* She recovered, attempting to accommodate her way out of guilt. He needed her help; he needed her to be strong. "But, I'll do what I can with the reservations, you know, just whatever, okay? Just, we can work it out and we'll have a great time. I'm looking forward to it, Scotty. I've been really looking forward to it."

"Me too, honey. We'll have a nice dinner. I promise. Okay? Talk to you tomorrow."

"Okay. I love you." *Desperate, I sound desperate.*

"Love you, too. Goodnight."

"Goodnight."

Scotty hung up. Janie put the receiver down. She could barely breathe, she had to stand up, walk around. *I'm not going to cry. It's not that big a deal. We're still going out. It's going to be nice.* She was choking, *a window, I just need air.* She ran to the window and threw it open, gasping for any oxygen that she could draw into her lungs. *The kids, I'll go to check on...*

The phone rang again, *Scotty,* she turned and leapt for the phone, *maybe he...* She collected herself, "Hello?"

"Hey," the deep bass of the voice probably vibrated the telephone line all the way to her house.

"Hi," Janie sighed impatiently, *did he have a-time-to-irritate-Janie-sense or something?,* grabbing a tissue from the nightstand, wiping her nose, "Do you know what time it is, Billy?"

"About 2 am," he answered. "You okay?"

"Yes. I'm fine. Why the hell are you calling me? It's late and I'm tired."

"You sounded like you were sniffing."

"I was, uh, sneezing, Billy," she lied. "Seriously, calls this late, not cool. Are you drunk?" Janie had noticed awhile back he had a 'tell,' most people would just think he was being deliberate, but Janie had figured out that Billy spoke extra slowly when he had had a couple, *like he was choosing each word especially for you.*

"Little," he admitted, then asked, "You were sneezing in your sleep? I didn't think that was possible."

"I wasn't asleep. Billy, why are you calling me?"

"I was bored."

"What? No company tonight?"

"Nah, didn't feel like it, too tired. I am on my own tonight. By myself. Plus I've got an early call and..."

"Then go to sleep."

"Take your own advice, dearie."

"Well, I can't with you people calling me."

"This late? Who'd call you this late at night?"

"Just you," Janie sighed, *I don't need to explain it, it's not like this is his business.* "How'd the show go?"

"Oh, good, really good. Thank you for asking me."

Billy asked, "How are the kids? They sleeping?"

"Yep."

"How'd bedtime go? I was thinking about you all right around 8 o'clock, wondering if they'd be in bed or trying to get another story out of you."

"I'm not the softie, that's you."

"Nuh-uh," Billy protested. "So," taking a deep breath, "I have to be on set at six, and it would be a waste of time to go to bed now, dontcha think?"

"No."

"Yes it totally would. Hey! I can come over there!" like he had just thought of the idea.

"Okay, you've crossed the line, buddy." Janie started in, her mild irritation turning into complete and total exasperation.

"What? You're awake, I'm awake," he laughed. "I'll bring breakfast. For you and me and I'll get something for the kids so you wouldn't even have to cook this morning. You like French toast. I can get you French toast."

"It's two am! And clearly you should NOT be driving."

"I'll get Del to take me. Okay then, see you in a few."

"NO! Don't you dare! You are not waking Del!" It was quiet on the other end; *he'd left, didn't he?* "Billy Smitts! Get back here! BILLY! Do not hang up this phone!"

He was laughing on the other end of the line, "Nah, I just, I'm just being a pain in the ass."

She heaved out a breath, "You've got that right."

"Well, you're the only one I see. I don't have any just regular friends…"

"...that you can remember their names after you call for a cab."

"You're funny."

"Yes, I am. Not for much longer though."

"I'm pushing it?"

"Pretty far."

"Okay, I'll go. Hey wait, did I talk to you about Ashley and her whole monsters thing?"

"Billy?"

"Yes, Janie."

"Are you trying now to come up with a pretense for calling me at two am after you've been drinking all night at your show?"

"Yes. Yes, I am."

"You're a little too late for that." She tried not to chuckle at his honest reply, *it would only encourage him.* "Okay, here's what I want you to do..."

"Anything for you."

"Okay then, go get two Tylenol, have them with a big glass of water, set your alarm and get into bed."

"Where did you come from, Janie Hadley?" he said intently. "You are, you are so good. Amazing, really. An amazing girl. Hey! 'Amazing Girl' – like a superhero."

"Yes, great, now, let's just say 'goodnight' and I will see you tomorrow evening. Wait, sorry, tonight."

"Okay. Tonight. But not now, right?"

"Not now."

"Okay. I hope you have sweet dreams, Janie."

"Thanks, Billy. You too."

"Thank you."

"Bye."

"Bye."

"Are you going to hang up?"

"Yes."

"Then do it."

"Okay. Goodnight, Janie," he sang into the receiver.

"Goodnight, Boozie." She clicked the receiver down, shaking her head. *How did I get myself into this? Really. A few months ago, had anyone told me I'd be fielding late night calls from a drunken rock star as he was trying to fend off boredom, I would have probably thought they were certifiably insane. And now, this is just part of my everyday life. Billy.* She undid the hooks of her bra and slipped the straps through her t-shirt sleeves. *Thank God I don't have to deal with this for much longer, right?* The thought made her sort of smirk to herself. She unbuttoned her jeans and slid them down her long legs. *It is not like I'll miss this. Or him.* She frowned at herself, *that pain in the ass?* smirking again.

Janie crawled over to her side of the bed, and pulled the covers over her. Over the course of that ridiculous phone call, her heart had settled back into place and she was able to breathe again. Maybe she could think a little more clearly. *Okay, it's okay, it's going to be okay, with Scotty. So maybe dinner wasn't exactly what I had hoped, but maybe, maybe when we take this trip... When he and the kids and I go to Sea World, maybe that's when it will start to get better. It's gotta go somewhere, right? Anywhere –*

The phone rang again. Janie rolled across the bed, picked the receiver off of the hook and wearily answered, "Yes?" wishing she could predict lottery numbers as easily as she could predict who was on the other end of this call.

"What should I do, my Amazing Girl," the words picked their way one by one over the telephone line, "if I don't have any Tylenol?"

Janie couldn't help herself - the tension of the day; the shit, *yeah, I am finally going to call it 'shit'* Scotty was putting her through, again, making her feel like she had to jump through hoops to get his attention away from paperwork and due diligence and clients and spreadsheets and everything else for a half a second; the fact that it seemed that she was living a whole life separate from her husband's, a life they were supposed to be sharing; that silent suffocation she felt at times was encompassing her whole existence; and now, tonight, the absolute, utter absurdity of the situation, this insanity. Janie couldn't help it.

She just started to laugh.

Chapter Fourteen
Janie's 199Sometime

Janie had always known what her currency was with her mother. She didn't realize until Junior year in college how fucked up it really was - when her mother used her refusal to do the Miss California pageant to cancel her summer plans to visit her dad. They wouldn't have the money to get through the summer if Janie didn't work.

"What about Joseph? Picked up anyone else yet?" Janie had sneered. Twenty is still such an evil age, but Janie couldn't stand her stepfather and any opportunity she had to put him down in her mother's eyes, she would take.

He's not like Daddy, Mom.

"Janie, Joseph is dedicated to your career. You don't work, Joseph doesn't get paid, darling. You know that."

Great agent. One fucking client and he married her mother so he could get her.

Janie had realized she had not been completely innocent in this game. She had learned how to play it and well - a pageant here, she got an envelope of money; a commercial, her mother had bought her a little used Volkswagen; a print job, and her mom had agreed to pay for on-campus housing. And if Janie felt her mom just had a little bit too much control, she'd just refuse to do anything more.

Until of course, her mother told her she couldn't see her father. *Checkmate.*

Janie never got those girls who spent their lives preparing for these pageants, *crazy dedication.* Janie had always treated it like a business deal - that's what she was becoming, *that's something to be proud of,* she would shame herself. She did the show and got paid, the "scholarship" money for coming in second, her mom and her stepdad could live off of that for a couple of months.

Janie actually enjoyed herself at that particular show; she fucked up pretty much everything on purpose, even going so far as to show up high on some good pot at her Personality Interview. Strangely enough, the judges seemed to like her, even as she laughed through most of the dumb questions and called one of them "Dude."

After the show, Janie's mom kept her promise. And she did get to go up north to the house where she grew up. But Janie didn't get to spend her yearly two months with her father.

Her father had died.

Janie had sleepwalked through the process of his wake, his cremation, his memorial service and her return to LA. But back in her mother's home, amongst the sashes, ribbons and trophies, Janie found a moment of intense clarity. *This isn't my life. I don't have to live it.* She packed up her things, and left her mother's home, driving steadily back north to the big house where she grew up, where her father had been found after about five days. The mailman had noticed that the same lights had been on for almost the whole week and the car had never left the driveway. Her dad had died alone, from complications of diabetes he had never known he had.

He had been alone.

Janie finished out her Junior year commuting two hours to class and back. She fought against the tide, flailing through the gamut of clichéd rebellious actions, refuting her mother's way of thinking, her way of life that had only survived because of the slot machine existence of a decent-looking daughter. Janie grew out that stupid Anchorwoman haircut that her mom had made her trim religiously every 6 weeks; she gleefully threw away the pageant paraphernalia. Janie found her breath, laughing as her head popped above the surface, out from under the hundreds of dollars worth of pageant gowns and shoes and pancake makeup and the endless supply of panty hose, nail polish, duct tape, hairspray and toupee glue.

Ridiculous, stupid, inane shit. Stupid way of life. Stupid way to raise a daughter, stupid way to ruin a family, stupid, stupid, stupid, selfish bitch.

Her mother had called and called her at the old house. She knew where she was, she warned over the answering machine. Sometimes, Janie would answer and hang up as soon as she heard the voice. Once Joseph had attempted to get through, she heard his voice and laughed. And hung up. The calls stopped and the last thing Janie had gotten from her mother was a bill forwarded to the house for her tuition for Senior year.

It was then that she met Scotty.

Chapter Fifteen
Del's Night Off

Billy decided to let Del have the night off so he could drive himself out to pick up Ashley. *Nothing new, nothing special, just felt like heading over alone tonight.* He settled into the plush leather of the driver's seat and agreed with himself that it was always smarter to arrive without a driver, less conspicuous. He turned on the radio and immediately his own voice popped out of the speakers.

Ugh. Something else, quickly. He reached unseeing into his Classics cd case, *yep, ole time rock n' roll,* pulled it out and probed the lips of the player gently until the shiny disc caught and slid from his strong fingers. He made himself not peek and Elton John's young voice began upon the theme of musical superheroes. *What do I have to do tonight after I get Ashley? Nothing really. Maybe I'll see what Janie's up to. If she wants company, if there's anything good on TV or maybe watch a movie or something, hell, she could do her laundry and we could hang out,* he laughed. *She's a good sport. She puts up with my shit. Well, honestly, she puts up with everyone's shit.* His thoughts turned darkly to Scott. *He is either the dumbest fuck I have ever met or he's got something seriously unbelievable on the side hidden away where no one, not even my own...*

Aw, you know what? Just forget it. Fuck him. Not worth thinking about.

Dumbass.
But Janie, such a good kid, you know, a good person.
You don't meet many good people nowadays. Genuinely
good people like that. And she's funny, that girl. Funny-
like-a-man funny.
Although, she isn't anything else like a man, right?
Well, no, but you couldn't help but somewhat notice
that. But she's cool. And she is so good for Ashley. And her
kids, she's brilliant with those kids. She's so patient, she
just deals with it all. She's just... She just discovers them,
she takes a couple of seconds to figure out who they are
and, I don't know, just brings it out.
Like that Austin kid, who likes to build stuff and Janie
ordered him that little construction kit. Or Ashley when
Janie gave her those markers, special just for my little girl?
Ashley just stared at them with this look, this amazed, sort
of wondrous look. Janie's just got it down, structure,
understanding, she's just cool. She gets it. Well, honestly,
she just gets everyone, too.
His voice swelled out of his chest and sang to Taupin's
lyrics, almost involuntarily, letting himself be drowned out
by the music coming from his stereo. His fingers popped on
the steering wheel, keeping alternate time and he turned
onto her street and a smile jumped to his face. *So, Janie's*
like this cool girl, a great pal. And being with her and the
kids has been good for me, like a little vacation from the
real world. I haven't felt this good... well, ever. She's good
to be with. You know, with the kids.
He pulled the sleek, black Mercedes into the driveway,
behind the white minivan. *We're good together with all*
those kids too, he congratulated himself. They could
practically run tag team tub and dinner time without a
single episode of fighting, bickering or whining. *From the*
kids anyway, he chuckled. *They would laugh for most of the*

two-hour homestretch. That girl can be so funny. She's a good friend, an incredibly good friend.

He swung his leg out of the car door and straightening up, he saw her in the doorway, holding open the screen for him and smiling. He almost didn't recognize her at first, except as the girl whose wallet he had lifted at the bar. Her dark sheet of hair had that funny bend in it from her ponytail and it fell softly across her shoulders and spilled down the soft curve of her breasts. The entirety of her makeup-less face was smiling, her lips, her eyes, her cheeks, her skin glowing in the early evening light. She was barefoot and a small bony knee peeked out of the rip in her soft blue jeans, that pair that just hugged those slim hips of hers and rode low under her little belly button. Her shirt lifted gently on the side of her outstretched arm as if in compliance with the lustiness of this moment. He saw the buttery skin, the smooth line of her stomach that curved down from just below her breasts. In the milliseconds before her hello, there flashed a brilliant image of him walking to her and pulling that shirt over her head and letting her chest fall against his. His hands implored him to do it, step closer, cup that warm flesh in his palms. His sharp intake of oxygen and the blood leaving his brain temporarily cleared the fog from his vision and he rocked backwards onto his heels.

Recovering slightly, he saw that she didn't look any different in the twilight of today than yesterday evening when he came to kiss Ashley goodnight and suck down a hot, strong coffee before a long night onstage. Janie had had dried mud on her cheek and her neck and a couple of her long dark hairs had stuck to it. He had gently pulled them away from her fine cheekbones and noticed the pale skin beneath it. Last night, Del had been watching and he had felt the big man's eyes on them. Billy had looked quickly away before he noticed the blood pulsing in the veins in his own neck.

It was just that last night, in that second, every instinct he had told him that it would have been much more natural if he had just put both of his hands in her hair, leaned in and kissed her goodbye, promising her that he'd run right back after the show that night, asking her to please stay up for him, than what had actually occurred - their awkward pulling away, their sudden self-consciousness, their tingling awareness of how close their bodies had actually been. The conflict of thought and reality had confused him momentarily then, but now, looking at her fully, he believed he could recognize what he saw and how he was responding.

Unaware of the fact that she was being made love to repeatedly in quite a few different ways, Janie gave him sort of a funny smirk, "You feeling okay today?"

"Yeah. Why?" He cleared his throat, freaked. *Could she see? Christ!*

"Just after the call. Last night. You were a little inebriated."

"Oh, yeah, the drunk dialing. Sorry." He pulled his lower lip from his teeth, confessing, "I haven't done that since I was a kid and I was after this girl and she wouldn't go out with me. I got Booze Guts and called her. It didn't help."

"Really? You?" Janie replied, a little amazed. "Well, I have to say, I've never been a victim before." She laughed, "You were pretty funny, and I needed a laugh…"

"You did? Well then, good. I did good…"

"…but don't ever, ever do it again."

"Okay, gotcha."

"Where's Del?"

"He's off tonight."

"Oh, shame, Ashley, Katie, Brian and I made him some cookies."

"I'll bring'em back to him. And again, thanks for keeping Ashley for the night, is she ready?"

"Oh, yes. Hold on, the phone. Her stuff is all ready to go, just let me grab this." She ran from the door to answer the urgent ringing.

"Okay." He cocked his head, watching her ass leaving him outside alone.

She yelled behind her, "You coming in?"

"Yep, be right there." The screen door snapped shut behind her. *Okay, there is no need to get weird now. It was just a quick couple of seconds, she'll be back to normal. I mean, that was what happened before.* He had seen her, he was drunk and the long hair and her tits, her face, and she looked beautiful and *hell, anything looks good when you are drunk,* and they talked and she was nice and funny and he had taken her wallet to find out who she was and he had come to her house and then they had made the deal. *And then they were friends. Good friends who helped each other, and discovered that they liked the same stuff and could talk or hang out or whatever. Like friends are supposed to do, right? Right. And they could laugh and play with the kids. So, it's no big deal.* He had seen her like this before, the weird dreams too, and that all went away pretty quickly, like the odd hangover he had had when he went to this house for the first time.

Inside, inside, walk inside. His feet tripped up the cement stairs and he walked in through the now vacant doorway.

He walked into the kitchen, and Janie came in with the phone to her ear and the kids trailing around her legs. Ashley leaped up at him and into his arms.

"Good day?" he hugged her tightly.

"Yes! I'm going to play! Bye!" She danced out of his grip, her blonde hair whirling as she grabbed Brian's hand and ran from her father.

The corner of Janie's lip curled downward as she hung up the phone, and her eyes looked a little red, a little swollen. Billy forgot all about his idiocy.

"What's up?" Billy, his face twisted into concern.

"Nothing, had plans, but they just fell through." *So much for ink.* She snuffed, clearing her throat.

"I thought you said you never got out?" he said incredulously.

It made her laugh a little, "Yes, can you believe it? Again! I had Mrs. Sawyer all ready to sit the kids and I was planning on scooting out just after you and the little girl left tonight."

"Oh, okay. Well, I, uh, have to get going pretty quick so…" He stumbled over his words.

"Well, don't hurry unless you have to." She exhaled. "Dammit, I was looking forward to this night out. Too bad, I guess." Feigning indifference from the disappointment, Janie didn't want Billy to see her hurt; she didn't want to see his face wrinkle with concern. He didn't need to waste that on her. "Yep, too bad; I'm all hopped up on coffee and nowhere to expel this extra awake-i-tude."

He smiled slightly, "You feel like hanging out?"

"Yeah, that'd be good. I've got plenty of food for Ashley and you. Oh, but wait, don't you have something?"

"Uh, no. That was just a ruse."

"A ruse?"

"Yes, I am internationally known, and I don't think it would do for my public image for me not to be having some type of plans for a Saturday evening."

"Ah, clearly I need a refresher on my PR strategies. So, should I put Ashley's sleeping bag back on the bed? She can park there until you go, then we'll just bag her up, fling her in the trunk and you can split."

"Perfect." He smiled again, right at her. His eyes poring into hers and she smiled right back.

Stacie heard Frank playing in the living room with the boys as she went over the bills in the kitchen. Stacie's listened to the finely choreographed routine, the kid noises stopped, the vacuum started and then exactly two minutes later, Stacie heard the sounds of Nick Junior coming on. In a few moments, Frank would amble in for his usual 'Hey! How was your day?' And Stacie wasn't really all up for that conversation yet again. She buried her head in the PacBell paperwork.

She knew Frank had come in, she could feel him standing in the doorway but he didn't speak for several minutes. When he did finally talk, he had to clear his throat before he began, "Stace-," Frank a-hemmed, "Stacie, I know what you've been doing. You know, out. What's been going on. With you."

Stacie's heart stopped momentarily to make the leap up into her throat. She had known for awhile that it really was just a matter of time; she planned to refute it, refute it all - *what good would it do for him to know? For them? Really?* In her head, she had always strategized that it would be simplest to answer these questions with a full out, 'Oh, Frank, what the hell are you talking about?' but this wasn't a question. It was a statement. And when she lifted her head to look up into his eyes, all she could answer was, "Oh."

"I know what has been going on, Stacie, and as your husband, I need to ask you to stop. Stop before you go too far. I can't let you do that to the boys. Or to me."

"Frankie, I…" Stacie began.

"I know it's been going on since he came around," Frankie interrupted. "I know you've been spending a lot of time with him and it's not like I don't understand the appeal."

"Wait," Stacie interrupted him, "He who, Frank?"

"Billy. Billy Smitts."

Stacie heaved a huge sigh and shook her head, Frankie began lamenting his inadequacies as a husband and pleading his case that he had always been loyal to her and that they could work it out if she would just… "Okay, Frank. Stop. Just right there."

"And God, I'm not him. God, I'm not even as good-looking as Scotty for Pete's sakes or a big business guy who wings off on huge important business trips and takes such good care of his family…"

"Okay, you can't even know the irony of that sentence."

"What?"

"If you are somehow worried about me and Billy Smitts being in love, don't. The retard hasn't even looked at me sideways. As far as Billy Smitts goes, I am not the one you should be worried about."

"What?" Frankie stopped, confused. "Who? Who should I be worried about?

"Janie."

Frank looked as though Stacie had just hit him in the face with a brick. "Janie?!"

"Yes. Janie. Janie and Billy Smitts."

"Janie?" *Never.*

"Billy Smitts and Janie Hadley."

"But Janie would never…"

Stacie had had enough, "Really, Frank? She wouldn't? Why not? Because she's perfect? Well, you know, what?

Maybe Janie isn't perfect. And maybe it is high fucking time everyone realized that."

"But…"

"No! You want me to prove it.? I'll prove it to you right now." Stacie grabbed her phone, "Call her. You always call her. Ask her, Frank. You ask her everything else."

Frank just shook his head.

"Fine," Stacie frowned, "I'll do it. She's supposed to be out with her husband tonight. But I can probably make a sure bet he canceled on her. But you know who won't? Billy. I bet you he'll be there, right now."

Frankie just stood there, dumbfounded. Stacie was disgusted, she dialed furiously, hitting the speakerphone. The phone rang and Janie picked up, her voice sounded happy, breathless, like she had been laughing too hard for too long, "Hello?"

"Hey Janie, it's Stace. I'm heading out for a few, you want to come with me? Frank can watch the kids."

"Oh, Stace, I'd love to," Janie still had a smile in her voice, the kids were giggling in the background, and a distinctly male tone was present, "but I think I'm in for the night."

Listen to her, Frank. Stacie pointed to the phone. "Are you sure? We'll just have a couple of drinks and then maybe see what's happening out in town."

"No Stacie. Thanks, have fun, okay. And be good."

"I'll try. You too."

Janie chuckled, "Call me tomorrow, okay?"

"Sure thing. Have a good night." Stacie hung up and turned to Frank. "Billy is there."

"How… how do you know that, Stacie? You're making assumptions. That could be her and Scotty with the kids."

"Have you ever, in all of your time knowing Scotty and Janie together, ever heard her like that with him? She's different, Frankie. It's like she's woken up."

Frankie just shook his pudgy little head, "But Janie, she wouldn't."

Stacie couldn't stand it. "You men, you are all so stupid. Janie isn't perfect. She's a human being, just like everyone else. *Like me.* She makes mistakes, she does stupid things and she had needs. She's not a robot who can just keep going on and on and on without recharging a battery, ever. She tries to make everyone believe that she is perfect, that she's got life all under control and you men, you see her making her way through it and you fall for it. But life isn't like that, it can't be. No matter how hard you try. It's messy. There are ugly feelings and dumb hopes and huge disappointments that you can't schedule away. And you can't pretend that they don't exist as you can sweep them all up and throw them all out and hope that no one ever looks in the trash bin because they'll see the great big mess we all live in. And her life, alone in that house all the time, with no one more than two little babies to keep her company and a husband who may or may not be on the other end of a phone line? You think that is really pretty to look at under the surface? You think there isn't a shitload of loneliness and sadness there?"

"But Janie, I just can't believe that she would ever, do that. That she would cheat on Scotty."

"She hasn't cheated on Scotty."

"What?"

"She doesn't... she isn't... I don't think she even knows how Billy feels," Stacie laughed ruefully.

She knew she had just rocked Frankie's world. The two people he had looked up to the most, the ones he always thought had everything anyone could ever want, who had planned their whole wonderful life together with their beautiful children in their great house. They were just like everyone else, ugly and afraid, and maybe, out of control. She could see he was trying to put something into words; he stuttered, "I just can't believe that she would ever let something like that happen, Stacie. She wouldn't ever let that happen. Not with what her mother did... not after all that she went through..."

"Maybe she is doing something, Frank, I don't know. But you know what? You can't judge her. You can't even blame her. Maybe it is wrong, maybe it is destructive but maybe she just needs to be reminded that she is more than just someone's mother or someone's wife. Maybe she just needs to be reminded that she is a real person, again. Not what everyone thinks, what everyone expects she should be."

Frank just put his hands over his eyes.

Stacie was exasperated. She couldn't make him see what was right in front of his face, everything she had just told him, everything it could mean about Janie, maybe, even about herself. She grabbed her bag. "You know what, Frankie? Believe what you want." She opened her kitchen door and looked back at him, "Maybe Janie isn't the one you should be worried about after all."

Stacie slammed the door behind her. Frank didn't move.

The rest of the routine with the kids went on without too much trouble. Stacie had called during the time when a round of stomach raspberries caused an issue. Janie and Billy had both refused him to blow on Janie's stomach: *Why not?* Katie and Ashley wanted to know. *They were part of the game; they should play by the same rules as the kids.* After hanging up the phone, Janie handled it all with graceful aplomb, explaining that it wouldn't be appropriate for someone else's daddy to do that to someone else's mommy. That seemed to settle the children down; a large word like "appropriate" usually put them in a pensive state.

But the effect of the idea told its impact a little while later, for tub time got a little more out of control than usual. Billy and Janie sat together on the floor, knees against the wall of the tub, monitoring the splashing to tubwater ratios when suddenly there was a spike in activity. In homage to last year's birthday trip to Sea World, Brian soaked the first five rows.

Janie burst into laughter, "Brian!" The boy looked over at his mom and stifled a little giggle in his prune-y fingers, but as his eyes glanced over at his buddy Billy, his small face froze. Billy was attempting recovery from a dream flashback when Janie looked at his stunned face, "Oh Brian that is probably an expensive shirt. Please don't do that again." Brian slunk back down into the water. She grabbed a towel and thankfully, flung it around her neck, then soaked up most of the water that had breached the sea wall.

Janie turned on her knees to the sopping wet man next to her. Billy's black Prada t-shirt hung from his shoulders and his hair had sprung up into immediate short curls. Janie half-smiled at him and pulled another towel down for his face. "That's about an hour's worth of primping down the tubes, huh?"

"I don't primp."

"You wear nail polish!"

"It's black!"

"I betcha you take more time to get ready than I do. And I was a pageant girl. C'mere."

"No." He was making a decided effort to not to look under, around, next to and beside the towel at the damp assets of the woman in front of him.

It surprised her that he wasn't taking the bait for her joke, "Are you seriously gonna be a baby about a little water? C'mere, take that shirt off."

"No. And I'm not being a baby."

"Yes, you are. Come here." She slid over to him, grabbed the hem of his shirt and pulled it over his head. He was nothing but white flesh over hard muscle. "I'll get you something dry, you're skinny enough, you can wear one of mine." She leaned over to whisper in his ear, "Toughen up, Smitts. Don't be such a pussy."

The spell broke again and he grabbed her wrist, laughing ominously, "You're getting it now dearie!" Billy picked her up, held her arms and leaned her far over the tub, as Janie screamed laughing and the children, in sheer delight, splashed out, "Katie! Ashley! Brian! Get her!"

Shirtless, Billy was helping the kids dry off as Janie changed. She beckoned the half-naked man into her room. "Here." She held up a t-shirt for him. "Good?"

"Good."

She rolled it up in her hands and flipped it over his head. He pushed his arms through, laughing, "I'm not one of the kids!"

"Sorry, habit."

"I know, Janie. It's a bad one."

They stood facing each other. It was a funny moment of indecision for Janie. Billy was notoriously a close talker who also didn't seem to mind silences. *I mean, he would almost be on top of whomever it was he was speaking to and when you watched him he wouldn't back away when the conversation stopped. He would just keep looking, listening for something, taking as much pleasure in it as in talking.* It had taken so much for her to get used to, but she had slowly begun to accept it, even enjoying his proximity and occasional close looks.

But these soft, quiet moments rattled her. Like last night, when he had grabbed a fistful of her hair behind her neck to clean some mud off, she had felt something akin to a great fear – not exactly frightening but something close, like the deep turns on a dark and fast drive. And now, every single one of her instincts, her overdeveloped flight impulses, were screaming at her to look away to, to leave the room, to *get out, flee!* She held out against them for a second, almost like a challenge, just to see if she could, looking right into his eyes. He smiled at her. She grinned back for a half an instant more.

It was all she could bring herself to bear.

She decided finally that it had to be irritation; he must be irritating her, "Get out of my way, Billy." She pushed past him and ran to the children for safety, "Kids! Underpants! 'Jamas! Pronto!"

Enough was enough, wasn't it? Just then, Billy could feel her. Her eyes, something in them, brought him back to that feeling from that day out in the yard. As much as he had tried to convince himself otherwise, he'd been cresting that wave for a while and just now, it was there. She was so close to him again - he found himself shaking. *What the hell?!* Anger, frustration flooded throughout him. *This is just un-fucking-fair. How can that man who gets to share this room with her come home every night and look at her and be able to feel that and not take her to bed with him? How could he see what she was and ignore it day after day? Did he not realize what he had, that I would fucking*

*give up everything I have ever had or done or seen to have
anything like this?*
    Or maybe, he really meant, *just to have this.*

    The final preparations were made for goodnights.
Stories were over; Billy had provided voice talent as well
as some impressive stuffed animal puppetry. Giggles were
calmed. Everyone had a cup of water, everyone had
brushed their teeth, and everyone had made a last potty run,
complete with hand-washing, Janie had double-checked
with Brian. Katie and Ashley were bunked down already in
Katie's room where Brian stood waiting to be carried into
his bunkbed after saying "Goodnights" to the girls. Well,
for Brian it was "Happy Birthday Goodnights."
    Janie had tucked and kissed each of the girls and finally
picked up little Brian, "Oh, Ashley, don't forget your
Daddy's kiss. Wendy's thimble to Peter. He needs it to be
strong, right?" Ashley leaped from her sleeping bag on the
trundle bed and kissed her father goodnight.
    Katie peeked out from her blankets, "Mama?" she
called.
    "What, sweetie?"
    "Could I give Billy Wendy's thimble, too?"
    "I want a kiss!" Brian said into her neck. "And he can
take me to bed."
    Janie was startled, she bit her lip, *it didn't feel... is this
crossing a...* but she couldn't think of any real reason not to
let them, or any excuse wouldn't make it seem like she was
being weird, "I guess so, if it's okay with you and, uh,
Ashley?" She looked at Billy, he didn't look at her, he
simply nodded. Ashley giggled and nodded, too.

Happily, Katie reached over as Billy knelt and she gave him a kiss, hugging him tightly around the neck. "Goodnight."

"Goodnight, girls." He took Brian from Janie's arms and left a fresh crop of giggles behind him. Janie shushed the two little friends as she shut out the light and closed the door behind her. She drew the corner of her lip down, watching Billy carrying her son to his room, Brian waving to her over the man's shoulder. It was so sweet to watch, and so rare that her children behaved like this with anyone but her, she was thankful to him for it, but, she couldn't shake a feeling that maybe this situation *...I don't know... wasn't how it was supposed to be.* Janie was so strict with her boundary lines, how had she let something slip by her? *What were they really doing here?* It wasn't bad, it didn't feel bad, it filled a little hole, loosed the knot in her neck, she could be grateful for that and *maybe Billy had just earned it.* She watched him lay Brian gently in his bed, cover him with his Bob the Builder blanket, lay his big, scarred, black-nailed hand on the little boy's cheek, give him a peck on the forehead and say, "Happy Birthday, Brian."

"Happy Birthday, Billy. Goodnight."

Janie leaned over and kissed her son, "Goodnight sweet boy." *It was okay, it was alright.*

"Goodnight, Mama. Happy Birthday."

"Thanks, baby."

As the kids were finally settled down, each kissed and tucked, a finally dry Janie expected to meet a fully-clothed Billy already settled in his place in the living room, but he was nowhere to be found. She looked around, "Where are you?"

He opened the back door, calling in brusquely, "On the porch."

Ooh, smoking outside, good. It's been weeks, I could have one. She grabbed the baby monitors and joined him on the back porch. "Gimme one."

"No." He wouldn't look at her, he dragged on the butt.

"What?" She put down the monitors.

"No."

She searched for his eyes, he pointedly avoided her face. "Can I ask you what is up your ass tonight?"

"Nothing." He flicked his cigarette over the railing and handed her the pack with his engraved platinum lighter. "Here." He opened the door to go back in.

"Are you leaving?" She stopped him.

"Is that what you expect me to do?" he said over his shoulder.

Huh? "You? I can't pay you to leave." She smiled, "Come on, have one with me." She was trying to keep this night friendly; she needed at least one nice thing to happen to her today. And as time had gone on, she'd come to rely on the fact that Billy would deliver for her, *he was normally such great company.* She decided to keep making an effort. Janie put the butt to her mouth and lighting it, grinned over at him conspiratorially, "Just don't tell Scotty, okay?"

"I will." He called back to her, "Next time I see him."

The alarms were ringing in Janie's head; she couldn't ignore his tone any longer. "What's this about, Billy?"

He turned on her. "When is he getting home?"

"Oh, Scotty? Tomorrow night. Last minute due diligence stuff." She shrugged, "An owner of the company – thems the breaks."

"Thems is. Seems like thems always is, doesn't it?" Sarcasm leaked out of his voice, turning it saccharine.

"Is there something you want to say?"

"Nope."

"Okay then."

They stood together in silence, eyeing each other.

Janie dragged and blew, crossing her arms in front of her, "You know I don't like this I'm-supposed-to-read-between-the-lines thing, Billy. So whatever you have to say, just say it."

He opened his mouth to speak.

She talked right over him, "Although, this is none of your business and I don't know why you would have an opinion about anything."

Billy paused, waiting for her to keep going, but then had to start out of sheer irritation from her last comment, "Why couldn't I have an opinion if I were to have one?"

"Who are you now? Stacie?"

He jumped on it, "Oh, you mean I'm not the only one who notices something's off?"

"Oh boy. Don't I have enough to deal with?" Janie looked at him, "I don't need this from you."

"You should be getting it from someone."

"What exactly are we talking about?"

"I don't know, Scotty's hours, his time away… It just seems weird."

"It's not weird. You keep odd hours working, don't you? This is making me dizzy." She flicked the butt over the railing too. *I can't even enjoy this one bad thing.*

"But I'm not married. Anymore." He turned away.

She asked calmly, "Billy, I think I know what you're trying to imply. To what end, I'm not sure. But I can't be bothered to listen to this, okay?"

He snapped back, "'Imply' is the wrong word, I'm not implying, I'm assuming I know."

"Okay then, I'm implying that you are making assumptions based on your own model of behavior."

"My behavior is not in question here."

"What is in question?"

His voice, exasperated, "Why are you alone? All the time? Is your husband an idiot? Does he possibly have something besides a business deal going on? Have you ever thought of that?"

"No. Why should I?"

"Because I think you could be misplacing trust."

"Misplacing trust? Could this be that you assume just because you live your life with an 'I like it, I want it, I have it' mentality everyone else does too?" Janie rubbed her neck. "The two of us knew when Scotty started this company that he'd be working a lot. And it isn't like this all the time."

"Really? I'm here everyday and I've seen him in the house maybe three times."

"He's been here more than three times."

"Before you've been asleep? In bed? Or on the couch? Because I've clocked more time on the couches with you than he has."

Janie paused, taking in that little bit of an observation, "Just what are you saying, Billy?"

"Who is here with you? Who eats with you, puts the kids to bed and sits down to watch TV? Who's been here for you and the kids?"

"Okay, you're absurd. You've been here a few weeks, a couple of months. Try years. Scotty has been providing for his family for years."

"Does Scotty's family even know who he is? Could the kids pick him out of a crowd?"

"His family knows that he is a man that we can rely on."

"I'm not?"

"What the hell are you saying?"

Billy, aggravated, flung up his hands, "I don't know. It just… you don't make sense. This situation you keep making excuses for makes no sense."

"I'll clear it up for you. Scotty is my husband. And that's it. That's all there is. This is what I chose, and I have to uphold it."

"Uphold it? What are you, a saint, some sort of martyr upholding the sacred trust?"

"No, I'm not a matryr and just… just shut up about something you couldn't know anything about." Janie walked past him to the door. He followed her, grabbing at her elbow.

"Why wouldn't I know anything about it? I was married."

Her anger splattered against him as she whirled to face him, "Not 'anymore,' right? Billy, this isn't VH1's version of marriage. There's no money, there's no coke and there are no 'birds.'"

"Say what you want. I do know what you are talking about. But if this lonely life is what you signed up for, you are wasting so much. There is so much more that you could be giving to other people who would cherish you. Who would just want to be near you for the sheer sake of being with you."

"I have to believe I am doing something right with my life, Billy. That I am doing something good and true and real. So, you know what? Save your speeches about me wasting myself here in this house. That there is some whole world that I will never know about. I've picked my world Billy, so save it. Save the bullshit lines for some blonde you'll pick up later."

"Will you just cut that out?" His dark voice growled from the depths of his throat, "You just don't get it – can't you understand what I am saying to you?"

"You don't approve of what you think my life is about."

"Well, okay then, what is it about?"

"For one thing, it's not about money or fame or having sad housewives and pretty little teenagers memorizing all my vital statistics from some web site or some rag newspaper. It's about life and dealing with what you make of that life, and making real choices and seeing them through." Janie's voice broke. She cleared her throat, collecting herself. "See, you? You aren't real, Billy," she poked his chest. "I am."

"I'm real. I'm more real than…"

Janie interrupted, "Than what?"

"Than anything you think you've got right now."

"Please, Billy, just stop." Janie rubbed her forehead, exasperated. "Do you know what it is to be married? I mean, when you said the vows, did you consider it a permanent arrangement? Because that's what it is supposed to be."

"Janie, there are circumstances…"

"No, see, there can't be interpretation. I'm not like you, or my mother, or Stacie. It's supposed to be for better or for worse. No matter what you feel today or tomorrow or the day after. You pick one, one partner and you have a family and you do what you can to make it work. Whatever it takes."

"Are you trying to convince yourself that is what you have? A partner?"

"Yeah, that's exactly what I have. Scott and I want the same things – a home, safety and security for our kids. It's what we work towards. Every day."

"What about you?"

"What about me?"

"What about you?"

"Well, Jesus, Billy! I've lived a life. What I want doesn't matter anymore, and Christ! I don't want to do anymore. At the end of the day, I've got laundry and dishes and I'm tired enough as it is. What more do you want?"

"I want to know what you want." His hands splayed out in front of him, he wanted to just grab her, *make her see,* "And how can you say you lived any kind of life? I mean, how much time passed before you traded Stage Mommy's rendition of life for Scotty's? Any? Did you have any time to even figure out what you thought life could be? For you?"

"And do you think maybe you would know? That you know me so well? How could you even think that you know anything about me?"

"Because I watch you. I listen to you. I pay attention to what you do and what you say. You don't think anyone does, but I do."

"And what do you see, what do you know, Almighty, All-Knowing William Smitts?!" Her voice was reaching the breaking point.

"Will you quiet down? The neighbors are going to hear you."

"I don't care, Billy. Let them hear us."

"Why? So they'll be finally convinced that there is, in fact, a man living here too?"

"I can't even dignify that."

"It's the truth! Everyone else sees it but you."

"What the fuck do you think you see here, Billy?"

"I see you. That's it. Every day."

"Yeah, you said that and it makes you the resident expert on all things Janie."

"I see a lot, dearie. A lot." He had to take a second; he had to calm down, this girl did stuff to him, "I see that you are kind, and funny, and probably one of the very few good people I will ever meet. I also see that all that goodness, that loyalty, that 'I must uphold it all' principle bullshit makes you into a gigantic, blind pain in the ass!" Billy spoke slowly, his voice building to level off at a plateau of intense frustration, "Anyone else would get this. Anyone else would see how bad of a situation this is and they'd get the hell out. But no, I get you."

"This isn't a 'bad situation,' Billy. I'm not unhappy."

"But you're not happy!"

"Who gets to be happy? Jesus, this is Life!"

"What the hell kind of person are you?! Who gives up on trying to be happy?! I think I get you, that I understand and then you turn around and say fucked up shit like this," he stopped himself, pulling his hand down his face. As much as he didn't want to, he could see the charm of her face even as she glared at him, her pretty mouth set, her chin tilted up, nostrils flaring, arching brows drawn low. If he wasn't so pissed off, he would have laughed. *I'm getting nowhere. I've got no Angle with her, ever.*

He did laugh, "Janie, you are beautiful, you know. You're like the kids that way; there's nothing you need. I think you are more beautiful than the women who have paid thousands of dollars to look like you do every day of your life. It's kind of dumb when you think about it. I look at you and I see that you are incredible, even when you've just slept on the couch all night, or when you've been playing outside with the kids, and your face and your clothes are dirty. And you've got sand under your fingernails and leaves in your hair. I love... I love seeing you like that. And it makes me feel like I'm a hell of a lucky man, because it's like something I've discovered, that

I noticed and I get to see it. When you are with those kids, you're alive that way." He pulled his fingers together across his brow. "God, it is stupid how beautiful you are."

Janie watched his face; she saw this look, a look of frustration sweetened, tempered with affection and *I don't know,* but it was close to something that in the back of her mind she had been trying to put away, wondering how it would feel, *did he ever look at those girls he spent his nights with like this?*, pretending for a half a second... and a panic arose in her, "No! No! See, you don't get to say that. You don't get to say those things!"

"What?"

"This, this isn't supposed to be for you."

"Why can't I feel... what?!"

"I choose. Because I choose who gets in. This is my house, this is my life. You, you're trying to get by that. You can't get by that, Billy."

"What are you trying to hide, Janie?"

"I'm not hiding!"

"Bullshit. You do everything you can to hide, you could possibly be the only beautiful woman I have ever met that practically begs people not to notice her. Why?"

She tried a different tactic, sarcasm could usually come to her rescue, chase this fear away, "Please, Billy. Is this one of your lines that you feed to your little conquests? Because honestly, it's pretty fucking lame."

He pressed on, "Is it because of your dear, old Stage Mommy? Or maybe it's Stacie? She seems to enjoy the benefits of playing dress up with you. Was it the agent, Janie? Did he like to see you, too? Look at that body and that face when you weren't anything more than really just a little girl?"

Her face flushed with anger, "Just shut up, Billy. You don't know shit."

"Why do you love them? Why do you love Scotty? He picks you up, plops you here with your kids and leaves you. Stacie, what has she ever done for you that doesn't help her out forty times over? Your mother, did she even bother to ask who you were or what you wanted out of life? What did these people do to deserve the leeway you give them? They take it willingly enough, hell, yeah, without a second thought. But why them? Do you want to know what I'm starting to think?"

"No. No, I don't," she insisted.

"I think it's easier for you that way."

"For chrissakes…" she rolled her eyes.

"Let me finish," he snapped at her. "You couldn't handle it, if someone loved you. Because if someone actually did, that would be pretty tough on you. You'd have to be more than just the girl backstage running the show that these jokers put on for the rest of the world, taking care of their kids, their lives. You'd have to go back to thinking about what you would be when you hit Center Stage. Not what they wanted to see, no. But really who you were. Or maybe what you wanted. You wouldn't know what to do. So, is this a matter of them using Janie or Janie using them? Maybe this is all just your fine orchestration."

She turned to him, making him stop. "Did you do a guest spot on 'Law and Order' or something? 'Orchestration?' Please."

He faced her, "Hell, Janie, why not? You enlisted the help of a young college boy named Scotty to help you shake off your mother's idea of how and when and where you should use that face and that body, didn't you?" he spat venomously. "Instead you found out that Scotty's version could be better. His version of Janie was nicer, a lot easier on you. Just fill in the blanks for the Perfect Wife, the Perfect Mother, for the Perfect Family. That really is a much better fit for someone like you, don't you think? Scotty had an easy job, it was typecasting."

"You don't know what you are talking about, Billy," she warned him quietly.

He ignored her. "It's the nurturing thing. I get it. It is you. It's what you need; it's what you want. But you put up with all that bullshit – Scotty, Stacie, your mom, God knows who else. But the kicker here, the real piece de resistance knocked you back, didn't it? It gave you everything you ever needed to complete the big wall you could hide behind."

"What the hell are you talking about?!"

He paused, "Kids, that's where you really got it. That's where you found your thing. You fell in love with them and you fell hard. It happens, hell, it happened to me. I didn't know what love was until I had my little girl. Trust me, I get it. And now, you don't have to go out searching for sad little strays that need someone to fulfill all of their needs. No more outside recruiting necessary. Scotty, Stacie, your mom, all of these people they came in under the wire. Lucky, lucky people. I just happened to be a latecomer, a wild card, 'dangerous' was the word you used. It makes more sense now. But in the kids' little world, you don't have to run the risk of making a mistake. I mean, you could pick up someone like me, someone who would want to be close to you, someone who'd like to help you, to want to take care of you, too. Kids - that's just so much safer. You can contain their world - it's so small - right here. You can be free there. With them. And let's be honest here, they are the only ones that really deserve what you give them, Janie. Not these other jackasses who are just sapping what they can out of you.

"So, while you are so busy with your little daycare-scheduled day and your art projects and your free playtime,

you don't have to think for one second about you. You
have your own safe little place where you can give every
little part of you loving those kids for, well, you've
probably got a few years, without anyone or anything,
especially you, disturbing the idea of the perfect little
family that Janie built. Someday, in some freak chance that
somehow got by you, that may all be gone and you won't
know what hit you. But up until then, until that day comes
you can assure yourself that you won't ever have to deal
with the woman that is Janie Hadley."

"Could you just once spare me the dramatics, Billy?
This speech would look so much more effective with
another cigarette in your hand, or maybe a glass of
bourbon. No, I'm sorry, Stoli's your drink. Let's see if next
time we can work in some good props." She started for the
door again.

"Could you for once just spare me the sarcasm, Janie?"

"All right then." She turned back, "Why don't we take a
look at what I see."

"Go to it."

"I pay attention to you too. And whatever you think
about me, or my situation here, at least I'm not trying to co-
opt someone else's perfect little family, using it for when it
can make you look good, maybe give you a good enough
story to get you laid again. You're trying to pretend you
have the perfect family too, Billy. But what's really great
for you, is that there's really no long-term obligation
involved. You can be Daddy here, and you don't ever have
to worry about all that pesky commitment crap that tends to
usually go along with it all. You get to keep riding that
fence between being a man and being a boy." Janie seethed,
"I can't say I blame you, we've made it perfect here for
you, really. You get to swoop in, play the hero for us and
the audience cheers, and we're grateful and we are so

happy you've come to our family. But at the end of the day, don't you just love the fact that you really don't have to stay? You don't have to. And you don't have to think about the bills, or whether the water heater is going to last another year, or what you would do if you couldn't stand to look at my face for another moment. No, you can always go home. You get to go home and bang the next hot little ass that shakes at you."

"What choice do I have, Janie? It's not like I can stay here with you!"

"Why would you ever want to? You're living the life, Billy Smitts. It's what you get to do. Every day."

"Well then, what's the problem, Janie? The two of us, we've got it so good - we should be happier than hell! I mean, at the end of the day, I get an empty house and an empty bed and no one who actually gives a shit about me and, hey look, so do you! Two sides of the same fucking coin, Janie."

"No it's not, Billy. My life… I'm not… I can't be anything like you."

"Yes, you are, Janie. The two of us are the 'How-To' section in a Defense Mechanism handbook. You can pretend that you've got it all, that you 'live the life.' I won't make believe. I can't anymore."

"I'm not making believe anything."

"Oh, really? You think you've got it all just perfect? You know what? On most counts, you're pretty damned close. You've got the nice house; you've got the beautiful kids; you've got a husband that brings home the bacon, it's everything anyone could have ever wanted, right? Right?" He finally grabbed her arms and pulled her close to where he could force her to look in his eyes. Blue locked onto black and his dark, rich voice grew low, "But think about this for just a second, underneath all of that good stuff, don't you find in the middle of the night as you lie there in your bed - and Janie, I don't care whether he's there with you or not - don't you feel that there is one big fucking piece missing? I mean, that there should be, somewhere in this whole big, long life, someone for just you. Shouldn't somebody get to have you? Shouldn't someone feel happy to have you? Shouldn't someone be on your side? Someone who looks out for you as you are taking care of everyone and everything else? Who is there for you, Janie? I'm looking around here and I'm not seeing a soul."

Janie pulled away from him. He let her go. She wanted more than anything to punch his face. And she could read in his eyes that he knew it. And that, above it all, broke her. It broke her open. *How could he see anything like that? How could he know?* She had to pull herself back. *Give me a second to think.*

He sighed, his voice soft now, "How do you keep going? I'm just starting to face this whole thing and I don't think I can make it much longer. The only relief I get is when I'm talking to you. No, I don't even have to be talking, just breathing your fucking air. I'm... I'm lost here, Janie. And I don't get it, how have you gone this far?"

She choked and turned from him. He wanted to reach for her again but he knew she wouldn't stand for that. She just held herself and the words stung her mouth as she poured them onto the wooden slats beneath her. "I... I don't know. I couldn't tell you how to do it, Billy. Not if I tried." She couldn't look at him. Her tears were hot. Through the baby monitors, they heard the phone began to ring. He watched her as she brushed those terminal mistakes away from her cheeks, opening the back door.

"Don't Janie. Just let it go."

"I can't let it go, Billy." She ran inside. The machine was just about to kick on when she picked it up, "Hello? Hello?"

Frankie was on the other end, his voice was barely recognizable, "Janie, I'm at the hospital."

"Frankie? What is it?"

"Um, Stacie was going out tonight. She called you, remember?"

"Yes, Frank, she called earlier, I couldn't make it tonight. What's going on?"

"She, uh, went out by herself and, uh, that guy, that Billy Sanderson guy, the one from your house, he was at the bar…" Frank staggered over the words. "He beat her up pretty bad, Janie. He, uh, really hurt her."

"Oh my God, Frank."

His voice cracked. "She wasn't outside for too long, one of the waitresses found her when she went out back for a smoke. And they picked up that guy - he wasn't that far. He told the cops she was a prostitute, a whore." Frank was lurching, panting like a marathon runner on the verge. "He said he was trying to get her friend's name, your name Janie, and he told them she wouldn't tell him."

"Oh Frank." Janie's eyes stung, her face contracted with pain.

"Janie, can you come? I need to go home and see to the kids. I don't want to leave her alone but I've just gotta run back there for an hour or so, or something. The babysitter can only stay for a couple more hours."

"Yes, Frank. I'll be right there. Just give me a few minutes to work this out."

"Thanks, Janie."

She hung up the receiver. *This crying was crap and stuff needed to get done.* Billy had followed her in, moving as close to her as he could get and as she spun to face him, her body slammed into his. He caught her arms and looked at her face. "What do we need to do?"

"Stacie... that guy, that Billy, he got her, he wanted my name, and he... he got her. I've got to go to the hospital." Tears were squeezing from the corners of her eyes and she looked away to try to regain herself.

"I'm going with you." He grabbed her chin and locked his eyes on hers. He was forcing the emotion from within her again and it angered her. *No one had the right to do this, especially not him.*

"No, you're not. I need someone to stay here with the kids until I can come back or Scotty gets here."

"What about your babysitter? Can she come?"

"No. It's too late. You need to stay. I will go." She wrangled away from his strong hands.

"By yourself."

"This is my fault, Billy."

"No, Janie, no it's not. Let me come with you. You can't do everything alone."

"Please don't make some kind of lonely woman, on her own, husband's absent-type comment. I've had enough. Okay? There are bigger things to deal with here. That guy, if the cops let him go, he could find his way here. Will you stay here or not?"

"No."

"Great, thanks."

Billy grabbed his phone, "I'm calling Del. I'm going with you. That guy could go to the hospital too." He dialed and Del answered. "Del, Janie and I need you, can you come and watch the kids? Good, thanks." He hung up, to Janie. "Del will be here in five minutes and then I'll drive you. You leave the keys and that way, if anything happens, Del can pack up the kids in the car seats."

"Jesus! Back off, Billy! This isn't your movie and I didn't ask you to be the hero."

"For chrissakes, Janie, I'm trying to be your friend." Fuming, Janie grabbed her purse as Billy continued. "Don't act like this is all some new experience for me. It's not, dearie. I'm a divorced father with a little girl. I know what real life is. And it isn't holing yourself up in your house, only letting people come and go when and if you think it is convenient for you. When you think you can let them in."

"I'm sorry, this is coming from you? Someone who was married for three years and now comes home to a different girl every night? Yeah, I can tell you're looking hard for something real in your life. When was the last time you actually tried to have a relationship, Billy?"

He yelled, "What do you think I am trying to do here?"

"What?"

"I am trying to have a relationship - a friendship, with you."

"Just, just stop! This is not your issue – stop making it about you."

"Fair enough. Let's go."

The black Mercedes sped through the streets, its contents sealed within the darkened windows. Janie could barely see out as she forced herself to look as far away from the profile to the left of her as she possibly could. Tears were starting to fall down her cheeks and she wasn't sure which ones were for poor Stacie and which ones were for her. *The asshole couldn't be right. About anything.* She monitored her breathing so that he wouldn't hear the sobs rising in her throat. It took all of her concentration to direct him to the hospital and maintain a steady voice. But he saw through her facade, and he grabbed her hand between shifting gears and held it, warm under his palm.

She let him, for about a minute. It seemed to be what she needed; she had siphoned some strength from this small contact. She pulled away from him, wiped her cheeks and straightened up, as if her potency had been regained.

Inside the hospital, Janie and Billy ran to the waiting Frank, who just stood there hugging himself. He hopped up and down a little when he saw them, holding his arms and biting his lip. "Thanks Janie. Thanks."

Billy watched Janie hold Frank's arm as she looked into his desperate eyes, "Where is she?"

Frank couldn't seem to let go of himself; he just nodded toward the window they were standing in front of.

Billy asked gently, "Is she conscious, Frank?"

He shook his head.

Janie, "How long do they think she will be like this?"

He shook his head again.

Janie, "Frank, did they give you something?"

He nodded.

"I think you need sleep. Should we call you a cab?"

Frank nodded but Billy interjected, "Let me take him." To Frank, "You can take a cab back in the early morning. Relieve us, okay?" To Janie, "Stay near Stacie. I'll be right back, and I'll call Del and let him know to stay until tomorrow."

"Okay," Janie nodded.

Billy grabbed her arms, and gave her a deep look, his brows drawn together, his voice, quiet, intimate, "Stay in her room, keep the call button and your cell with you. I'll be right back. I promise." A smile cracked the corners of her mouth and impulsively, he kissed her forehead.

She turned to the window and opened Stacie's door as her hero whisked off on his black horse.

It was hard to tell where the lines of makeup began and the bruises and crusted blood stopped. They hadn't begun to wash her face except to clean away the slashes on her cheeks to sew them up. Stacie went to the sink and wet a face cloth. She sat on the edge of the bed and gently wiped around the swollen eye sockets and the lip that had burst through its own skin. And when the small square had no visible white left, she smoothed back the hair around the flap of skin that extended her forehead back into the bandages. She reached into the hard shell around the small cool hand to touch Stacie's fingertips.

This was how he found her; he stopped at the window and tapped. She went to the door and closed it behind her in the hallway.

"Hey."

"Hey."

"We cool?"

"Yup."

She reached for his hand, her fingers alighting on his for a second and pulling away. He grabbed for them and held on. It was if all the blood in his body was rushing to visit the nerves of this one location, heightening the sensation. He could feel the bumps of her knuckles, the ring on her finger, the round tips of her nails through the thick skin of his palm, his thumb wrapped underneath. He was attempting sympathy, trying his best to be what she needed, to be an empathetic friend to her, but this touch was making him heady. He ran his thumb over her knuckles and watched her face. She didn't pull away from him; she kept her gaze steady, blinking.

I could. I could do it. He took her hand in both of his and she bit her lip.

Now.

And then his arms completely enfolded her body, her face buried in his chest and for the two of them, it was a relief.

It was only a moment until someone recognized him.

A voice rang out in the darkened hallway, "Hey, is that...?"

He felt her tear away from the whole of his body as she put her head down and walked to the nurses' station. Hanging his own head in defeat, he took a deep breath and spun on the toothy orderly with an engaging smile and a hand out, "How's it going?"

"Wow, you really are, you're Billy Smitts." Such a recognitive smile on such a toothy person just beamed enthusiasm and Billy swung into action.

"Yep. What's your name?"

"Jason. I loved your last CD, Mr. Smitts. And I saw "Criminal Law" like twelve times."

"Thank you, thank you. You work here?" An arm around Jason the Orderly, he led him away from Stacie's window.

"Yeah, and I really liked all those albums you did in the nineties. Your music, man, especially your first stuff, it inspires me."

"Glad to hear it. Let me ask you something. Do you think you could do me a favor?" Charm was leaping from the tenor peaks and sliding down the bass hollows of his dark, sugary voice. And Jason the Orderly followed its course with every word, nodding in entranced compliance. "Could you please keep it quiet that I am here? I am visiting a friend and I need to respect her privacy." They turned further down the hallway, towards the elevators.

"Of course, Mr. Smitts. I totally get it."

"Call me Billy." They stopped in front of the sleek doors and Billy, hitting the up button, pushed Jason to arm's length with a firm hand on his shoulder. He worked the Angle this guy would most appreciate. "And you'd be doing me a complete favor and quite possibly helping me, you know, along, with my lady friend." A conspiratorial raise of those dark, scarred eyebrows sealed the deal and elicited a knowing guffaw from the toothy orderly that temporarily covered his largest assets.

"Totally. I could totally say I helped Billy Smitts score!"

"Yes, but nothing said tonight. Big favor, thank you."

"No problem, not tonight, yeah. Absolutely not. Lips sealed." The orderly pursed his lips, forcing them to cover more than they could truly handle and locking them with a key. The elevator doors opened and Billy gently forced the young man inside. Jason the Orderly, his lips quivering against the strain, grinned and held his fist out. Billy knocked it with his own in gratitude, his large silver rings rapping the orderly's knuckles.

Janie, standing at the glass outside of Stacie's room, heard heavy footsteps coming down the hallway and she tensed.

When Billy swung around the corner, he saw her face awash with relief. "You okay?" he picked up the pace to get to her.

"Yeah, just relieved it's the right Billy." She turned back to the window. And he came behind her. The second of relief she felt at his reappearance returned to trepidation; it was fear but of a slightly different kind. *He was close, close again, and all I want is for him to stay there.*

But I can't, I shouldn't.

His arms came around her and pulled her against him. He was taking a liberty, he knew it, and she tensed for just a moment, but he could feel her apprehension melting away. She let herself lean into him. He pressed his face to her hair and inhaled long and deep. "What did the nurses say?"

"They said that if she makes it through the night, she should be okay. They are worried about internal bleeding though and scarring. They are having a couple of the plastic surgeons who stitched her face come back in tomorrow morning to go over the, uh…" Her words faltered a bit and his arms squeezed her slightly. "…the wounds to her hands and arms." She stopped again. "Apparently, that was a sign that she fought him."

"Good for her," he rumbled softly.

Janie smiled ruefully, "Not to be lame, but Stacie, I don't think, she isn't the type who would give up. Her life was what she wanted it to be, all the time, she made it fun."

"Hey, I'm… I am sorry about earlier. It all sounded like I don't think well of you and trust me, nothing has ever been further from the truth. I was just frustrated, I guess. This hasn't been an easy…"

"Please no, okay? Let's not talk about it. I don't want to. Just nothing outside of this hospital for tonight, okay?"

He nodded against her head, "Anything you want."

He felt her take a deep breath, "We're just here tonight." *He was here right now, wasn't he? There was no mistaking that. He had been there for awhile now. No one else was, were they?* Why did she have to hold out all the time? Couldn't she ever get a break? *Just for me, just once.* She felt that she had to, she felt she needed to for once, let herself surrender. *For maybe just a second.* "You and me."

She turned to him within the circle of his arms, looking straight into his blue eyes. Her hands slid into his hair at the back of his neck and she lifted her face to his. He was shocked; elation, relief, desire completely overwhelmed him. She registered his surprise and quickly withdrew, embarrassed. *No, no, no.* He recovered her quickly, almost bouncing her off his chest in his assertion of will. His arms surrounded her and suddenly, his mouth found hers. It was sweet and soft and warm and persistent. The blood rush ripped through her body and a hushed moan escaped her throat. Janie broke away for a moment, touching her forehead to his, breathing in his breath, "I wanted to say, for your help, I'm sorry, you have been so good to us, to me, and I mean I appreciate…" she whispered as he gently held her face in his hand, brushing his mouth up along her cheek where he lay grateful, soft kisses. The release of this contact between them was overpowering him. Her eyes closed and she let herself soak in the sweetness, until she finally laid her hand atop his, pulling back from him, her voice hot in her mouth, "There is nowhere for us to go, Billy."

He stepped back, his breathing fast and shallow, he raised his hand to tip her chin and look into her black eyes, "Then we'll just have to stay right here." He leaned in closer, not breaking the stare and gently placed his lips to hers again, his tongue tasting her own, their eyes both slightly open.

And down the hallway, just beyond the nurses' station, a very quiet orderly held up his cell phone in the direction of the darkened hallway and snapped a photo that later, after a phone call or two, a man named Ian would ensure would put him through all three years of nurses' training. *If he could just get her name.*

They didn't speak for most of the night; too many words between them would break the spell. She let him hold her. Once or twice, she got up and went to Stacie, moments later coming back to him. He would watch as a small, almost thankful smile broke through her sad expression when her beautiful eyes met his. Janie would come to him, wrapping her arms around him, pressing herself softly into the hard lines of his body and she would sigh when his arms came around her.

Summoning a discipline he didn't know he possessed, Billy didn't let himself feel all of that overwhelming joy that welled up in him again and again as he tasted her skin, felt her body warm against his. But he did let himself hope that maybe daylight just wouldn't come.

Even with the hospital staff, the ambulance drivers, the town police, that little shit orderly, the bar owners and even the wait-staff as non-forthcoming, Ian ran the story anyway. The cops wouldn't release that Billy Sanderson nor would they let him talk on the phone, had his one call already – these small town police were really quite quaint. So, Ian sighed, looked at his nails, no name. But still, good press.

Ian had also been trying to get a direct hold on his dear client all night but alas, no answer on the cell. Del wouldn't take his call and Ian couldn't wait around to get up there to investigate himself. *It'd be better to get whole little Hospital Honey thing out while the gun still smoking and Billy hadn't moved on to something else a little more, ahem, typical.* Anyway, when his client, Billy Smitts, saw a return on a Bad-Boy-And-The-Pretty-Small-Town-Girl story, Ian would definitely be expecting a thank you call.

Frankie found the two of them in the morning, asleep upright in the chairs in the hallway, Janie's dark head on Billy's shoulder, her face nestled into his neck. They slept side by side, her legs across his lap, his arms and his black leather coat wrapped protectively around her. Frankie tapped Billy on the shoulder. "You two need to get out of here."

Janie awoke with a start, quickly disentangling herself from Billy, "What is it, Frank? Is it something with Stacie?"

"Nothing has changed with Stacie, there's no bleeding. And I am grateful that you stayed last night but I mean, you guys have to get out of here."

"What's wrong, Frank?" Billy yawned, and stretched, standing at her side.

"You're on the local news this morning. There are some people waiting for you outside - photographers, LA people. Security is keeping them outside. They're at the entrance trying to keep them all in one place. There's some picture some kid took with his cell phone of you two here, uh, together."

"Oh my God." Jane's stomach sank to her knees as she stood, blood filling her head. *The kids, Scotty...*

"Listen, I don't know what is going on but I can't think of why you would do this here."

"I'm sorry, Frank. I wasn't meaning to be disrespectful to you or Stacie or careless with the responsibility you gave me or..."

"No, Janie, you know, don't worry about that. I'm just surprised," Frank responded. "I mean, yeah, Stacie, you know, I get it. But you, I never would have thought, ever."
Billy watched her crestfallen face as the temper of the

words hit her. Frank went on, "Listen, Janie, take my car. It's parked out back and I think you two can get out without too much trouble."

She quickly hid her face from Frank as he handed her the keys. She strode toward the elevators, "Thanks, bye, Frank. I'll call… be back later."

Billy ran and caught her arm; she pulled it free and kept walking. "You can't go that way."

"Yes, I can." Billy had to jog to keep up with her long-legged, purposeful strides.

"Frank's car is in the back. Listen, I can get us out of this."

"No 'us,' Billy. There can't be an 'us.'"

"Janie, stop now," Billy demanded, "I need you to listen to me."

The bark in his voice stopped her, she screeched to a halt, "I've got the kids… and you and Del need to get out of my house… and my husband is coming home tonight… and his brother…"

"I know. This is a disaster," he said more gently, he touched his fingers to her cheek, attempting anything to shadow the intimacy she allowed him just a few hours before.

For only a second more would she let herself respond to his touch, tears jumping from her closed eyes. A second, and she pulled away, putting her hand to her mouth. *What am I doing?*

He perceived her flight impulse and grabbed her arms, "Janie, right now, just listen to me, okay?" She nodded and he continued, "My car is out front. Let me go out there and deal with the photographers and all the crap and you can go out the back, they might be back there but if you don't say anything and just take Frank's car and go home, it should be okay. Just send Ashley home with Del. I promise you,

you won't have to deal with any of this. This stuff is all me. I've got it. I will take care of it. Okay?"

"Okay," and she whirled to run, he stepped in front of her starting gate.

"Come here." He reached for her, again. *Please.*

"No, Billy. Christ! Are you just stupid? We... I can't." She ran around him and turned down the hallway, out of sight.

It wasn't the slowly dawning light of the day that awakened them both from their midsummer night, carried them away from Neverland, just the brief, harsh flash of a single camera bulb that had brought their reality so sharply back into focus.

Billy Smitts put on his leather coat, sunglasses, sucked in a deep breath, cracked his neck and waited for the elevator doors to open into the lobby. The throng of photographers, straining at the arms of the security detail, snapping his photo as soon as he strode out and through the outer doors, as they hoped to catch him with this mystery woman from the orderly's pixilated digital picture, were distinctly disappointed to catch the star alone. Still, it was good to get a picture so early in the day. And after they'd at least gotten the celebrity goods, maybe they'd have a look around for her. Someone had to know who she was.

"WhereissheBilly?WhoissheBilly?Howoldisshe?Isshea nactressasinger?What'shernameBilly?Whatdoesyourexthin kaboutthis?Howaboutyourkid?Isthegirlpregnant?Whywerey outwoatthehospitalBilly?"

His smile was truly heart-stopping. He tipped his sunglasses further up onto his nose, lighting a cigarette and saying nothing as he moved the swarm to his car, closed the door and slowly drove from the hospital parking lot. That smile fell from his face and he sped away. The only place he had to go to was back to the empty rented house.

Chapter Sixteen
Kenmore or Maytag?

Somehow this peroxide blond boy had sucked her temporarily into some sort of crazy fantasy world. Today, she woke up, got in her brother-in-law's car and Janie knew that free playtime was over. She just needed to definitely shake this feeling off. She had let it get to the point where his presence had begun to affect her and his words... *The guy's a Hollywood bullshit artist, an oversexed rock star cliché, an, an actor – of all the people in the goddamned world, how did I let him get to me?*

Last night, comforting her at the window as Stacie lay unconscious, his bass voice had vibrated its way into her chest and made her heart and lungs resonate with its deep variants. His arms had locked her within an impassible fortress about her shoulders and when he spoke, his breath had felt hot against her neck. She shamed herself for responding so readily to such an offer of warmth, a few words, especially at a time like this. *And after my mom and dad, and everything that I said last night, that he had said about him... about... me.*

There was no excuse ready for her; Stacie could have made up about a thousand for her if she had been let in on any of it. If Stacie even had an inkling of what Janie was not even going to think, she would judge and make wrong assumptions and tell her that there wasn't anything wrong with what she was feeling and why couldn't she have this, "Janie, you've denied yourself everything else?"

Janie had never felt as physically protected like what she had felt in that hallway all last night, ever before in her life. *That someone could be there, for her.* She hadn't felt those blood rush moments, those warm riptides, the sweetly physical results of some intense emotion that had coursed throughout her body, in what seemed like years.

And he was just so damned pretty to look at, and funny, and an asshole, and occasionally sweet, and kind, and a complete pain in the ass and just so damned pretty.

But she was what she was. And she knew it was time to end this part of the story - a dangerous, impossible fairytale that could end in nothing but bad for everyone.

He had taken her mind off of the things which made up her life - the base component of whom she was and who she had wanted to become since she was a kid – a mother and a wife of a hardworking, well-meaning man. And the little devil of Stacie sat on her shoulder and whispered in her ear, "a hardworking, well-meaning man who checked out on you and the kids emotionally about two years back. I mean, hell, he isn't even around to see what is going on in his own house."

Shut up, Stacie. I know what's right. And I'm not the one lying in the hospital bed, unconscious, clinging to the prayers of the people around you that you don't become just another Oprah Exclusive, 'Women Who Aren't Home Where They Should Be and End Up in Comas Because They Are Stupid.'

"Funny thing is, I'm not the stupid one here, Janie."

Why didn't you just give the guy my name?

"You think that would have stopped him from doing this? I was being smart for once. I was protecting my friend. But it seems as though, I might have been in the wrong location for that."

Again, I say, 'Shut up Stacie.' You're just mad because I blew you off.

"Who'd you blow me off for, Janie?"

No one.

"Bullshit. He was there with Ashley wasn't he?"

He was picking her up.

"And finally it occurred to you that you didn't have to spend another night alone, in your big old house, after the kids were in bed asleep."

Scotty was coming home and we were supposed to go out together again finally and then he called and said he had to go away...

"Again. And Billy was there, happy to be there, with you. And maybe you finally noticed that something in his face when he looks at you."

Nothing, there's nothing.

"Really? Not even that hopeful look? That you knew that if you just asked him to stay, he would and that look would turn into that smile and his face would become that masterpiece of bone and flesh and tendon and color that is only there for you. And its there everyday, at your door after all the other kids and their parents leave. I'm not mad at you for blowing me off for him. I would have done it too and I'm not half as lonely as you are. I definitely would have stayed, with that luscious thing waiting at my doorstep, practically begging me to please love him – hell yeah. Only I think I would have done it about two months ago."

But it isn't right, Stacie.

"But didn't you make his decision to stay easy? You had everything for the kids and it would be simple for you to feed Ashley too and then there was plenty and why not?"

Because, because...
"Because what?"
Because I am a married woman with two children who need me and I am not going to pretend Billy could ever be a part of my real life. He is a client. I am here to help him with his daughter.
"His daughter?"
Ashley is so sweet and needs a real, stable influence, which I can give her. It's what he's paying me for, it is what I do. I take care of kids. I can help her. Yes, Billy is nice, he is funny, he is attentive to me, but, think about this all realistically. Think about what he is and what I am and what would I ever be to a man who can do, who can have whatever he wants?
"Something he wants to have. Janie, he's in lo..."
No! No! Stop! It can't. At most, MOST, I'm a friend, a convenient friend. And maybe someone who might be giving him something he used to have and right now, he thinks he wants to have it, maybe for his daughter.
"I would say, he wants it for himself."
Please, I've got to look at this rationally. I can't, I can't act like this, my life, my children are at stake. I can't be... No, I am nothing more than a, a new handy appliance, like a stupid dishwasher - you know? Something that makes life so much easier for a little while? And every day after you get it, you look at it, you pore over the instructions, you take care of it and appreciate every feature, every little thing about it until the day you forget it was ever not there. And then it is just like everything else. You don't notice it again until it is broken, and then you're pissed because you've gotta take the time or spend the money and get the crappy old thing fixed, or maybe you just replace it.
And it is stupid to even think about how he would be, or what he would do, which he wouldn't. And when it comes

right down to it, I couldn't. I couldn't sacrifice everyone else for something so ridiculous and far-fetched and stupid. A rock star? I'm so fucking stupid. And maybe, he'd find that when he goes back to his real world, he's gotta go back there. Because he'll see, he'll know that all that he feels now, what he thinks he wants, what he believes when he sees me really is just, unfounded.

You know what? I can't even pretend it would be okay to think about how it would be or what it would feel like. I have to believe I know who I am.

"Yes, my dear Janie. You are *another* man's appliance."

Chapter Seventeen
Another Man's Appliance

Billy pulled into the long driveway of his rented house, past the photographers at the wall, and drove just beyond their sight into the courtyard behind the house. Just a quick flip through his missed calls on his cell phone gave him some clear evidence as to who was behind the little fiasco this morning.

Fucking Ian Dormande.

Fucking Billy Sanderson.

Fucking Scott Hadley.

Fucking bunch of stupid men.

He slammed the car door, the tail of his leather trench caught in the car door practically knocking him back onto his ass, a growl of frustration turned into a full-throated roar, ripping his coat away from the sealed door. It wouldn't give way and he repeatedly kicked the door of his beautiful car. *You – son – of – a - bitch!* Hurt at the physical assault, the car door surrendered its hold on the leather and Billy stomped up the back garden stairs to his kitchen door. Del was waiting in the doorway.

"Where is Ashley?" Billy snarled.

"I just made her a snack and now she is playing in her room." Del said. His head held high upon a massive throne of crossed arms as he stared down at Billy.

"Well, then."

"Well then." And that was when Del punched his boss, the famous singer/actor, Mr. Billy Smitts, in the face, for the second time. Billy felt an immediate crunching sensation directly behind his nose. Billy lurched backwards down the stairway. He yelled involuntarily, "OW!" in pain and indignation.

Del watched him regain his balance in the driveway, turned his enormous form, muttering, "Stupid asshole." And shut the kitchen door behind him.

Billy ran up the stairs, attempting to stop the blood flow, and ripped the door open. "You've got something to say to me, Delbert? Just say it! I've had a pretty shitty morning all ready!"

"I've got plenty to say to you, Mr. Smitts," handing Billy a paper towel.

Applying the paper towel to his nose, it quickly red with blood. "Oh now it's 'Mr. Smitts' again. What happened to 'stupid asshole?'"

"You are a stupid asshole, Mr. Smitts." Handing him a dish towel filled with ice, "At least when it comes to her."

"Me?! How am I the stupid asshole here? I am not the one leaving her alone, to rot in that house! That Scotty I'm-A-Dumbass Hadley is the stupid asshole! He doesn't know, doesn't appreciate, what he's got! And what does he think? A woman like that no one is seriously going to notice?! He's just lucky it hasn't happened to her before! It is a testament to Janie's sheer sense of duty and loyalty to that dumb fuck that got her and him this far!"

Del looked pensive. "He may not deserve her, Mr. Smitts. But you don't either."

"Why, Del? Why don't I? I put in time. I like who she is. She is funny and sweet and strong as hell. And she's GORGEOUS – I haven't seen a body like that outside of LA, ever! And her face, her hair, she's beautiful! Why does no one seem to notice that? They just show up at her house and expect her to just give to them whatever they need. And she does! And I'm there and I am trying to help her. I'm trying to be her friend. Why do I not deserve it?"

"You're not trying to be her friend. You're trying to get her to like you. You want to deserve her; you want to be her hero."

"No, Del, okay. Yeah, I want her to like me. I want to help her." Billy gestured, the bloody ice pack in his hand. "I do want to be her hero – maybe you do get that part – but, I want to be there. With her, doing things with her, just being next to her is good enough." He stopped. "I feel like I am the man I was supposed to be with Janie. I'm not pretending, Del, this isn't acting. The man I want to be - that good guy – that man is who I am when I am with her."

"Mr. Smitts, you don't live in her world. You're vacationing in it. And you are so damned selfish, you have put her in a position that will do nothing but hurt her. She has been clear from the beginning that she isn't available. She is married. 'Mrs. Hadley,' remember? No, no you don't. She must have thrown you completely off your game that night, Mr. Smitts, because for once, you didn't really listen. You don't care about her life outside of you. You just want her to be there to give you some kind of life you decided you liked, that made you comfortable. But this is not your life. It's hers and you've intruded on her property. You're nothing but a trespasser." Del continued. "So don't give me this bullshit about how no one else gets her and all they do is take from her without even knowing she's there because that is exactly what you are doing too."

"Bullshit, Del, no, that's not it. You're not… you're not getting it. I can't explain it. Why can't I explain it?" Billy sat, his head down, his nose bleeding, ice packed against his face.

"Mr. Smitts, please, you can't just take what you want wherever you go. You can't do that to real people. I know you really like the girl – you've been infatuated with her since the beginning. And I know how much you want her. I do, I can see it when you look at her. And I know that she's everything all these other women you've ever had in your life are not…"

Billy couldn't take this anymore, *why couldn't anyone understand?* Christ, he didn't understand it himself. It made no fucking sense. None of this did. Billy had to say it, he couldn't stop himself as much as he wanted to. It burst from him like fodder from the mouth of a cannon, "It's not fucking infatuation! This isn't some puppy-dog bullshit! And it's not just that I wanna fuck this girl and she won't let me – it's beyond all that! Jesus Christ, it's insane. I lo… shit, man. Janie. I'm in l…" His shoulders dropped, and he resigned himself to the truth, the truth of what he felt, of what he had been feeling, of what it had to be, but he couldn't finish his sentence. Not here. Not to Del.

Del stopped short; the cannon shot hit him hard. Del never thought Mr. Smitts would be in so deep that he would actually acknowledge what the hell this all was about, never mind ever coming close to admitting it. "Oh Christ, Mr. Smitts."

Billy looked tired, "Del, please, please, just help me."

Del took a deep breath, "I can't. I can't help you. Not with that, Mr. Smitts. I'm sorry."

"Jesus, Del," Billy sighed, "can't I just bring her here?"

Del thought, he thought hard. "No."

"Why not?"

Del shook his massive head, "What do you plan on doing, Mr. Smitts? Are you going to go to her, shove her husband out of the way and explain that she could just leave all of it behind, so you could be with her? Take her

home to a rented house around the corner and just never
leave? Or what - bring her to LA? You want her to just
drop her entire life, everything she has built for herself, her
husband, her children, her business, her home, for the slim
chance you would be?"

"I'm not a slim chance for her! And I would never
expect her to leave the kids. We could be a family. Hell,
my kid, her kids, our kids, trust me, we've practiced the
whole situation over and over again and it works! I could
make her happy, Del. Happy. I could do it, I know I could.
I want to."

"It would make you happy, too, wouldn't it? Happy as
hell. But you've got a lot less to lose. You wouldn't be the
one breaking up a family; you'd be getting one free of
charge."

"Yes, so what? It's what I want. It's everything anyone
would want, it's what we're all looking for, isn't it? It's not
unselfish. I understand that." He muttered, almost to
himself, "But it's her, Del. Janie. Janie fills all the holes."

Del sighed, "Mr. Smitts... Billy, if this is really how
you feel..."

"Yes, this is really how I feel! Jesus Christ, Del, do you
know how hard this is? Do you have any idea?"

"Just listen to me, Mr. Smitts. Listen. You have to
realize that you fell for the woman for pretty much every
reason that she could never go with you - her dedication to
her family, her children - their life, their happiness - her
strength, that she's just a 'regular girl' - if that even makes
sense. You screwed yourself. She wouldn't come home
with you, Mr. Smitts, even if she really wanted to. She
would never put her family through that. She would never
let them suffer for anything or anyone. You've got to know
that. You can see that when you look at her. And I think
that if by some remote chance she did leave with you, I

think then she wouldn't be the woman that you are so blindly in love with."

Billy glanced up at Del's words, his chin then dropping again, "Oh crap, Del." He ran his hands through his hair. "This is too fucking stupid. I am a stupid asshole."

"Yeah, a little bit," Del sighed. "But I wouldn't do what I just did if you weren't somewhat redeemable, Mr. Smitts."

"All right, Del. I get it. Okay. I get it," Billy surrendered. Del rubbed his hands together and got up to leave but Billy stopped him, "Please, if there's nothing else I can do, I have to… Del, put a cap on Ian, any of those pricks, now. Tell him anything he knows about her, if it's published, I'll come down on him like a fucking freight train. Buy the pictures, any of the information they have on her, please. Just get it and bury it. I promised her, Del and I can't let them, I can't let them… make it cheap… you know. I won't let them sell her."

"I've got it, Mr. Smitts." Del said gently to his boss. Billy nodded ruefully, painfully, in appreciation. Del spoke softly, but his voice was authoritative, fatherly, "You know what you have to do, Mr. Smitts. For her. Think about her, who she is, what her real life is like. If you know anything about her at all, you know you've got to just leave her, her family, all that, leave it alone. You've played with her long enough; it's time to go home now." Del watched as Billy, his head down, nodded.

Satisfied, Del left the kitchen, pleased his wisdom had been spoken and that he essentially had been given carte-blanche to finally kick Ian's ass.

Only a moment passed until Billy had gone out the door.

Chapter Eighteen
Stay At Home

Del had been pulling out of the driveway when Janie slowed in front of the house. He waved to her and she sheepishly waved back. He rolled down the window and she responded in kind.

"Janie, they don't know who you are yet and I will do my best to make sure they don't find out."

"Thank you, Del. Mr. Hadley is home I see?" Indicating the white sedan in the driveway behind the minivan.

"Yes, ma'am."

"Okay, thanks Del. You've been a nice friend."

"Thank you, Janie. Good luck."

Janie nodded and swung herself out of the car. Scott was standing at the door and she took a huge breath. "Hi." She said awkwardly.

"Come in."

"Please, Scott. The kids."

"They are across the street. With Mrs. Sawyer. Please come in the house."

She walked by him, entering the kitchen.

There was the morning paper on the table and there was a blurry photo of her and Billy on the front page.

"There's no mistake in that picture is there. That is you. Last night. Can I ask how long has this been going on?"

"There was only the kiss. Kissing. Last night."

"And this one happened to be caught on film."

"Yes."

He interrogated, "And I should believe that?"

"Yes."

"Okay." Scott stood feet apart, leaning against the counter. Janie sat at the table. "Why?"

"Why what, Scott?"

"Why should I believe that's it? I mean, I really have got to be stupid, don't I? Inviting a guy like that into our house? He's here all the time! He's stayed overnight for chrissakes! Have you slept with him?"

"No."

"Well then what the hell is this about, Janie?"

Janie took a deep breath. "I've done my best with what I've got, Scott. Billy, Billy and I were friends. I had a friend. Hell, for most of the time, I didn't even like the guy. You convinced me to make nice with him, to ease the business relationship."

"So this is my fault?" Scotty jabbed a finger at the paper.

"No. Yes. No. I don't know. I just know that you aren't here, ever, and I needed a friend, Scotty. I needed someone to be there and he was standing where you were supposed to be. I needed a *real* partner. And I let my guard down just once and that was my fault, Scott, but…"

"I think he had something to do with it. I mean, it's Billy Smitts."

"It's not like that… it's not because of who he is. It's because of you and me and him and me and you aren't here and…"

"Me?" he stopped her, "Janie, how does this include me? I'm not here. I haven't been here to be involved in this problem."

"No! You haven't!"

"Then how can you blame me, Janie? How the hell can you blame me?"

"Scotty," Janie sighed, if he could just stop, he could see, she could show him. "I know I've lost every right to be mad or indignant about any of this. I am the guilty party. It's just now, this morning, and the kids aren't here and maybe I hoped we, you and I, we could talk about it. And maybe I could tell you, hope you might listen to the fact that I need someone here. I need someone to share this with. It's been so hard here, by myself. And you, you're my husband and you are the one I should be living through this with. What can I do to make it our life?"

"Our life? Janie, this is supposed to be our life. This is what we've talked about; this is what we've planned. You are responsible for this. Maybe I can't blame him because really Janie, this is you. You did this... I trusted you. I've always trusted you." He paused, "That's why I have been able to accomplish so much in my work, because I had you to take care of me and my home and my children. I could trust that you would take care of it all. You made it easy for me." Janie looked up at Scott's face, tracks of tears had lined his cheeks but his eyes were hard, glistening.

Maybe I made it easy for you to forget me, Scott.

"But Janie, right now I don't think now I can trust you."

Janie just stared at him and he wouldn't look back at her.

He inhaled deeply, "And I don't think I can stay here right now."

Janie was, for a moment, shocked, but then realized she had no real reason to be.

Of course, Janie nodded.

So for the last time, she straightened herself, she could do this, one more time, she could be strong, she could do it for them, for all of them, "I understand."

"You do?"

"Yes, I get it. You go do what you've gotta do and I'll be here, okay." Janie wiped her nose. "Where are you going to stay?" *Mustbestrong. Mustbestrong. Maybe hewon'tsee. Maybehewon'tunderstandbutstillI'lldowhatI haveto.*

"I'll be at the office. Bed's in there and a shower. I've got clothes and stuff," Scotty seemed relieved.

"Okay."

"Janie, let the kids stay at Mrs. Sawyer's tonight, okay? If reporters show up, I don't want…"

"I know." She would have to take care of everything.

"Okay," Scott hugged her. "I'll call the kids tomorrow morning." She nodded over his shoulder.

"Okay, bye."

"I'm sorry, Scott." He turned to her, nodded, walked out the side door. She was left there, in her house, alone. *What does it matter anymore?*

Life will go according to plan.

She chose this life. She did. Janie didn't have anyone to blame but herself. Scotty was right. He was really right -she knew the man she married, she had chosen him because he had promised to give her kids and a home and peace and wasn't that what love was supposed to be? And still for all the pledges of love and support and harmony and quiet that he, her mother would have given Janie if she would just do, pose, get, dance, say, live, be, have what they needed, what they wanted, she was still waiting patiently for one of them, someone, anyone to deliver what she needed, what she wanted - as a child, as a girl, as a wife, as a mother, as a woman. If she played the game by the rules they had so clearly laid out for her, why couldn't she ever win? Get the grand prize, cross the finish line and get the big check?

Because maybe it wasn't their game, maybe it never had been.

Janie was the fuel source. She was the power. She was who they needed more than she needed them. And after thirty-four years of pulling herself through this daily shit, this perpetual forward motion of a life that was set up for her, carrying everyone and everything she had ever cared about along with her whether they wanted to go or not, Janie found that today, finally, maybe she just didn't have enough strength to do this all alone anymore. She had to stop, even if it was just for another moment or two.

She finally let drop her last façade of strength; every last degree of force was finally exhausted. Janie's knees crumpled beneath her. She sunk into her chair and silently began to cry.

Chapter Nineteen
Billy and Janie

Billy had driven past her house twelve times in the past two hours. He had taken Del's car to be less conspicuous – he knew the ins and outs of publicity and now was no time to be stupid.

The only cars in her driveway were Frankie's car and the minivan. There were no signs of life in the house. He had debated on waiting until Scott was there to finally talk to him, man to man, but the sky was beginning to get dark and it seemed like maybe he had missed his chance.

He finally decided to head back to his rented house; his face was throbbing, although he counted himself lucky. He had hired Del and knew full that the big man had been holding back. Billy got to the end of Janie's street and was about to pull out onto the main road when it came upon him. He swerved into traffic and u-turned down the street. *Fuck Del.*

He ran from the car, up the stairs and flung the door open into the kitchen.

Janie ran into the dining room as he was turning the corner of the kitchen and stopped short. "Hi."

His fervor paled at such a small greeting, "Hi."

"I was thinking it was…" she stopped, "Your face…"

"It's nothing," he assured her. "He's gone isn't he?"

Janie nodded.

"For good?" He couldn't let himself hope.

"I don't know, Billy. He just said he couldn't handle it right now and needed to get some perspective. I don't know…"

"Well, there's a surprise. Scotty's gone."

"Billy…"

He began posturing, "I know, Janie, but really, the man isn't smart. He leaves you alone all the time. And now, when it is crisis time, he leaves you alone again. He runs. You think he's invested in you and his family, he can just pick up and go like that? Doesn't that tell you something about him?"

"Please, Billy. I can't right now…"

He paced the kitchen, "And I can make a pretty bet that he didn't take the kids with him. Why would he? I mean, his kids barely know who he is."

"Billy, stop."

"So of course, he's just leaves 'em here for you to take care of, like you do all the time. It makes so much more sense doesn't it? Hell, Janie, it's actually like nothing happened. You're better off with him gone."

"Billy." The notes in her voice stopped him short and he looked at her. She stood there, her arms clinging to themselves and her face was about to burst with pain. His eyes widened and he went to her, enclosing her in his arms. Her sobs were long and hard and wrenched the whole of her entire body.

Billy realized, "I'm sorry, Janie. I'm so sorry. I'm sorry. I'm sorry. Janie. I'm so sorry." He held her; and he couldn't take any more away from her.

Maybe he had taken it all.

Janie had quieted. Billy stood still, holding her to him for as long as she needed, until she pulled away. She didn't. She merely shifted her weight, sighing softly, "You have to leave Billy."

The back of his throat ached, strangling his voice, "Okay." *Del was right.* He knew. He had known all along. Billy closed his eyes, awaiting the painful moment when she would begin to pull away.

But she lingered, nestling her face into his neck, breathing deeply, inhaling the scent of his skin - it satisfied something in her. He had put his hand in her hair and run his fingers down its entire length, trying to soothe her. Exhausted, empty, she drew off some strength from the touch he had offered and decided she knew exactly what she needed, what she wanted to do.

Her hands moved first, unlocking her grip around his waist. He prepared for the loss, but instead, he felt her small hands slide firmly up to his shoulder blades. He was disconcerted for a second, if he hadn't become so hyper-aware of her entire being over the last few months, he might not have felt the first kiss. But of course, he did. It burned. It was soft and faint, but he suffered it through his entire body.

Janie turned her face, her mouth brushing along his neck, the tender skin of her lips catching on the dark shadows of stubble. She breathed softly, pressing her mouth again and again over a slow line up his throat to his ear. She listened to his breathing quicken, she felt his chest begin to heave against hers.

"Janie," he whispered, "What are you doing?"

"No questions." *Just love me.* Her hands slipped up and over his chest to his arms, sliding his coat off his beautifully muscled shoulders. It dropped to the floor behind him. She could feel the hard flesh, the heat under his shirt, comfort, the sweet warmth he offered her. She needed it. She needed something. She needed what only he had given her. *No one else.* She looked at his mouth and took his lips between her own, wetting them gently with her tongue.

He whimpered softly, trying desperately to maintain control, but after their long night together last night, he had very little strength left. Her kiss overtook him, he couldn't help but follow it, her mouth was so sweet, her tongue was so soft and it was Janie. *Janie. Janie.* He put his arms around her, drawing her close.

Her hands were under his shirt, traveling up and then down, lifting the hem and pulling it up, breaking contact to get it over his head, careful of his broken nose, his blackening eye. She stood back, looking at his face as she lay her hands on his chest, his skin was softer than she had imagined, lying smoothly over the ripples of muscle she tripped her fingers over. She moved in close to taste it. She touched a finger to the silver ring embedded into his left nipple and looked up at him again. Her eyes were full, dark, warm, sad, determined. He slavered miserably, his breath coming in short, sharp bursts, his arms dangling at his sides.

Janie stepped away. In a panic, in a frenzy, he almost lurched at her to take her in his arms again, but he stopped himself, watching as she slowly pulled her t-shirt over her head and unhooked her bra, sliding the straps off of her arms, dropping it to the floor, quickly forgotten. She went to him again, pressing skin against skin.

Billy was shaking, he was at the end of his rope. "Janie, you have to know how I feel… I've never wanted… I'm not…" He grabbed her elbows, pushing her to arms length, looking into her eyes, "I'm not man enough to stop this."

Janie was shaking too. She couldn't help it, in the depth of the silence of her house, she felt that now, for a few moments, she could feel joy. He was the only one who could give it to her - he was the only one who had. She was willing to cross all of her own lines for it, eager to. But she was frightened about what she wanted, about wanting it so much, about needing it, from him. "Yes, you are, Billy. But I am asking you not to stop it."

He looked at her face a moment more. She saw his faint resolve begin to crumble and she watched his eyes move over her naked breasts, his grip on her arms softened and she took his hand, lacing his fingers in her own and led him willingly up the stairs to her bedroom - the bedroom she shared with her husband, where she had cried alone at night, suffocating under the pressure of the sea-like stillness even as he lay next to her in the dark. The place where she would always lay alone, and now perhaps literally, for the rest of her life, except for tonight. She wouldn't be alone tonight.

She finished undressing the two of them, standing over her bed. She waited - she had taken him this far. *Please.*

He moved toward her, words caught in his throat and he was unable to focus on everything he saw, everything he felt, everything he was thinking. *If ever I had a chance, this is it. If ever I wanted to tell her, the time is now.* He took her face into his hand, twining a strand of her long dark hair between his fingers, he searched her beautiful face; he knew her every expression. He knew what it looked like while she slept, and when she was working in the kitchen and she would bite her lip in concentration, or when one of the children would be hurt or sad and her brows would draw down and then up as she gathered them to her in madonna-ic sympathy. He wanted now to memorize how her body would react, as he touched her, as he kissed her, as he moved inside of her. He kissed her expressive mouth, her firm cheeks, her eyelids that were just beginning to crinkle softly into fine spun webs at the corners, down her nose, and back to her mouth. He stopped, and she smiled, opening her closed eyes. He gazed into their blackness, admitting, knowing there would be no answer, but needing for her to know, "I love you, Janie."

She looked at him fully, "I know you do." She lay down on the bed. He followed her, stretching out next to her, drawing her to him. And he began to make love to her.

It shattered them both.

Their eyes locked, and as the tender throbbing subsided, their breathing slowed, they found that neither of them could say a word. She took his face in her hands and kissed him sweetly. It made him smile into her kiss, relieved.

He stayed inside of her for as long as he could, drawing out the time of their inevitable separation. He held her close, embedded his face in her hair, feeling himself drift, her breathing steady and even. One thought came into his head as he lay pressed against her, *this is where we both belong.*

They woke throughout the night, finding each other in the dark, with tenderness, with seething ferocity. He intended with every fiber of his being to keep her with him in Neverland, convincing her with every touch, each kiss, each stroke, that he loved her. And when she called his name he knew she had to feel it.

"Janie?"

"Yes?"

"I want to stay with you."

"You can't."

"Then come with me."

"I can't."

"Why?" his dark voice rough.

"Billy, this is it. This is all we can have, a little time to just pretend that this is how life could be."

"It could, Janie. It can, I can give you, if you…"

"No, no it wouldn't. You know it."

He looked down, "Whatever you say to me, or do, you won't convince me."

"Your life and my life? A rock star and a stay at home mom? That's just silly. You know that. You lead the kind of life I never wanted to have. And I won't pretend I can follow you. I'm not a little schoolgirl. As I think I may have just proven to you, a couple of times."

"Don't. Don't joke."

"Why? Why not? That's what we do. What else is there? My husband has decided to leave me here for something I did last night, which in comparison to now, was nothing. For once, I took something for me - it was wrong of me to do it - and it could cost me everything, my life. And now, I've been with another man in my husband's bed while my two little children sleep across the street. You know I am going to be guilty for the rest of my life and I've come to the point where I don't think I care. But, for them, it all has to be for them. I have to do what I can, Billy. They're innocent in all this. They should never pay for anything I've done, the choices I've made. I spent twenty years of my life trying to make up for a life my mother never had. I won't do that to them. And those babies, they're not just mine, they are his too. They deserve everything I can possibly give them. What else am I supposed to do?"

"You know what my answer to that would be."

She sighed, "What we just did, Billy, it wasn't right. But I needed you and you were there and that is more than anyone has ever given me before. You've been my friend. So I took one more thing, one more day for me, you gave it to me, but that's it, that's all I can do. It's the only thing I'll probably ever have and I'll happily give the rest to them. It's what I do, isn't it? They need it, Billy."

"So do I."

"They were here first."

He didn't speak for a few minutes, finally asking, "Let me stay until morning."

"Be with me until then."

They slept again. Janie's eyes opened as the sun started to peer into the windows; she listened to his soft snoring and smiled for a moment, tears tracking slow lines down her cheeks.

This is it.

She woke him with her mouth, watching his face, putting a finger to his lips as his eyes opened. He was quickly ready for her but she lingered a moment more. She pulled herself astride and eased him inside of her, taking as much pleasure for herself as she was giving to him. She watched his beautiful, broken face as she moved over him, enjoying his responses to her. She smiled down at him, leaning in, arching back, finally putting his hands on her hips. He was eager, gripping her tightly. Janie looked into his eyes as they both strained against each other, "I love you," she whispered. He stopped moving, his eyes filling, he moved his mouth to speak but she stopped him again, "Don't." Her heart was in her throat. She was not sure if she meant what she just said, not even sure really what it meant, but she had to say it. The words had just come out. She knew that she was doing what she had to, consummating all that he had come to mean to her, everything he had earned. She felt she owed it to him, and she felt that more than anything else, she owed it to herself. Billy reached up and pulled her down to kiss her, moving inside of her again. She flexed her muscles and kneaded them both to orgasm and he called to her through the haze of feeling and sweat and light and moisture.

It was early morning and she held him for as long as she thought she could allow herself. The day would come and if she lingered in his arms, she would lose courage, she'd crumble and things would be worse than they already were. If she acted now, she could stop before this killed her, before it changed everything in her real life. "Time for breakfast," pulling herself from his grasp, she slid off of her side of the bed to her dresser, slipping on a t-shirt and underpants, pulling her bathrobe over her like armor.

He watched her pick up his pants and boxer briefs and lay them on the end of the bed and she left him, turning down the hall to the bathroom. So it would seem, regardless of what he had said, what she had said, what they had just done, what they felt, what they knew together, Billy knew he'd lost his chance. *But,* he mused, *I don't think I ever really had one to begin with.*

He dressed quietly, she came in as he was finishing up, went to him and buckled his belt, looking into his face, reaching up to his injured eye, kissing him lightly, "Come down." She tried to smile and took his hand, leading him to the kitchen. She picked up the shirt and set his coat aside and busied herself with coffee, bacon, eggs. He pulled the shirt on, sat at the table and picked up the newspaper, she smiled over at him, occasionally catching him looking at her.

They ate ravenously together, "That's what a night of sex will get you," she grinned. She was trying to make this as easy as possible and she was grateful to him for going along. But it was getting harder by the second, seeing him at her table, knowing what he was, how he felt, she wanted nothing more than to go to him again and take him back upstairs *and good God, to hell with everyone else.*

He chuckled at her comment, eating heartily, swigging his coffee. But finally, realizing that the faster he went, the sooner it would all be over, his actions slowed. With all deliberate speed, he came to the end, swept his plate clean, picked up his emptied dish and lay it in the sink next to his coffee cup. He said over his shoulder. "No dishwasher, yet. Maybe soon," he turned to her. His voice broke and its sharp edges stabbed her, "Time to go."

She was grateful again for his incredible strength. Watching him finish his breakfast, she didn't know what to do next, what to say, where they were supposed to go, her determination had reached the breaking point. *He did it. For me. My hero came through again.*

"Yes." She nodded thankfully, standing up and picking up his coat. He took it in his arm. "Goodbye, Billy."

He didn't speak, he just nodded, his lips drawn back in a painful smile. He looked away. His eyes drowned in their sockets. His throat burned.

"Will you…" she croaked, clearing her throat, steadying her voice, "Will you kiss me goodbye?"

And he came to her; he took her into his arms, and kissed her. He couldn't speak to her, couldn't say the words he wanted, he couldn't even look at her, but he could do this. And he could finish this up the way she wanted to.

And then he let her go, turned from her, got into Del's car and drove away.

Janie stood at the side door of her house, leaning her head against the frame of the screen.

And she ached.

Del saw a haggard, swollen-faced Billy rolling in at six-thirty in the morning. "Everything okay, Mr. Smitts?"

"Yes, Del. Pack up the house. We're going to LA."

"Good. Good decision, Mr. Smitts," Del nodded. "Can I ask where you've been all night with my car?"

Billy turned to him, looked him full in the face, trying to be sincere, to play the part, "Sorry, Del, I was just out… driving."

"Good, using some time to think. So everything's okay?"

"Yes, Del." Billy cracked his neck, straightening his shoulders, "You were right, I have to leave her… leave her alone. It is time to go home."

They couldn't disentangle their lives slowly. Billy left Janie's house and had a new nanny for Ashley before noon – an old lady, with glowing references up the wazoo. Del and Bobby packed up the rented house and left for LA, Ashley and nanny in tow.

Nanny Sarah promised her sad little charge that she could make a picture for Janie and Katie and Brian as soon as they got to the big house and then they could mail it at the post office as their first adventure together. Ashley brightened up considerably at the idea of an adventure and sat back in her booster seat to think about it for awhile.

Billy drove back by himself.

Janie's check was written for the balance of the full amount for the maximum months agreed upon and mailed from his accountant's office. The check was cashed and returned a few weeks later to the accountant with Scott's signature on the back.

Janie packed up Ashley's toys and clothes and finally the dry black Prada t-shirt into a box and mailed it to the address on the check. The accountant was good enough to forward it to the LA house. Del opened the box and put everything away before Billy got back home late that night.

Ian did get a story across the wire the very next afternoon. The pic would have to wait until he got a decent shot from Billy later this week. But Del had assured him it would come. The story would go out on next week's grocery store racks and newsstands across America. It was so much better than he had expected and he was starting to send calls from the trades directly to his personal assistant, which would cause an absolute clamor for Billy. *Negative attention. Two weeks in a row!* Coupled with the fact that the article reported that Billy's camp had demanded silence would make it even hotter!

This had worked out far better than the Hospital Honey story. Really. He wasn't able to get a name, no new pictures and no clues as to the woman's identity – *I mean, nothing* - no addresses, no canceled checks, no license plate numbers – and he personally ran every single one in the hospital parking lot. But it worked out all for the best anyway. *I mean, that would have been a hell of a lot of evidence against him, right?*

When Del had called that morning, Ian had been half-expecting to finally get some answers about the pretty girl's identity, when instead he had received a very politely phrased what could only be called death threat, or so it very politely sounded. Del wasn't hard to read.

"Hello?" Ian sang into the phone.

"Ian, Del Marks."

"Hello Delbert. How are things up north? Good? Did Billy have a nice morning?"

Del, evenly, "Yes. He did."

"Can I speak to him? I'm sure he'd love to talk to me." Ian was buzzing on the smell of the press ink.

"Actually, he's out. Don't bother, he won't answer his cell phone but he did tell me to give you a ring."

"Oh he shouldn't have, although he really should considering how much press I got off very little info, you naughty boys. You just tell him I'm a size eight - well, my ring finger is anyway and I prefer a platinum setting."

"Hm, well, actually Ian. Mr. Smitts told me to handle everything concerning this week's press releases."

Odd, but Ian rolled with it, "He did? Okay, what do you have for me? A name, maybe. An interview with the girl, dare to dream? She was just so cute, from what I could see - a little country maid. Does she have a headshot, perchance?" he thought, "Probably not, in LA that would be a given, but most likely not up there. Either way, if I could get an address, I can have someone up to her place we could put a tail and get some nice candids to start out. We want her to look good, at least, at first. Haha! So good for press. Billy was really smart this time. She could totally change his image! Getting pretty tired of the ladies man/bad boy thing, honestly! So what have you got?"

"Not much, Ian. Just a very, very clear set of directions."

"Okay?"

"Well, I need you to listen very closely, Ian. Get some paper and a pen."

"I have it right here, Delbert," he dug.

"Mr. Smitts has requested that I personally take over coverage of this story. He has asked that any further inquiries into the woman's identity, any photos that may turn up or history you may unearth are to be turned over to me." Del wanted him to hear the warning in his voice, "No double files, no lost folders, no numbers in your Rolodex. As a matter of fact, you'll need to call off your dogs up here now."

"Wha... why would I do that?" Ian was absolutely flabbergasted, *please, who does he think he's talking to?* "And you know, those photographers are not mine. They're not under my control."

"No, but you can have them removed. You do work for Mr. Smitts, correct?"

"Yes, but this isn't PR, that's security detail," Ian scoffed.

"No. Actually this is a very big mess you will need to clean up."

"Okay, there's gotta be something I'm not getting." Ian was suspicious, but not enough to be upset, he just didn't like the tone of Del's voice. *It sounded too, happy.*

"I've done a little research this morning and Patient Privacy laws in hospitals are a lot stricter than I had realized. And so it would seem, the laws can extend to visitors of patients in the hospital. Now the photo was taken inside the hospital by an employee who received a faxed contract for the digital file of Mr. Smitts and the woman he was with, indicating that payment would be wired to his bank account upon receipt of the picture. Herein lies our little PR problem - the hospital has legal obligations to its patients and apparently those patients' visitors to protect their privacy. The employee, in lieu of termination or suit, has already agreed to tell the hospital precisely who would convince him, for what seemed to be a significant amount of cash, to violate state and federal laws against hospital privacy, which means a suit will be brought by the hospital itself, the insurance company for the patient, and a federal agency that serves to protect the HIPA Act of 2003. The employee handed over a fax. The fax was from Empire PR and the signature is yours." And for the first time, Del was enjoying every second of an Ian conversation. He smiled to himself as he delivered the death blow, "So the lawyers for the hospital and the insurance companies as well as this government agency, they want some answers. And they will get them. They won't be coming after the Enquirer, they won't go after the Sun, or US Magazine and now, it would seem they won't even be going after your PR firm. Your firm has already issued a statement saying, and I quote, 'never would any of our representatives put their valued clients in a position that would damage the reputations our firm works so hard to protect and uphold. If Ian Dormande was in fact in contact with these publications or the purveyor of the illegal digital file, it can only be assumed he was acting not on behalf of Empire Public Relations, but should be held solely responsible for any criminal act.'

"Now, the real ironic thing is, even if in two, three years, these inquiries end and the evidence does abdicate you, the woman's identity will never be disclosed to you. So not only would you lose a story, be sued personally, most likely fired for making an indiscriminate call against the contract your PR firm has with my boss, the federal government could watch you for the rest of your career in Public Relations to, you know, ensure that while you are held in suit, you don't do anything like that again."

"Oh my God." If Ian could actually turn pale under the layers of Mystic Tan, he would have.

"Yeah, so, you might want to get off the phone with me and call off the dogs, they're not going to help your impending suit when they confiscate your cell phone bill."

"How... how... how do I fix it, Del? What do I do?" Ian stuttered.

"I didn't get that far in my research," Del remarked casually.

"But, I... I..." Ian sounded like he was about to cry.

Del let the prick stew for just a couple of seconds more, before dangling the carrot in front of him, "I have an idea that could help you though. It's just a story, not even true really..." Ian laughed nervously, and Del continued, "but if you run it, I could persuade Mr. Smitts to at least try and save your job."

Ian snuffed, relieved, "Okay, yes, what, what have you got for me?"

"Well, it is pretty juicy and represents Mr. Smitts' more should we say 'dangerous' side."

Del could hear Ian's highly bleached smile over the phone lines, "My favorite one, personally. And best to maintain that hard edge, really. He is supposed to be totally bad boy punk."

Stacie came out of her last surgery within two more days of Billy leaving. Frankie was there waiting for her with Janie with the kids. The plastic surgeons had done a wonderful job and told her she would be left with minimal scarring. Stacie reached for Frankie and held him for a very long time. Janie hid her tears tidying up a small collar and wiping a nose or two.

Billy Sanderson sat in his jail cell. He had been denied bail because of his prior arrest so he was stuck in this stupid hole for another week until his trial started. *Unbe-frigging-lievable.* The guard had been nice enough at least to give him some stuff to read. GrossUnshoweredPainfully SoberBilly rifled through the week's worth of papers, Newsweek, Time, bo-ring shit, but *wait a second, what the fuck is this?* His own mug, more appropriately, mug-shot was staring at him from page two in the US Magazine right across from a much larger and terrifically gruesome candid photo of our favorite rock star/movie star with a bandaged up nose and a purpley-yellow black eye. Across the top of the page was written: BAD BOY BILLY IN BRAWL WITH LOCAL BUM!!

GrossUnshoweredElatedBilly stood on his bunk and screamed until the guards came and had to hold him down to then cuff him up against the bars. It was only a County Holding – they had no where to put him. Billy Sanderson wouldn't stop yelling and laughing so fricking loud. He had a smile on his face that no amount of taps with the bat would touch. The guy just kept saying over and over again, laughing in some sort of ridiculous satisfaction, "I'm the 'LOCAL BUM' you bastards! Not one of you fucks believed me, did you?! IT WAS ME!! ME AND BILLY SMITTS RIGHT HERE IN BLACK AND WHITE!! I'M THE BUM! HA!"

Scotty did come back. Two weeks later, he came back a very apologetic man and slightly ashamed of how far he had let things get away from him. He told Janie that he knew he could trust her and he always would love her if she would let him.

She said okay.

She never told him anything else. She couldn't. Janie would never let anything ruin their lives together, the life they had planned to have.

Billy laid off the blondes, the redheads and the brunettes, too, for, what Del considered, a hell of a long while. In fact, Del clocked it at just over six months before he noticed a pretty little yellow-haired bird lighting into a cab first thing in the morning. He went straight away to collect his money from Bobby.

He could have known it was coming though. The night before the first bird of Billy's springtime arrived, Del noticed Billy locking himself in his room with what looked like a letter, just a single crumpled piece of paper and an opened envelope. Earlier in that afternoon, Del had noticed Billy staring at that same envelope, tapping it slowly against the kitchen table. Del didn't get a chance to look at it himself but he had a pretty good idea who it was from.

But that night, up in his sanctuary, Billy was alone, not to be disturbed. It was just like in the old days when the boss was writing his music. But Del didn't hear any guitar or the piano at all, just some tones of the boss' voice he didn't think he had ever heard before.

So that next day, the pretty little thing. *A good old-fashioned meaningless fuck to cleanse the system, right?*

Yeah, so, it didn't help at all, but hell, it passed some time, didn't it?

Just like it always had before.

So after that, work. Billy threw himself into getting roles and producing an album for some new talent he had scouted out during his last trip to New York. He felt okay. Well, maybe not okay, but he was working, he was out among people. *Being alone got a little claustrophobic sometimes, too many stupid thoughts.*

Ashley was doing fine with Nanny Sarah. He spent a lot of time with her when he could work out of his home studio. And they had gone to Disneyland together last week; he met up with Stacie and her littlest boy.

Well, Billy had actually paid for Stacie and her family to go. He needed to see someone, someone close, at least.

They arranged to meet while Frank was on the Matterhorn with Benji. Stacie didn't say anything important, but took his addresses. He pretended to be glad when she told him Scotty had come home not long after he had left and that things seemed to be patching up. Billy searched her face for any clue she knew about his night alone with Janie at the house. Stacie would be pretty easy to read, and he could tell she didn't know a thing. He almost hoped she did, at least then he would know Janie had talked about him, thought about him, maybe told someone else that she loved him.

So other than work and Ashley, he did what he could to fill up all of the many other hours of the day. But it was hard, and the days had somehow become ridiculously long.

At first, Billy had feared that he was wearing the memories of Janie down to nothing; he was spending too much time with them. He did his best to just put them away until he had a clearer head. But sheer determination wouldn't stop up the flow. He was pretty much screwed.

It seemed that every little thing he did throughout his day was soaked with memory, or not even that, just maybe the idea that she could be there with him and get it all - all the jokes, the questions, the teasing comments he would have thought to make to her if she were just there, next to him. *Stuff she'd get.*

See, that was it, that was the problem - he could still see her, he could still know what her reactions would be, he could still hear her laugh, and, *I'm such a dumb fuck,* he could still feel her. *Christ I can't even drive by a fucking playground without laughing. And then feeling like complete shit.* It was all he could do to try and keep going, to keep moving.

But he would, especially after what she wrote to him, the letter he just got the other day, and what that stupid little piece of paper, a few little lines gave to him. It was,

well, it was something. She was still making him so fucking
mad, and ridiculously frustrated, and insanely hopeful. But
the funniest damned thing about that letter, the strangely
ironic thing about it was, she was still making him feel
better. *So, you know what?* He could do it. He could keep
going. *I mean, what else can I do?* He put the letter away
for now, tucking it into a gray lockbox he kept inside the
grand piano in his bedroom. No one would look in there, no
one would see. The letter nestled right next to a small
picture that he had ripped off of that poster the kids had
pasted together for him at her house. He could have that,
couldn't he?

There was really nowhere to go from there. There
wasn't any recourse. There wasn't a way for him to tell her,
to see her, to yell at her, to love her, to thank her. He hadn't
lost her to him so much as he really lost her to them. *And
against the kids, I didn't stand a chance,* he smirked. So
Billy just went on. He worked, went to premieres, hosted
read-throughs at his house, and brought some pretties home
to bang away the frustration. He went back to what he
knew, living through most of the days in his old routine
again. And he decided that, even if for nothing more than
that, it was good to be a star.

'Living the life.'

For now, it would just have to do.

Del and Bobby talked about Janie every once in a blue
moon, mostly when they drank Nanny Sarah's coffee. It
was weak and tasteless. If they even thought the boss was
in ear shot, they shut up immediately. He never mentioned
her but Bobby and Del could tell he was bad off, he missed
her. Del did what he could to take good care of his boss,

did what he figured Mr. Smitts would want to do - make her happy.

About two weeks after the move back to LA, Del took a couple of days off and drove up to the town. He parked in front of a beautiful glass building. Slowly and quietly, Del made his way to the third floor and politely asked the receptionist where he might find Scott Hadley. She rang him and soon Scott appeared. After the initial shock and Del's polite request to speak to him, Scott showed him in.

"Are you home yet?"

"No. Although it isn't any of your or your boss' business."

"My boss doesn't know I am here."

"Oh really?" Scott said nervously. "So why are you here?"

"I am here to tell you something that you might not realize."

"And what would that be, uh…?"

"Del."

"Yes, Del. I remember now."

"I am here to tell you that you, Scott Hadley, are one stupid asshole." It had worked for Del before.

"Excuse me?"

"It was a mistake. Janie made a mistake."

"Yeah, I'd say, a big one."

"I don't think you are considering the huge role you played in all of this, Mr. Hadley."

"Me? I wasn't the man, your boss, who was coming to my house everyday, trying to seduce my wife! And she's the one who gave in! Doesn't anyone get that?!"

"You are the husband of a woman who after years of neglect from her husband was so loyal to you that she gave up on a chance with Billy Smitts. Billy Smitts - a guy who could have any piece of ass he wanted just by walking in a

room and pointing. And he loved Janie. He loved her. He
paid attention to her, like she was a real person. He was
there for her and the kids. Where were you? He was doing
your job!"

"I was doing my job!"

"You have a wife!"

"I know that!"

"No you don't. You have someone who cooks and
cleans for you and takes care of your children. That's called
a maid, or a nanny. You pay them, they do their job and
they leave. I've hired plenty of them, I know. You have a
wife, a real woman who is supposed to matter to you as a
man, not just a provider or a boss, as a man, as a person, for
chrissakes. And that woman cares about you so much that
she is willing to give up a man who loves her like you
should, to let you go rather than to cause you pain, and who
is suffering right now because of a momentary lapse in her
resolve."

He picks up the paper, now weeks old, with the picture
of Billy and Janie. "How do I know that this was just
momentary? How can I believe that?"

"I don't know, Mr. Hadley. But you need to know that a
person can only be so strong, and you gave the girl nothing
to hold on to. And still, up until that night, she'd given you
all of her. And you know what? You'd forgotten all about
her. You've forgotten what it is like without her there.
Without her taking care of everything in your life that
makes it worth living. Let me ask you, who is there right
now, with your kids? Who is there right now, making your
bed and washing your shirts and paying your bills just so
that you can stay here and hide from her? You, my friend,
are a stupid asshole." Del got up to leave. "And don't think
he isn't waiting for you to knock off or something. Billy's
counting on you overworking yourself into a very early

grave. Because as soon as you are in a casket, he'll be at her door."

"Is that some kind of a threat?"

"Let's pretend it is," Del smiled. "Be a man, Scott Hadley. Go home to your wife and your children. Take a look at how beautiful they are and count yourself one lucky asshole."

Del deftly made his way through the small glass door, pleased with himself, never realizing that he didn't know the entire truth about Billy and Janie. Janie would have been ashamed if he had.

At Stacie's urging, Janie decided to sit down and write Billy a letter. After all that she had done, Janie didn't think it was a good idea, but Stacie reminded her that she didn't have to mail it. She assured Janie that you could just write and write and write and never send it, or if you wanted, only share parts of it that you could decide would be constructive for the other person to know. It was just a technique her and Frank's therapist had taught them to work out problems they had without hurting each other.

Stacie had finally settled in to being settled down and she was really happy for the first time in her life. Her scars were almost invisible and she had her last cast off in time for a surprise trip to Disneyland last week with the kids and Frank.

Janie was happy for them, still amazed at how they had gotten through so much. Scotty had been doing really well though, he had been spending some serious time with Janie and the kids and it had been nice. Things were still not at ease between the two of them, as if they weren't used to living together, the house had suddenly become smaller. There were days that they bumped into each other, or they barely spoke, except maybe a polite word or two over the heads of the chattering kids at the table. But Janie thought at least now they were completely united in a common goal of preserving some kind of normalcy for the sake of the children.

Their family, their kids - it was all that they had planned together; it was the life they had talked about having together, wasn't it? And although there were times that she couldn't bring herself to look at her husband – the unspoken guilt that there were moments she had happily lived outside of her marriage, her unapologetic selfishness to possess the one man who had given her joy without a price, lay over her like an autumn rust – still she knew she was doing what she had to do.

Janie refused to do what her mother had done to her. She couldn't take away her children from their father, leaving him to chase a life she'd never have, using them to get closer to her own dreams. A fourteen year old girl pulled from her home, to go live in Los Angeles with her mother and an agent and to live among people, "people in the know" her mom had assured her, who encouraged her mother, who pawed at Janie and swore to her stepfather that if they "could get a hold of her," they could really "do something with her," her mother beaming proudly over her. She had imagined that her children would have become like she, only seeing her father in the summers. A scant seven months together in this house before he died when she was a Junior in college. No matter how Janie felt, what she wanted, or needed, she knew she wouldn't let anything like that ever happen to her children. It was far too late for her, but she wouldn't ever stop making the world right for them.

And she could. Knowing Billy, together with him that night, Janie realized that regardless of what happened, of where they would go and what would come of both of their very different lives, she could believe that maybe she wasn't really alone anymore. That maybe there was someone who had wanted to, well, *had wanted to love her, in some small, insanely ridiculous way,* she smiled, *in a way that belonged to only her. It was something at least.* More than she had had before.

Just so funny, of all the people in the goddamned world...

Scotty did seem to be trying to make up for his mistakes, Janie would try too. He was just so different than she remembered him, or maybe than how she had imagined he would be, someday. At least, she *thought* it was him that was different.

She decided she would allow herself only a little more selfishness in the big long life that would be hers. Janie would write her letter that night.

Scotty had given her the night off from the kids. She thought she might go visit Stacie but she decided against it. She drove to the beach and parked at the Marina. Six months had passed since the morning that Billy had left but the feeling of him was fresh upon her – not just the memory she recalled in those dark nights, savoring the moments he had given her only for herself, but his friendship, his easy laugh, that incredible voice, their absurd bickering and *well, just him.*

So, Janie wrote until about two in the morning, picked out the last page of the very long letter, sealed it in an envelope and mailed it to a Los Angeles address Stacie had given her this morning.

I never got a chance to thank you, Billy. You were my hero.

My love to you always, Janie.

Acknowledgements

I would like to thank everyone who contributed, helped, supported throughout the course of this effort. I realize that I was insane during the initial weeks of this project and without you, I am not sure if we could have survived it all. I would like to thank Peter, Anna and Pete for being more things "in heaven and earth… than could be dreamt of in…" my "…philosophy" (Bill, the O.G. of Dialogue). Leah Miles, a veritable font of continuous inspiration and dauntless support. Ace proofer Kathleen McDonald and Kerrin Cuffe for being there to take me out and to listen to my story that first crazy week, Laureen LoGiudice and Donna Lane for being the first to read, for taking the time and being willing to understand the story in its infancy. Brent Sprague as an integral and loving part of my support group – I knew I'd love you from the beginning. Mary Phelan for offering great insight into the book-reading world, brilliant comments, alcohol-induced enthusiasm and being responsible for all around best pal duties. Andreana Osborn for "getting" Janie, and falling as madly in love with the ridiculous Mr. Smitts as I did. Sean Bishop, my story mentor and true friend - gossip and coffee is always waiting for you. Paul Mailloux, without whom my husband would be very bored and me and my fine Tennessee whiskey would be very lonely. Eileen Fitzgerald, J.D. Scrimgeour. Renee Stock for offering some killer commentary as well as some kick-ass writing soundtrack suggestions. Bryce Ambo for amazing design help. Christy Nelson, hair and makeup and Rosa Razavi, photography. Larry Lowe, the man responsible for most of our circle's success in life. Jay Wolf, Paul Rutter, Ron LeBrasseur for actually talking to me about my writing. Grimace, dirt and mcb, whose motivation got this bad boy up and running. The Ramp Rats as the original source of my first story inspiration, without you, I wouldn't be writing this one. Charlotte, Janie, Jimmy, Mark, Jay, Beth, and all of the kids; all of the Phelans and formerly Phelans, way too many to name. Jesse Fraser, Helen Blatchford, the Fraser girls, Jeanne Moulton and all of the Taylors. The Agony Productions crew – I adore you and yet I believe you all to be imaginary. Jesse Gahm-Diaz, Kristen Contois and the kids. Leon, Mugwump & Melba.

And to Eunice and Jim Blatchford, to whom I dedicate this book. I love you and I thank you.

Using the words that made me fall in love with my husband so long ago, "You're wonderful."

About the Author

What can we say about Sarah Phelan? She claims to be something of an intellectual, but you know what? She's really not. She's really just a great big nerd with a closeted love of Star Trek, comic book characters and computers - yeah, you might see Shakespeare, Steinbeck, Morrison and Garcia-Marquez on her bookshelf but do you know how she's really spending her time? She's riding on a Hippity Hop, chatting on internet message boards and ogling Joe on Blues Clues. She shouldn't even pretend to be a grown up anymore, there's no point.

Anyway, the daughter of Eunice and Jim Blatchford, Sarah grew up as the spoiled baby of the family with two sisters, Charlotte and Jane, and a brother, Jimmy, in Lynn, Massachusetts. She currently resides back in that very city after a five year exodus to Los Angeles where she was married to Peter, also a native of Lynn. They met in Drama Club in high school, believe it or not, but that is a long and complicated story best not relayed to the children, ever. Peter and Sarah have two incredibly gorgeous kids, Peter Junior and Anna. Sarah claims she is raising them with her own odd little formula of "Comic Book Morality" hoping that one day, her kids either a.) become superheroes or b.) have a really good comic book collection that they can sell if they fall on hard times. They are good investments, you know.

Sarah graduated from Regis College in Weston, Massachusetts but her whole college experience is a wee bit hazy, coming back to her mostly through flashbacks and weird dreams. I told you it wasn't a story for the kids. And she is currently enrolled in what she calls the Writing Masters in Thirty Years program at Salem State in Salem, Massachusetts.

She writes mostly for her own amusement, as I am sure by now you can tell. She would be a full time, practicing vegetarian but the seductive lure of bacon is way too strong. And steak, who doesn't love steak? Well, real vegetarians, I guess. Sarah loves her family, her animals, her incredible friends, books, music and being a true theater geek.

You could stop by her house but she's been known to cut people's arms off with a light saber for interrupting a princess tea party. Also, she'll claim that she'd love for you to come by if you were interested in talking about the irony of Shakespeare bookending "A Midsummer Nights Dream" with the relationship of Theseus and Hippolyta, saying she's starved for adult conversation, but you know what? You'll go over there and I swear within fifteen minutes she'll have you talking about the merits of Batman under the label of "super" hero, how she always thought Riker was a dink until she saw the movies, and how the addition of Spike in Season Five was great for the cast but did very little for his character arc. And you'll have to sit there and listen, because she'll feed you.

Blanket Fort Publishing Quick Order Form

Fax Orders: Send this Form to: 925-402-8280
Email Orders: saeph47@excite.com
Postal Orders: Blanket Fort Publishing, 117 Lakeview Avenue, Lynn, MA 01904

Please send me more information about (check ✓ all that apply):

❏   Ordering Stay At Home
❏   **Book Club Appearances** *(or call 781.632.1824 to invite the Author to Your Book Club Meeting for **Stay At Home**!)*
❏   Events
❏   Book Signings

Name: _____
Address: _____
City: _____
State: _____
Zip: _____
Telephone: _____
Email: _____

Sales Tax: Please add 5% sales tax for Orders Shipped to Massachusetts addresses.
Shipping by US Post, please add $3.85 for the first two books, $2.00 for each additional book.

Payment:
❏   Check
❏   Paypal to Blanket Fort Publishing at saeph47@excite.com
❏   Visa
❏   Master Card

Card Number: _____
Name on Card: _____
Expiration Date: _____

You may return the book for up to a full year after the purchase date for a full refund!

www.billysmitts.com